ChangelingPress.com

Data/Thorn Duet
A Bones MC Romance
Marteeka Karland

Data/Thorn Duet

Marteeka Karland

All rights reserved.
Copyright ©2021 Marteeka Karland

ISBN: 9798452792895

Publisher:
Changeling Press LLC
315 N. Centre St.
Martinsburg, WV 25404
ChangelingPress.com

Printed in the U.S.A.

Editor: Katriena Knights
Cover Artist: Marteeka Karland, Angela Knight

The individual stories in this anthology have been previously released in E-Book format.

No part of this publication may be reproduced or shared by any electronic or mechanical means, including but not limited to reprinting, photocopying, or digital reproduction, without prior written permission from Changeling Press LLC.

This book contains sexually explicit scenes and adult language which some may find offensive and which is not appropriate for a young audience. Changeling Press books are for sale to adults, only, as defined by the laws of the country in which you made your purchase.

Table of Contents

Data (Bones MC 8) 4
    Chapter One 5
    Chapter Two 20
    Chapter Three 36
    Chapter Four 49
    Chapter Five 62
    Chapter Six 80
    Chapter Seven 100
Thorn (Salvation's Bane MC 3) 120
    Chapter One 121
    Chapter Two 139
    Chapter Three 155
    Chapter Four 171
    Chapter Five 188
    Chapter Six 201
    Chapter Seven 221
    Epilogue 242
Marteeka Karland 251
Changeling Press E-Books 252

Data (Bones MC 8)

Marteeka Karland

Zora: I live a life of wealth and luxury. There isn't anything I can't have. Except my freedom. So I turned to the computer for friendship. And that's where I met my match. And when my life suddenly falls apart, he's the one to find me. But he'll also be the one to rip my heart in two.

Data: I'm not good with people. It's why I stick to my computers. When my online partner and friend ends up in trouble, there's no way I'm letting her go it alone. I was expecting a mature woman when I pulled up in front of her house. But the girl is barely eighteen.

And I friggin' want her. To make matters worse, she's been targeted by elite members of global organized crime. I'm confident I can keep her safe from that danger. I'm less sure I can keep her safe from me. She's already had one unwanted relationship with an older man. She doesn't need a man like me. One who will rule her to make her mine. And kill anyone in my way to keep her safe.

Chapter One

The day was about as perfect as it could get. Zora Hightower relaxed by the pool of her husband's sprawling Nashville estate sipping the sweetest, most refreshing glass of sweet tea she'd ever had in her life.

"Can I get you something else, Mrs. Hightower?" Renee, one of the assistants in the kitchen, asked her.

"No, thank you, Renee. And please, call me Zora. Who made the tea?"

"Anna, as always." Renee smiled.

"Please tell her she's outdone herself. It's absolutely wonderful."

"Of course, Mrs. Hightower."

"Zora."

The older woman paused, seeming to debate saying something. Then she stepped closer to Zora. "Ma'am, if there's ever anything I can do for you…" She trailed off, giving her a look that said she meant more than what she was saying. "…don't hesitate to tell me." Then, Renee smiled, as always, before leaving her side.

Zora tried desperately to concentrate on the luxuries she had and forget why she had them. Sipping sweet tea by the pool. The warm summer breeze tickling her damp body. Breathe in. Breathe out.

Fuck.

It didn't matter what she did. The image of Gordon Sandlin, her husband of all of six weeks, filled her vision. He wasn't a particularly large man, but he was mean. Their wedding night had been the worst experience of her life and had been repeated three or four times a week since. He hadn't insisted she take his name, though. She'd assumed she would, but he hadn't insisted and she hadn't brought it up. She'd also learned quickly not to hide from him when he came for her. Pretending everything was all right was the only way she knew to deal with her new life.

Well, that wasn't true. There was one other thing.

Immediately, she stood and crossed to the umbrella-shaded table next to her. She had her laptop set up there with a sunscreen so she could use it outside if she felt like it. Another luxury. Her new husband had insisted she not work. Probably to keep a tight leash on her. As such, she'd had time to help an online friend with some information digging recently. She'd pretended to like to game and had more than one on her laptop in various stages of play in case Gordon decided to check on her.

Though she enjoyed games on occasion, her favorite thing, that which took the anxiety away from her life even for a brief time, was her continued correspondence with an online friend. The man was some kind of intelligence person she'd found by accident when she'd hacked his system purely for fun. They'd struck up a friendship, and now she occasionally helped him dig up information. It was something she enjoyed. And, really, the guy was just too sweet. More importantly, he helped take her mind off her current situation.

Fab Z-Na: Got anything for me today?

D Bonez: Always got something for you, cutie.

Fab Z-Na: *giggle* Work, you naughty boy. Do you have work?

D Bonez: Some consider it work. I think you'd consider it play.

Fab Z-Na: D!!! I'm serious! Much as I love this absolutely awesome sweet tea and the pool, I'm hungry for some digging!

D Bonez: Oh. Shit. Sorry, sugar. All the bad guys caught for the moment.

Zora thought about pouting a little. He always seemed to get a kick out of that. As much as she loved flirting with D, she really was in the mood for some work. With him. She and D were awesome on the computer together. She'd learned so much from him, but she'd taught him a trick or two as well.

Fab Z-Na: Look. I'm bored. You know that can only come to no good. Surely you've got something. Help a bitch out!

D Bonez: Nope. I was about to take a much-needed break. Planning on a short vacation with my daughter and some friends.

Fab Z-Na: Oh! Sounds fun! Have a great time. If anyone deserves it, it's you.

There was a pause. Zora was about to disconnect the secure chat when another message popped up.

D Bonez: You wanna join us? Would be great to meet the face behind that brilliant mind of yours.

Would she ever. Unfortunately, she was certain her husband wouldn't approve. Secondly, no matter how much she was tempted, no matter how much she wished she hadn't married Gordon in the first place, flirting was all she was willing to do, and even that was crossing a line she shouldn't. This was her mess. She'd figure it out. Dragging sweet D into her problems wasn't something she could do.

Fab Z-Na: I'd love to. Can't though. Plans.

D Bonez: Never said when we were going, cutie.

Fab Z-Na: I know. Truthfully? I'm married. One of those arranged things, you know. But still.

D Bonez: Wow. You should have mentioned that. I hope I've not made you uncomfortable.

Fab Z-Na: NO! I just don't like giving out personal information. Wouldn't have said anything except I thought you should have a truthful explanation.

D Bonez: Baby, you don't owe me. If anything, the reverse is true. You've helped me a lot over the last couple of years.

Fab Z-Na: Years? Has it been that long??? I thought we just met up a couple of weeks ago. ??

D Bonez: Time flies when you're having fun.

Fab Z-Na: Yeah. I guess it does. You have a wonderful time. Show me pictures and tell me all about it when you get back.

D Bonz: Will do, cutie.

Zora disconnected the chat with a wistful sigh. She'd met D when she got caught snooping on his private network. She'd wanted to see where it led. At first, he'd been angry. With himself. Not her. Then they'd struck up a friendship and he'd tightened his security. She'd never been able to get into it again. But he'd given her a way to communicate with him when she wanted to.

Why couldn't she have married a man like D? If she was lucky, Gordon would be gone again tonight. He'd taken great delight in humiliating her during sex and seemed to enjoy it for the first few weeks. Thankfully, the last eight or ten days, he'd only been home for brief amounts of time. In fact, the only reason he'd been home as often as he had was, as he put it, "If I've gotta give your old man half my Goddamned fortune, I'm gonna at least have the satisfaction of knowing that *he* knows I'm fucking his daughter." A statement he'd backed up every single time by taking pictures during the act and sending them to her father.

Zora had never been so humiliated in her life. She hated Gordon, but because of the arrangement he had with her father, she was powerless to do anything about it. Both of them had made it sound like her father's life was at stake. All Gordon had mentioned was money, though. She was beginning to think it was in her best interest to throw caution to the wind and do a little digging on her own. She'd prefer D's help, but she could do it without him, and she didn't want to drag him into her private mess.

With a sigh, she took another long pull of the tea before going to the pool and diving in. When her mind wouldn't settle, swimming laps sometimes helped. She hoped it would this time.

Gordon was a real estate investor. Zora's father had been in business with him for years, but the two had had a falling out just a month before her father told her she'd be marrying Gordon. The particulars hadn't seemed important at the time in the wake of the news. At first, she'd protested, but her father had become angry and, for the first time in her life, he'd struck her -- a hard, backhanded blow that'd sent her spinning.

"You'll do what I damned well tell you to! Gordon agreed to marry you, and you'll do it! Do you hear me?"

His anger had shocked her. She'd felt like whatever had happened between them was her fault for questioning him. Looking back, that was likely exactly why he'd done it.

The wedding hadn't been a big church affair, or even a small ceremony at the courthouse. A friend of her father's had shown up at the house an hour later along with Gordon, and they'd simply signed the marriage license and the certificate. No vows. No words of love or even affection. Gordon had simply given her dad a smug, angry look and had kissed her so aggressively she'd nearly gagged. Then Gordon and her dad had gone to his study where Gordon had opened a laptop. He'd placed his thumb on the screen, tapped a few keys, then turned it to her father so he could inspect whatever was on the screen before Gordon slammed the thing shut.

"There. Done. Make this fucking go away."

"It was your power-hungry greed that got us into this mess in the first place," her father said.

"And your Goddamned job to make it fucking go away! You benefit or hurt from this as much as I do. *Fix it!*"

Zora had been so shell-shocked she'd nearly missed the whole exchange, but they hadn't bothered to hide it from her. As a rule, she was quiet and submissive. She never put a toe out of line. Never drew attention to herself. Because of that, people tended to underestimate her and sometimes forget she existed at all. She knew then she'd have to look into whatever was going on. She just couldn't do it immediately. If she made a mistake -- like she had when D had caught her two years earlier -- it might not end so well for her. She'd decided the time was right. She was going to figure out what was going on. She'd just have to be careful.

The one thing Zora was good at was anything to do with the Internet or a computer. She was a hacker. So far, she'd only used her powers for good, but she was ready to get her hands dirty on this one. Her new husband was nothing if not predictable. It was twelve-thirty now. That meant he'd be getting back from lunch and would be at his office. She knew because she'd hacked his phone and set up a tracker. The purpose had been so she always knew where he was and, more importantly, when he got home. She always tried to be ready for him when he got home. And by ready, she meant doing something vigorous so he would leave her alone. He didn't like sweat or anything to do with working out. If she was on the treadmill, he wouldn't touch her until she'd had a shower. Likewise if she were swimming. He hated the chlorine smell.

She checked his location on her phone before beginning her task. Hacking into his company and, more importantly, his personnel files.

It took some doing, but she managed to get past the company's security and into Gordon's personal server. She'd been preparing for this since that first night he'd... well, since their wedding night. It had been a painstaking process, but it was paying off now. What she found was one scheme after another. Cooked books. Shady deals. Offshore accounts. Shit she'd never even heard of but knew was wrong because the math didn't add up. But that wasn't what concerned her the most. Hell, what got her attention was a stray footprint. A tiny bit of code that shouldn't be there. She supposed that, to most people, it wouldn't be noticed. But she wasn't most people.

Zora had hacked enough for fun to know each hacker had a signature, just like a bomb maker or a sniper. Sometimes it was intentional. Sometimes it was like a tell. They didn't even realize they were doing it until they got caught and someone explained how. It could also be a trap. Or even a setup.

She debated on whether or not to follow it. Then she found the same footprint on Gordon's personal server, and her curiosity got the better of her. Yeah, no way she couldn't dig further. The files being targeted were all financial in nature. The date the hacker had accessed them was about two months prior, shortly before Gordon and her dad had their falling out. Then, by accident, she stumbled onto a second footprint. This one had attempted to erase or alter certain files but either thought better of it or had been hasty and sloppy. She retrieved the files for study later. If someone else was interested, she was interested. But she suspected the interested party was the government, and that both her dad and Gordon were in deep shit.

Careful to blend her digital footprint in with the ones already there, Zora painstakingly made her way out of the system without setting off any alarms. It took several hours, and Gordon would soon be on his way home, assuming he did come home tonight. She uploaded everything she'd found to a private cloud and removed any evidence from her laptop that she could. It might not hold up to top-level computer geeks if they went looking to see if she'd breached the company's security, but it would fool most people.

That done, she shut down her system and dove into the pool.

* * *

Data watched as Zora went offline. How had he not known she was married? He'd tried to respect her privacy, but he really should have found out at least the basic information about her. She was so intelligent with computers and code, and with her ease of getting through any network undetected he'd always figured she had his level of experience, which meant she was close to his age. But what did he really know about her? If she was in an arranged marriage she could be of another nationality, but her English was flawless. He'd spoken to her a few times over voice messaging, and if anything she had a pleasant Southern accent. She'd sounded younger than he thought she was, but it struck him then how little he actually knew about her.

Which set his curiosity ablaze. Not good with a hacker. So he'd gone digging.

He knew her real name. He'd contented himself with that. Fab Z-Na was Zora Hightower. Before now, her name had been enough. Well, that *and* knowing without a doubt she couldn't breach his firewall again. He'd watched her try several times when she thought he wasn't looking and had been satisfied with the results. Her attempts had been genuine and not something designed to throw him off, and his security had held fast. But now, he had to know more. Mainly because he'd grown attached to the spunky hacker. He'd never seen a picture of her. He'd knew next to nothing about her. But she was a hard worker, super intelligent, and now he had this image of her in a loveless marriage. It just didn't seem right.

Drawing in a deep breath, he took the plunge. First, he did the easy stuff. Social media and public records provided all he needed, really. And he felt like he should shoot himself now, because he was getting ready to commit an unpardonable sin.

The woman -- girl, really -- was absolutely, *stunningly* gorgeous. She tried to downplay her looks by hiding behind overly large glasses and fixing her long, caramel-colored hair so it partially hid her face, but there was no denying her beauty. There was not a single picture of her with makeup or in formal wear. No wedding announcement. No pictures of her with her husband or even with him as her boyfriend before they were married. Her infrequent posts had stopped almost two months ago. She had a few friends -- less than a hundred and fifty -- and very few of them commented on her posts. But what was getting him into trouble was her age. The last post on her feed, two months before, was the only post that had more than a handful of "likes." Wishing her a happy *eighteenth birthday*.

Data sat back heavily, stunned to his core. "Fuck. Me."

"Something wrong?" The voice coming from the entrance to his office startled him. The man was as quiet as they came. Big, gruff, with the biggest heart of any man Data had ever met, Stunner stood awkwardly just outside his office. He looked decidedly uncomfortable, but wouldn't pass on by knowing one of his brothers might be in need of help.

"Hey, Stunner. How's Suzie?" At the mention of the teen, Stunner's features softened. Melted was probably a more accurate term. The man had appointed himself her protector from the second he'd seen her. Now she rarely left his side unless it was to study or do something with the ol' ladies.

"Good. Wants a lesson." He was referring to Data teaching the girl the inner workings of the net. How to hack. How to keep from getting hacked. Probably not something Angel, her teacher and Cain's wife, would approve of. But she wanted to learn it, and Data loved to teach her.

"Anytime she's ready. I'll clear my day for her."

Stunner nodded once, then turned to go before stopping again. "Something wrong?" he asked again.

Data sighed, scrubbing his hands over his face. "I'm not sure."

The big man looked down the hall like he wanted to head on, but instead ducked inside and shut the door. "What can I do to help?"

Data snorted. "Good Goddamned question." He thought about not saying anything, but he and Stunner had developed a rapport. The big man was surprisingly insightful when you could get him to say more than two words. Data slid a tablet across his desk. Stunner picked it up and looked at the images. He scrolled through, taking his time with each image. Through it all, his face remained impassive.

Finally he looked up at Data. "Pretty girl. That your woman?"

Data opened his mouth, then closed it. He cleared his throat, then tried again. "Stunner, did you see her age?"

"Yeah. She's legal. That the girl you're always talkin' to? The one helpin' you out?"

"It is. For the record, she's not 'my woman.' But I think she might... Well, she might need our help."

"Our?" Stunner tossed the tablet lightly back onto the desk before crossing those impossibly muscled arms over an equally massive chest. "You gonna get Cain to let us go after her?"

"No," Data said on impulse. "I'm gonna dig a little deeper. See if I can learn more about her."

"I'd've thought a man like you would've known everything there was to know about the girl already."

"I should've," he acknowledged. "But she seemed to want her privacy, and I didn't want to push. Had no reason to push. We had a good thing goin'."

"Somethin' happen to change that?"

"I don't know," Data said, tired frustration coming out. "She says she's married and that it was an arranged marriage. Now, she could be perfectly happy, or she could be lying to me. But none of what I found on her social media says anything about a boyfriend or a wedding. You saw where I found the public record of her marriage to Gordon Sandlin. He's in his fifties, for Christ's sake!"

Stunner shrugged. "Maybe it's a money thing. Ain't that Sandlin guy rich or something?"

"Yeah. Or something." Data sighed. "It's none of my business. I guess I got a little obsessed with an online persona." He gave the younger man a rueful smile. "Happens all the time. I'm sure she's fine."

"But you've got a bad feeling."

Data shook his head. "Forget it. I'm probably just jealous. Can't deny the kid's a looker. But she's definitely too young for the likes of me. Even if she were interested."

"Seems like you're in a little deep if this is the first time you've seen her and you're trying to lay a claim on her."

"Old and silly. Maybe a little lonely. She's the first woman in my life I've had any kind of connection with. I guess it's the computers. Hell, I didn't even feel much of anything for Darcy's mother. And this girl is younger than Darcy."

"Did you know she was that young?"

"No. She was so intelligent and seemed to have so much experience with networks and security systems, I just assumed she was older."

Stunner stood. "Go with your gut." He nodded once as if agreeing with what he'd just said, then left Data's office abruptly.

Go with your gut...

Well, his gut was screaming at him that something was off. With a sigh, he powered up his computer with its bank of monitors. It was time for some serious work. He hoped Suzie took a couple of days before she decided she was ready for another lesson, because Data had the feeling he was going to be occupied for a while.

An hour later, a message notification flashed from his private chat room with Zora.

Fab Z-Na: Hi

D Bonez: You good?

It was a full minute before she responded back. Data was afraid she wasn't going to answer. Maybe this was just a social thing. She didn't usually make small talk other than to touch base on Saturdays, but maybe she'd gotten bored.

Fab Z-Na: You know. Don't you.

D Bonez: That you're married to one of the wealthiest men in the area? That his business is in trouble? That you were basically sold to him by your father to cover money given your father by Sandlin? Yeah, cutie. I know. I'm still digging into why your father needed that money, but my guess is it's not going to matter for long.

Fab Z-Na: Feds are looking into it. Something about financial practices and defrauding the federal government.

D Bonez: What do you need?

There was another silence. Data knew without question he'd give her whatever she asked for. He hadn't thoroughly investigated the matter, but Zora was an innocent in this. He'd give her whatever she wanted. Money. Safety. A fucking Labradoodle if she said she needed it. He didn't care.

Fab Z-Na: I don't know. I mean, if the feds come in, they're going to take everything both of them have. I could care less about Gordon, or even my dad, but I refuse to be homeless and I refuse to keep things that were paid for by other people.

D Bonez: You gonna leave?

Fab Z-Na: Yes. First, I'm going to send you some files. I hate using you like this. I don't want anything to come back on you. But you have more contacts than I do and I wouldn't have a clue who to send them to anyway.

D Bonez: Files?

Fab Z-Na: Yes. From Gordon's office. I hacked into his system and found some things. It looks like someone is already on to him, though. I cloned his hard drive so I didn't miss anything. I don't understand it all. I'm a computer geek, not an accountant. But it all looks shady to me.

D Bonez: Send it to me. I'll take care of it.

Fab Z-Na: I appreciate it. I may be off the grid for a while, but I'll let you know when I'm settled.

D Bonez: No fucking way! You tell me where you're going and what you're doing. I'll meet you and make sure you're safe.

Fab Z-Na: I appreciate it, D, but this isn't up for debate. I'm already involving you way more than I should.

D Bonez: You're just making things more difficult for me, Zora. I'll spend hours finding you I could be using to plan your defense. Now, fucking tell me where you're going!

Pause.

Fab Z-Na: I found a little place in Kentucky. It's not big. Just a couple of acres and a small house. I worked out a deal to rent the place from the owner until we could close on me buying it. I'm calling it pay for sexual favors from my soon-to-be-former husband. It's not enough for him to notice. Auditors might miss it, but I doubt they'll get in a twist over it.

D Bonez: You get me the address. Ditch your phone. Buy you a burner phone and text me the address. I expect that to happen today. Understand me?

Fab Z-Na: I don't remember you being so bossy. Who are you? LOL

D Bonez: I'm your friend. And I'm not nearly as bossy as my boss.

Fab Z-Na: I'll be in touch.

D Bonez: You better…

Before they signed off, Data gave her his cell number. It was the first time either of them had shared personal contact information. He hoped she did as he'd told her to. If she did, he had a chance of getting her to safety before her husband or the feds found her. He had the feeling her father and her husband knew more about her computer skills than she was aware of. A testament of her youth. She was covering her tracks pretty well, but the adults in her life were much better at being crooks than she was. From everything Data had found, they were setting Zora up to take the fall.

Not. Fucking. Happening.

Chapter Two

Setting up the money transfer went off without a hitch. Zora used several pre-paid debit cards to transfer the money she needed. Not very efficient, but quick, and something the company did from time to time for employee bonuses, so the bank wouldn't balk. Thank God she'd continued to dig into the stuff she'd downloaded. Though she wasn't an accountant, she knew software, and the bonuses weren't something they'd tried to hide or code. By the time she got done, she was confident it looked like the money transfers came from the company's accounting department.

Transportation was a problem. Busses didn't stop anywhere near where she needed to go. She managed to get a ride to Lexington, and from there, she hopped six different Uber rides steadily south until she reached her destination.

Meeting with the elderly couple who were selling her the house was a pleasant experience, and the property was everything Zora could have hoped for. An older farmhouse with two bedrooms and one bath. Enough land for a garden. Good, sturdy buildings for storage. Once she bought a cheap car, she'd be set. All she needed was a job, which was no problem because she could work from home. With her skills, she thought she could figure something out. She'd made a deal with the couple to rent for three months, then close on the house. The guy was a retired Realtor so they weren't going through a company and could work things out on their own terms. It would allow her time to set up a bank account and transfer the money from the debit cards. She paid them the three months' rent, then went in to open the bank account.

Next thing she had to do was secure transportation. The little town she was planning on calling home had several used-car dealers. Once her money started posting to her bank account, she was free to go shopping. She settled on a seven-year-old car with more than a hundred thousand miles on it. Not the best of choices -- certainly not as good as the Corvette she'd left behind -- but it was cheap, and it would get her from point A to point B.

She also had to find a lawyer who could start the divorce process for her. She was done being that bastard's wife. No matter what trouble her father was in, she wasn't letting Gordon touch her ever again.

All this had taken several days. Closer to two weeks. It wasn't until it was way too late that she'd remembered she was supposed to buy a burner phone and text D. She knew it was too late because, while she sat on the front porch in the little swing, a flock of big motorcycles pulled into her driveway. And by flock, she meant ten or twelve. They made the most awful racket ever, and her first thought was to message her friend. Problem was, she didn't have a phone of any kind now.

One by one, the riders shut off the bikes but didn't get off them. Only one man took off his helmet and approached the house, a horrible scowl on his bearded face. Zora quickly jumped up and went inside. She tried to close the door, but the man was on her already. He didn't grab her but shoved his foot inside the door so she couldn't shut it.

She squealed, shoving her weight against the door. Like that was going to help if the man really wanted in. She was so slight there wasn't enough of her to deter him.

"Zora, stop," he barked.

She was so shocked he knew her name, she obeyed. Then she blinked several times. "D?"

"Data," he corrected. "And you are in so much trouble, you can't even conceive." As angry as he sounded, Zora thought he'd pull her outside, but he didn't. He held open the screen door and stepped back so she could come back outside the house. When she didn't readily comply, he raised an eyebrow. "I will carry you if you don't come out on your own."

She swallowed but did as he said. Why, she had no idea. Of all the ways she'd envisioned meeting her online friend, this wasn't it. And what was with all the bikes? She'd also thought he was closer to her age. Sure, the remark about spending time with his daughter had registered, but she'd just assumed his daughter was a child. She hadn't asked and he hadn't volunteered, but when she'd imagined what he might look like, it was as a college guy. Maybe slightly older. The reality couldn't have been further from the truth.

This man -- Data -- was in his forties, bearded, and heavily muscled. He *towered* over her. She was only five foot three, so she guessed he was at least six-three or -four. Looking at the men behind him on their bikes, talking amongst themselves, she noticed they glanced toward Zora and Data occasionally. They were all just as big and just as strong. Just as intimidating.

Data gestured for her to go back to her perch on the swing where she'd been before, and he took one of the chairs next to her. For long, long moments, he sat looking at her, his forearms resting on his thighs, fingers laced together.

"Um," she cleared her throat. "You, uh, want some tea? I've got soda, too."

Nothing.

"I'd offer beer, but I don't --"

"Why the fuck didn't you do what I told you to?" He didn't raise his voice, but the message was the same. Data wasn't happy with her. At fucking all. "Where's your phone?"

"I left it at back at Gordon's house," she squeaked.

"And the burner I told you to buy? You know, the one you were supposed to use to text me with your location so I knew where you were and had a way to contact you?"

"I forgot it, OK?" Her voice was firm and a little irritated. There. She'd found her spine. Finally. Mostly.

"Do you have your computer?"

"Yeah. But I've been so busy trying to get myself set up here, I haven't been online."

"Believe me, I'm fully aware. I've had our private chat open for days. I had the program set to notify my cell if you came online. My phone has been by my side or in my fuckin' pocket constantly." The more he talked, the louder he got, his anger obviously building. He didn't shout at her, but his frustration with her was more than obvious. Finally, he closed his eyes and took a deep breath before continuing. "I was fuckin' worried sick."

She blinked several times. "What? Why would you worry about me? I can take care of myself."

"I'm aware. Doesn't change the fact I like knowin' you're good." There was silence between them. An uncomfortable one where she fidgeted and he just stared at her, his expression unreadable but intense. "Did it ever occur to you I might care about your wellbeing?"

Of course. She got it now. Just like everyone else in her life, he worried about her abilities being taken away from him. And be Goddamned, it hurt. "I'm sure you could find any number of hackers willing and able to help when you need it," she said, unable to keep the pain from her voice no matter how much she wanted to act like it didn't bother her. "Hell, you're much better than I ever thought about being. It's not like I put you in a bind."

He sat up straight. "What the fuck did you just say to me?"

She shrank back. This wasn't her D. This man was scary. And an asshole, but she wasn't saying that out loud. "I said it wasn't like I put you in a bind."

"Data!" One of the men called warningly from his bike in her driveway. "Simmer the fuck down, brother." That was surprising, but not unwelcome.

Data scrubbed a hand over his face before stroking the front of his beard-covered chin with a couple of fingers. "Look," he said. "Did it ever occur to you I might be worried about more than your abilities with a computer? Maybe I was concerned about my friend. Ever fuckin' think of that?"

"I… Your… friend?"

"Yeah. My friend." Data shoved himself out of the chair and held out his hand for her. "Come here, cutie."

It was that nickname that made her stupid hand land in his and her body allow him to pull her to her feet. The next thing she knew, he'd wrapped her up in those strong arms and hugged her tightly. She was so much shorter than him, he just picked her straight up, her legs dangling in the air.

Holy. Shit. Had she ever been touched like this before? It was a fucking hug! Not a nasty, sweaty, trapping of her body by a man intent on raping her under the guise of marriage, but a real, true, *affectionate* hug. A man she only knew from the Internet had wrapped arms as thick as her thighs around her entire body, picked her up off the ground, and put her in a fucking bear hug that was both sweet and fierce. He held her like he'd never let her go. For any reason in the world. His chin rested on top of her head briefly before she felt his lips in her hair as he kissed the top of her head.

"I thought they'd done something horrible to you, cutie. I couldn't find you until you opened that fuckin' bank account. I thought you hadn't gotten away fast enough."

There were so many questions, so many things she needed to ask him, but all she could register was the feeling of his arms, and his scent. Both surrounded her. Every breath she took brought more of that addictive scent. There was the faint scent of gasoline where he'd been riding the bike, but there was also a clean, fresh scent of wind and rain. Wild man. It was just as intense as the first impression he made on her. This man was raw. Untamed. He wasn't the sweet, mild-mannered computer geek she'd often thought of when she communicated with him. He was... larger than life. A man straight out of a fairytale. And for those few moments he held her so tightly, so... possessively, Zora felt like she'd finally, *finally* found the place she belonged.

Tears sprang from her eyes before she even registered she was going to cry. She didn't know what to do with this. Zora had always felt like she'd been searching for something. She was an only child. Her parents were never the affectionate type. In fact, she'd often thought of her nannies as more like parents than either her mother or father. But even those women had never given her the affection Zora had always needed or wanted. And still, what she'd always wanted and what she was experiencing now were two completely different things. She just couldn't identify what the difference was.

He only held her for a few seconds. To Zora it seemed like a lifetime, yet she knew a lifetime could never be enough. It was something she knew she'd never forget. No matter what happened after, this moment would forever be etched into her memory.

The guys around them hooted.

"I think you're scarin' her off, brother."

"Don't worry, girl. We won't let him take too big a bite outta ya."

"Jesus, Data! Let the girl breathe, will ya?"

Then it was over. Data let her go. Her D. He set her back down and took those arms away, and she wanted with everything in her to protest, to scream a resounding "NO!" and jump right back into them. Instead, she just stood there, gaping up at him, not knowing what to say.

He scowled at the men, flipping them off. "Come on," he said. "Let's go inside and talk where these assholes won't bother us."

"I -- O-OK."

She fumbled with the storm door until he reached around her, his big hand sliding over her smaller one. Zora looked up at him, and he grinned at her. She felt like a star-struck teenager. Only instead of a rock star or a movie star, D was there. A rough-around-the-edges biker. A super-intelligent hacker as well as a warrior. Larger than life. There was no way any man could live up to the image that was snowballing inside her head. No way. She was setting herself -- and him -- up for a huge fall. It wasn't fair to him, especially when he had no idea what was going on in her head. And all of this in the space of a minute.

Fuck.

* * *

Data knew he needed to pull himself together. He knew Zora had no idea what to do with a man like him. She was probably terrified of him now. Which only made him want to protect her that much more.

"I'm not here to hurt you, cutie," he said, trying to do what he could to put her at ease. "I want you safe. More importantly, I want you to *feel* safe." He put a hand on the small of her back, urging her to sit down on the sectional that served as her only furniture in the small living room. He took a seat beside her. Unable to stop himself, Data took his hand in hers. It was so tiny. Like holding a child's hand. Which only served to remind him of their age difference. Immediately, he let her hand go, patting the back of it before pulling away so it didn't seem like he didn't want to touch her. He could see the confusion on her lovely face. No. Confusion wasn't the right word. It was something else. A complex mixture of something he couldn't identify, but he could see she wasn't unhappy he was here. She just didn't know what to do with him and his brothers.

"I -- I know you won't hurt me." Her voice was soft. She looked up at him, her large, luminous hazel eyes framed with deep black eyelashes. Christ, she was lovely! How the fuck was he supposed to fight this? It was so inappropriate he couldn't even imagine how deep a pit in hell he was digging for himself. Unbidden, his cock stiffened behind his jeans. How the fuck was he supposed to carry on a conversation when she was looking at him like he'd hung the fucking moon?

Data cleared his throat. "Uh, good. That's good." He tried again. "Look, I'm here to take you back with me. Err, us. Back to the clubhouse."

"But I don't need to go anywhere," she said. "I'm renting this house for a few months until I get my finances in order, but, honestly, I'm good."

"No, cutie. You don't understand." Just thinking about the trouble she was in helped quell his lust for her, but his balls still ached. "It's not the feds after Gordon and your father."

"Are you sure? I didn't have time to dig too deep into it, but everything pointed to some kind of cyber division. It had a..." She waved her hand around a little. "I don't know, an institutional feel to it. Something learned. Not something that came naturally. And definitely not someone being careful. When the feds investigate, they don't normally care if the people they're investigating know or not. By the time something like this is found, it's way too late."

"I agree," he said but patted her hand again when she would have continued. "But I also wasn't taking any chances. You told me to give those files to someone I thought could get to the bottom of this. Well, the president of Bones, the MC we all belong to," he gestured out the window at the men patiently waiting for them, "is friends with one of the men who own Argent Tech in Rockwell, Illinois. I knew if there was something we were missing, he could find it."

Her eyes got wide. "Argent Tech? Holy shit! You know those guys?"

Data grinned. "If I say yes will that score me points, cutie?"

Sweet. Baby. Jesus.

The girl had the most beautiful smile. He'd thought she was beautiful before, but the excitement on her face almost made him forget the reason for her smile. It wasn't because of him. It was because his president knew some super-rich geniuses.

"You know, I'm kind of a bigshot tech geek myself."

She got an uncertain look on her face, like she was afraid she'd messed up somehow. "I-I didn't mean…"

He chuckled, not wanting her uncomfortable. "Relax, cutie. I know they're bigshots."

"But you are, too," she said quietly.

"And so are you, cutie. They just have way more money than either of us."

"Yeah. I guess so." She took a breath, clearly trying to put the awkwardness behind her but unsure how to do it. "So, you said it wasn't the feds. Who then?"

He scrubbed the back of his neck. "Well, that's the hard part. It's kind of one of those things where it's a friend of a friend who has a cousin who knows of someone who might be involved. But Azriel thinks an organization called the Brotherhood is involved in it. Thinks they have someone working for them with their hands in this."

"I don't understand."

"I know. And it's hard to explain 'cause I don't understand all of it myself. I know the Brotherhood is like the end-all be-all of organized crime. They control pretty much everything going on in the world to do with money and if they don't, they squash whoever does and take control. They're the power behind… well, everything. No. it's more than that. They're the power behind the *muscle* behind the power behind the power… so to speak. They started out as vigilantes, but over the centuries they kind of morphed."

"*Centuries?*" Her eyes got wide.

"Yeah. Like I said. I don't pretend to understand it, but Azriel belonged to them for a while. The bottom line is, it's not the feds messin' around. And it's not your dad or Sandlin they're after."

She blinked, clearly not getting what he was trying to say. "So, who then?"

Data didn't want to be the one to do this. He didn't want to see what happened when she realized how much danger she was in. But there was no one else. "You, cutie. They're trying to set you up to take the fall for Gordon's misdeeds."

At first she just stared at him. Then she looked confused. "Me? That doesn't make any sense."

"Like I said, it's a long, drawn-out chain, but Azriel thinks you're taking the fall for Gordon. Someone in a front-level link in the chain of the Brotherhood has either been bought out or betrayed their masters. Which means they're trying to build an airtight case against you to present to the Brotherhood. Which means, if it happens, the Brotherhood will be sending someone to… take care of you as they see fit."

Her eyes got wide, and the color drained from her face.

Data could see the panic seizing hold, and it twisted something inside him. "There's a lot of stuff that will probably happen between then and now," he said, hoping to calm her as much as he could given the situation. "Azriel says these guys are smart. Despite being vicious, they're not usually indiscriminate in their dealings with others. The information they receive will be looked at by several different people. Azriel says that, if he can get what I sent him to the right person within the Brotherhood, they'll see it for what it is and will take the appropriate action on whomever was involved in the deceit."

Her lower lip quivered, but Zora held her ground. Data admired her for it even more. She might not understand all the variables, but she understood the gravity of the situation. "That's why I had to marry Gordon," she said. "Dad was always Gordon's fixer. Dad often remarked on how he'd been fixing Gordon's messes since college." She ducked her head. "Gordon must have been close to being caught in something my dad had to fix for him. If it's as big as you say, it all kind of makes sense now."

When she didn't elaborate, Data leaned in to catch her gaze. He didn't want to touch her or get into her personal space, but he needed the information she had. Once she met his gaze, he smiled at her. "I need to know what you know, cutie. I can help you better if you'll tell me."

"It's embarrassing," she admitted. "On our wedding night, Gordon said that, if Dad was getting half his fortune, Dad was going to know Gordon was... um... having sex with his daughter." She cleared her throat. "Anyway, I got the impression my dad's life was at stake if I didn't do what I was told."

"Not following, honey. You're gonna have to dumb it down." It was a phrase they often used together if one didn't understand what the other was talking about. Whoever was explaining would make it as simple as possible, even if it meant over simplifying.

"This is pure speculation," she said, "but based on what I was able to gather hacking into Gordon's system and our conversations and conversations I overheard between Dad and Gordon, I'm wondering if I wasn't part of the transaction."

"Still not following." But he was getting a sick feeling in his stomach.

"If Gordon did something big enough and hard enough for Dad to get him out of it, he'd have to pay Dad more. I've heard them negotiate with each other on more than one occasion. Also, if Dad had to pay someone else to get involved with the clean-up, there'd be more of a fee because obviously Dad's not eating that cost. Though they'd been partners since college, Dad wasn't smart enough to partner with Gordon on business sense. While dad was the fixer, he couldn't make the money like Gordon could. So, Gordon hired him. He paid him well -- we all had anything we wanted -- but I've heard Dad complain many times at how Gordon would be nothing without him, and he should be paying Dad more. If whatever price Dad asked was too much -- in this case, half Gordon's fortune apparently -- Gordon would have either made a counteroffer…"

"Or asked for something more." Data was following now. "Bastard ever indicate he wanted you?"

"Oh yeah. Several times, especially when he was drinking. Once he even put his hand up my skirt at a New Year's Eve party. I was barely sixteen at the time."

"Your dad know?"

"Yes. He told Gordon to leave me alone and told me Gordon didn't mean anything by it. He was drunk. He said he'd take care of it. I think that was more to get me to just shut up about it than it was to fix the problem. I'd been angry and threw a drink in Gordon's face. Dad was actually more angry about my outburst than the fact his business partner had groped his underage daughter, but then Dad probably knew he could use Gordon's obsession with me to his advantage someday."

"Much as I can understand an obsession with you, cutie, running his hand up your skirt doesn't constitute an obsession. Assault? Definitely. What else did the bastard do?"

"That was the only time he ever touched me before we got married, but he was always looking for excuses for me to be near him. He insisted I intern for him every summer after that. I was supposed to be learning how real estate markets worked and how investors knew when to buy and sell and all that boring stuff, but he mostly had me in his office typing up property listings and so on. He never actually touched me, but he always had an excuse to be right next to me. If he knew about my skill with the computer back then, he didn't say anything. Though, looking back, it was probably when he established my entrance into his system. You know. Just in case."

"How could he have known your dad would go for that? I wouldn't let my partner fuck over my daughter like that. I'd kill the sumbitch first."

"Because you're not *my* dad," she muttered. "Dad was always disappointed I wasn't a boy." She shook her head. "No... disappointment isn't the right word. Angry? Yeah, that might be a better word." She waved her hand dismissively, as if it didn't matter, when anyone looking at her could see it most certainly mattered. "Anyway, he and Gordon were in it for the long haul. Wives. Children. Nothing else mattered but how much money they could make. How much power they had." She took a breath. "Starting at that first stupid party, Gordon pushed me. Never far enough for me to go past my father to the cops or anything. Just hard enough that we were together and seen in public.

Six months ago, I went as his 'date' to a charity event my mother hosted. For all intents and purposes, it looks like we've been together for a couple of years."

"Except your social media has nothing of him on it. I know that for a fact because I scoured it. His has plenty of pictures of you. Some of you together, usually at one event or another. I see where you're going with the whole being photographed together thing, but you didn't have images of the two of you as a couple."

"I also don't post very often. Could look like I just don't like it. In any case, if there's money missing and Gordon took it, he's already got a plan in place to make it look like it's me. By marrying me the second there was trouble, he might be able to throw something together to make it look like I'd robbed him, or that I tried to get around the prenup I had to sign. You know. To get even with him."

Data thought about it for a while. "Juvenile, and more than a little disconcerting that a man could allow this to happen to his daughter, but given what Azriel told me, and what you found, I can at least see the likelihood of you being right."

She gave a shuddering breath, absently picking up a decorative pillow in the middle of the sectional and hugging it to her for comfort. "So, what do I do now?"

"Well, *we* head back to the Bones clubhouse. I don't want you here by yourself."

"I appreciate your concern, I really do, but I've involved you in my mess way more than I should have. I know I'm probably not ready to face something like this on my own, but I refuse to put you or any of your friends in danger."

He snorted. "OK, then." He said, standing up. "Will you at least see me out? Walk me to my bike?"

To his utter shock, she just smiled warmly at him. "Of course, D. You'll never know how much I appreciate you coming after me. I'm not sure I can ever remember anyone worrying over me like you have."

Data merely smiled as he stood. He ushered her outside, making sure her front door was locked as he pulled it closed quietly. She was too busy nervously eying the other bikers to notice what he was doing. Once they were to his bike, she turned to him, a polite but sincere smile on her face. She opened her mouth, probably to tell him good-bye, when he lifted her and set her on the bike.

"Wha --?"

"Helmet," he said, shoving it on her head. Men all around them roared with laughter as they started their bikes. He climbed on while she was still deciding what to do and started the big Harley, revving it a couple of times. Then he grabbed her arms and pulled them around his waist, turning to glance at her over his shoulder. "Hang on, cutie." He had to raise his voice to be heard over the noise, but she must have gotten the gist. The second he took off, she squealed and tightened her grip around his waist.

Chapter Three

All the way to the clubhouse, Zora knew she should protest. She should have hopped off that bike every time they'd stopped at a red light or stop sign, but she hadn't. Instead, she'd clung to Data like her life depended on it. And it just might have. It had taken them about an hour to arrive, and several men and women had met them in the parking lot. Surprisingly, there were a couple of young children as well as some older teenagers in the crowd as well.

"You're back!"

Zora looked around to see a girl about fifteen or sixteen bounding up to Data. She literally jumped into his arms. Had Data not caught her, she'd have either knocked him over or bounced off him. Well, except that she wrapped her arms and legs around him so tightly it was a wonder the big man could breathe.

"Hey there, glitter face! You look after Stunner while I was gone?"

She pulled back and nodded vigorously before hugging him tightly once more. "Uh huh! I also gots a *big* surprise for you!" She looked like a teenager, but she spoke and acted almost childlike.

Data simply held her close, patting her back several times like a doting father might a daughter he loved. Was this his daughter? The one he was taking a vacation to spend time with? Seemed about right.

"You do? Must be a big deal for you to be so excited."

"It is! So big I wanted to be the one to tell you first!"

A warm chuckle filled the air, and Zora felt a pang of something like jealousy when there was no reason for it. First, she and Data weren't a couple.

Second, assuming this was his daughter and he'd been gone looking for Zora, he probably had missed the girl. Third, he could damned well show affection to anyone he chose. Probably did. He was a kind man. She knew that firsthand. Though she felt awkward, she tried not to shift her feet once she'd climbed off the bike and removed her helmet.

"First things first, Suzie. I brought someone home with me. Don't you want to meet her?"

Suzie climbed down from Data quickly, putting her hands behind her back and looking at the ground as she murmured, "Hi." Obviously, the girl was shy around strangers.

Zora knew how the girl felt. She wanted to disappear too. "Hey there," she managed to squeak out as she gave the girl -- Suzie -- a little wave. "I'm Zora."

Suzie looked up then. "I like that name. It's pretty cool." Though she sounded like a child, she had the figure of a young woman. In fact, she thought Suzie might not be much younger than she was.

"Thanks. I like your name, too. Reminds me of summertime." Zora shrugged, feeling a little foolish. "I don't know why, it just does. Summer is my favorite season."

The girl smiled, big this time. "Me, too. I love swimming and you get to swim lots in summer."

"So, tell me," Data said, squatting down so he was more on Suzie's level, not towering over her. He looked much less intimidating that way, especially when he smiled. "What's your big surprise?"

A deep rumble sounded in the background. Just a single grunt really. Looking up at the porch to the big clubhouse, Zora saw an absolutely *huge* man frowning down at Suzie. He had long, shaggy brown hair and a full beard. Something sparkled in his beard, making it twinkle like a disco ball. "Suzie." All he said was her name, but it was obviously a warning.

"Uh oh," Data whispered loudly. "He seems like he's in a bit of a snit."

Suzie sighed, her face falling. "I only ever done what you told me to do if I wanted to help." Her voice was small, forlorn. A child who'd gotten caught doing something naughty.

"Well, if I told you to do it, it can't be as bad as all that. What's got Stunner in such a foul mood? Wait!" Data held up a finger in a "eureka!" gesture. "He couldn't get all the glitter out of his beard again. You didn't really use superglue this time, did you?" He looked up at Stunner as if to plead her case. "'Cause I was only jokin' about that. Mostly."

The big man cleared his throat then said, "She hacked Giovanni." His voice sounded rough. Like he didn't use it much.

If anything Data's smile got bigger. "Right." He looked at Suzie as if sharing a big joke. "Now, tell me what you really did. Did you spill soda on my favorite keyboard again?"

The girl's face fell. "No. I -- I really did get into Gio's system. The outer part of it, anyway. Somebody stopped me before I got any further."

Data sat -- or rather fell over -- on his ass. "You... what?"

"Yep. She hacked Giovanni." Another man stepped down from the porch, a wry grin on his face. "Azriel's been blowin' up the Goddamned phone for hours now."

"She's just a child, Cain." A slight woman in a pale pink skirt and a white blouse took the man's arm as she spoke to him. Cain patted her hand and smiled down at her tenderly.

"I know, Angel." He turned back to Suzie and Data. "Don't change the fact that, in the middle of an investigation, Azriel is having to soothe the delicate sensibilities of his tech guy."

"He's just upset that another girl beat him at his own game." Angel huffed. "And if Azriel is having to take time out of an investigation for this, I suggest he tell his tech guy to suck it up and grow a pair. Suzie could really help them if they'd take her seriously." Several men in the yard barked out laughter.

"Probably," Cain agreed. "Whatever, though, Azriel's constant calls are givin' me a fuckin' headache." He made a gesture, waving his hand from Data to Suzie to indicate he was talking to both of them. "Better get this shit under control."

Suzie burst into tears and ran down the sidewalk between the big clubhouse and the garage. Stunner glared at Cain before he went after her. The look he gave Cain should have frozen his blood. Instead, Cain gave a snort, his eyes carrying a good deal of mirth in them.

"Kid's got more brains than I know what to do with." He chuckled.

"Well, that's what I'm for," Angel huffed. "And you don't deal with it by intimidating her."

"Are you fuckin' kiddin' me?" Data finally managed to splutter. "Suzie broke into Giovanni's first line of defense?"

"Oh, yeah," Cain said. "You should have heard the likes of all the stuff going off in your office. You'll probably need to do some shit with your command center." Cain grinned at him now, not in the least upset. Apparently, they were just trying to impress upon Suzie the seriousness of what she'd done. They just didn't know how to actually go about it without laughing. Data wasn't certain if it was at his expense or Giovanni's.

"What happened with my rig?" Data got to his feet slowly, dread creeping into his face.

"Well, she let out a screech, then started unplugging everything. And I mean *everything*. No computer, router, or TV was safe. Anything that could possibly connect to the Internet, she cut. Some of it literally. She'd even started working on cell phones before Stunner threw her over his shoulder and took her to her room. Not sure what happened there, but she calmed down somewhat. More importantly, she stopped cutting cords to shit when she couldn't immediately find where they plugged in."

"This sounds like a bad time," Zora said softly, hoping only Data would hear. Unfortunately, that wasn't the case at all. "I can call a cab or something to get a ride home."

"On the contrary," Angel said, her face beaming. "You're exactly what Suzie needs."

"I'm sorry?"

"Of course! Data told us all about you. How you're smart and crazy good with computers. Suzie would love to have you to work with when Data is busy." The other woman hurried over to her side and pulled Zora into a big hug. "It's the perfect way to keep both your minds occupied."

"I need to be helping Data," Zora insisted. "This is my mess. He shouldn't have to do all the work."

"No," Data said. "But I won't be. And Angel's right. Besides, I think you're the perfect person to engage Suzie." He glanced toward the way the teenager had gone, a worried expression on his handsome face. "She's fragile in so many ways, but more intelligent than anyone realized."

"How old is she?"

"Just turned seventeen," Cain said. "She and the boys, Cliff and Daniel, came to us when Suzie was eleven. All of them had been abused. Suzie most of all, though the boys tried to shield her from most of it. Took her beatings most of the time, from what we've been able to get out of them. But... other abuses, they weren't always able to prevent." Cain pulled Angel into his arms, as if he needed the comfort more than she did.

"When they first got here, Suzie would hardly speak at all. I coaxed her back a little, but it was Stunner she really bonded with."

"And he with her," Data offered. "He has his own demons, but with Suzie he's a different man."

"Sounds like they need each other." Zora remembered the slight admonishment from Stunner in the form of a grunt and just her name. "Was he angry with her earlier?"

Data shook his head. "No. Not sure there's anything Suzie could do that would anger him. Hell, he lets her put glitter in his beard when she needs to be a kid and play."

"A few years ago, not too long after she got here, a prospect made fun of her. Called her behavior embarrassing and stuff," Cain said. "Told her he was making Stunner look like a fool or some shit by putting glitter in his hair and decorating the whole clubhouse double time for Christmas." The president of Bones looked like he remembered the whole incident fondly. Until Angel slapped his arm none too gently.

"Cain! Stunner beat that prospect to a bloody pulp! How can you laugh about it?"

"Well, the kid learned his lesson."

"Right." Angel rolled her eyes. "He learned not to fuck with Suzie anywhere Stunner could hear."

He shrugged. "Same result."

"Uh, actually…" A young man about mid to late twenties approached them. "You remember when Pig left?"

Cain tilted his head, looking at the guy curiously. "Yeah, Daniel. So?"

"So, he left 'cause Cliff beat the shit out of him again, and actually cut him. Told him next time he so much as looked at Suzie he'd cut his balls off."

Again, Cain grinned. "Yeah. Heard about that."

"Cain!" Angel looked horrified. Whether it was from her man's response or the threat Zora had no idea.

"What? Even Arkham said the little bastard should'a been nutted right there. He's just lucky it wasn't Stunner who got a hold of him."

Angel let out an exasperated sigh, then looked at Zora. "The men around here are barbarians on their good days." Then she smiled. "Come on. Let me show you around and introduce you to everyone."

* * *

The rest of the day passed in a whirlwind. Zora met so many people she would never be able to keep them all straight. She'd spent about an hour with Angel and some of the other women in the club, but all of them were "ol' ladies" of one club member or another. There were other women she met, but they weren't in the same group. Club girls, they were called. The only non-club girl who wasn't attached to a patched member was Suzie. All the club girls were friendly enough, but they didn't seem to welcome the ol' ladies or Zora into their group any more than the ol' ladies wanted to hang around the club girls.

Supper was a huge affair with grilled burgers, tenderloin, chicken, and hotdogs out by the pool. Data had been absent most of the time, but emerged just in time to snag one of the last burgers before the club girls cleaned up the mess.

Zora was so relieved to see him. Angel had been wonderful, and she'd gotten to talk with Suzie a little more, but she wanted her D. The man she'd grown to respect and care for, and quite possibly developed a crush on.

Then, like a breath of fresh air, she caught his scent. She turned, and he was striding toward her. At first there was a look of welcoming. Like he'd missed her as much as she'd missed him. Then, his expression just shut down. He'd stopped in front of her and gave her a tight smile.

"Everything OK?" she asked, wanting the man who'd swooped in and brought her to safety whether she'd wanted him to or not. He hadn't been mean about it, simply got her to do what he wanted by not giving her much of a choice. Or any choice, really.

"Yep. Had a few cords that needed replacing where Suzie had cut them, but no damage done I couldn't fix."

"That's good. I can help you set things back up if you want. I'm pretty good --"

"No need. I got it all fixed. You enjoying the party?"

"Um, yeah. Everyone's nice and the food is wonderful."

"Good," he said, nodding, obviously uncomfortable. "That's good." Then he looked over her shoulder, raised a hand in the air to wave someone toward them. "Let me know if you need anything. Angel should be able to set you up with a nice room until we get all this sorted out." Then he excused himself and was gone.

Zora looked over her shoulder and saw who he'd flagged down. One of the club girls. She thought her name was Mercedes? Or was it Topaz? She had no idea. All she knew was that Data had grabbed her arm and escorted her off. The woman giggled as they walked away.

Had Data punched her in the gut, Zora couldn't have been more shocked, surprised, and hurt. She hadn't expected them to live happily ever after, but she'd thought he'd maybe spend some time with her. Get to know her outside of their online relationship. He'd seemed to genuinely care about her, but obviously not the way she cared about him. A single tear escaped and slid down her cheek as she watched them go. Data gave the woman a roguish grin. That was the last she saw of them as they slipped into the crowd.

"Hey, little lady." A deep, soft voice with a drawling Southern accent brought her out of the trance she'd been drawn into. She turned, and the biggest man she'd ever seen stood behind her, his hands on his hips and a huge smile on his face. He was African American, and hugely muscled with a shaved head. His skin gleamed in the moonlight from the humid night air. "You look like you're lost."

"Yeah," she said, taking in a shuddering breath. "I guess I am."

"Data not bein' good to you?"

"No, he's wonderful. I'd be all alone with who knows what kind of people after me if he hadn't brought me here. I'm in his debt." She couldn't blame

Data for her stupid crush. He'd never led her on. Sure, they'd flirted from time to time, but nothing heavy, and he'd done nothing to continue that once they'd met.

His smile faltered, and a small frown appeared. "Then who made you cry? You point me in the right direction and I'll take care of 'em."

She couldn't help but let go some of the melancholy she felt. "While I appreciate the offer, making someone cry isn't a punishable offense. Besides, I'm responsible for my own feelings. This is no one's fault but my own."

"Not buying it, little miss. But I'll let go. For now." He offered her his hand. "I'm Shadow," he said. "Come on. They've always got a good movie goin' in the war room when nothin' big's happenin'. If it's too violent, you can pull rank as a visitor and make the boys watch a chick flick or something." He chuckled. "Nothing better than when someone gets to pull rank and the guys have to watch chick flicks."

"Wouldn't they just leave if they didn't want to watch it?"

"Nah. Mainly, they like watching the girls watch them. If they want to watch a movie for the actual content they'll go to a fuckin' theater."

The "war room," as Shadow'd called it, was packed with men and women all watching some silly romantic comedy.

"Looks like someone beat us to it," he said with a sigh. When she looked up at him, he'd looked like he'd just lost his favorite toy. "Fuck," he muttered.

"Wasn't this your goal? To get the guys to watch a chick flick?"

"Well, yeah. But half the fun is listening to them groan when they have to change it."

He took her hand and guided her to a corner with an empty love seat facing the insanely huge TV. It was more like a screen from a theater, it was so big, taking up one entire wall. They'd just sat down when Zora caught sight of the woman Data had left the party with. Sitting beside her, his arm over the back of her chair, was the man himself. Her stomach plunged. Could she sit here and watch this? What if he leaned in and kissed her?

Zora shook herself. It wasn't like it was any of her business. Or like he'd committed to her or even kissed her. They were friends. He was worried about her. Nothing more. Didn't keep her from feeling like she couldn't breathe.

"Shadow," she whispered, her voice catching. "C-can we just go?"

The big man glanced at her sharply, then narrowed his eyes and let his gaze move around the room. Zora started to get up, but Shadow stopped her with a hand on her thigh. He let out a breath when he saw Data with the woman. "Motherfucker," he muttered.

"Have you seen this one already, Zora?" His voice was still that soft, Southern drawl. Smooth as molasses, but it carried. Data glanced over his shoulder, and Zora immediately dropped her head.

"I -- no. I just..." She started to speak but Shadow leaned in and whispered in her ear.

"Just play along with me, little miss."

His voice and the soft breath of air at her ear made her shiver. It tickled her, and she couldn't help but giggle. When she did, she couldn't help a self-conscious look toward Data. He was looking back over his shoulder again. She barely had time to register his frown before Shadow, with a soft chuckle, cupped her cheek gently in his big hand and kissed her.

It was a gentle kiss, but full on the mouth. He coaxed her a little, and she found herself kissing him back. There was no tongue or anything heavy, just his lips sliding over hers until she felt herself relax into his arms. She hadn't even been aware he'd slid one arm around her. When he ended the kiss, he brushed his nose against hers affectionately. "You can thank me later, little Zora."

She was just trying to puzzle that out when she found herself being hauled out of her seat by one arm. "Ouch! Hey, stop that!"

"Data, if you bruise that sweet girl's arm, I will throw you a fuckin' beatin' the likes of which you've never seen." Shadow didn't look so pleasant anymore. Instead, there was a cold-blooded killer looking up at Data with death in his eyes.

Making a visible effort to calm down, Data let go of her arm, but pulled her solidly against him. "Noted, brother."

"Brother or not, you hurt her in any way, no one will ever find your body."

"You're right. I should have been more gentle with her." He brushed a kiss over Zora's head. "I'm so sorry, cutie. We'll look at your arm when we get up to my room. If I bruised you, I'll present myself back to Shadow for punishment."

"Stop it," she snapped. "Just stop." Shadow didn't take his gaze from Data, so Zora stepped between them. She turned to Shadow. "Can we please go?"

"Oh, no you don't, cutie," Data said, taking her hand this time and dragging her away from Shadow and out into the hallway. "You're comin' with me."

"I came with Shadow. You're being rude."

"Not as rude as I'll be if he hurts you again, little miss." Shadow wasn't quiet with his threat, and the whole room erupted in laughter. Data flipped them off as he urged her on.

"Where're we going?" she asked, dragging her feet a little. As much as she wanted to go with him, there had to be some ground rules. Some guidelines. *Expectations*. "You and I both have a date back there. I think we need to just go back --"

"Not fuckin' happening, cutie," he growled. He probably tagged on the "cutie" to keep from sounding so gruff, but it didn't really help.

"You're not being reasonable."

"No," he said, abruptly stopping and turning her to face him. He had her by both shoulders, hunched over so he was looking down at her face to face. "I'm not. But when I see you I'm not a reasonable person. For the record, I don't like you kissing other men."

"You think I liked you with your arm around another woman?" He'd raised his voice so she followed suite. "Tit for tat, I'd say."

"Oh, I plan on gettin' a little tit and givin' you a big tat before it's over, cutie," he muttered, then pulled her into his arms and kissed her.

Chapter Four

If Data lost his sanity over Zora, the first person he was killing was Shadow. The bastard had known there was something between Data and the little hacker. Fuck. Everyone probably knew. And he couldn't give a good Goddamn.

As his mouth moved over Zora's, Data swore he'd found something he'd been looking for his entire life. Kissing her was peace as much as it was war. Part of him wanted to take her to his room to hide her away from anyone who might hurt her. Another part of him wanted to tie her to his bed and see just how long they could both last before they passed out from pleasure. The sweetness of her breath, the way she moved against him as he deepened the kiss, was more than a mere man could handle.

"I am *so fucked*," he muttered before slipping his tongue into her mouth. Zora whimpered and clutched at his T-shirt. God, she was so fucking sweet. Her body molded against his on her own. When that happened, there was no way for him not to wrap his arms around her and hold her as tight as he could.

Sweet God above, she kissed him back. Her little tongue tangled with his, accepting his thrusts. She was untutored, but allowed him to lead, and fuck, she learned fast. Her little whimpers and moans sang in the hallway as he backed her up against the wall. He urged her legs up and around his waist as he mashed himself against her body.

Data had one hand fisted in her hair and the other around her waist. She gasped when he pulled her head back sharply to look into her eyes. He needed to see her. Needed to see for himself that she was good with this. If she was frightened or disgusted, he'd find a way to end it. If not, God help him because he was going to fuck her into oblivion. Age difference be damned.

Her eyes were closed, but her lips parted. "Look at me, Zora," he growled, tightening his hold on her hair. "Look at me now!"

With a little gasp, she did. Her pupils were dilated, her eyes glazed. Her cheeks were flushed, and her breath came in little gasps. Data looked into her eyes until he was certain she saw him. Really saw him.

"I want you, girl. Want to take you to my room and fuck the shit outta you." As words went, they weren't the most soothing. In fact, if he was trying to scare her that should do it.

"D," she gasped. "Data."

They stared at each other for long, long moments. The longer he gazed into her eyes, trying to figure out what to do, the more confused he became.

"Well? What do you have to say?"

She got a dreamy look on her face. Almost like she was high. "How many times will you do it?"

He didn't hesitate. "As many times as it takes. All fuckin' night. All the next fuckin' day. And the fuckin' day after that. I'll fuck you 'til I get my fill."

A giggle escaped. "Promise?"

"Goddamn," he muttered. He was trying to scare her off. Wasn't he? "Come on." He picked her up, cradling her against him as he carried her further down the hall and around the corner to his office.

His room was adjacent to his office. In fact, the only way into his room was through his workspace. He locked both his office door and the door to his room. When he had her inside, he pressed her up against the door and kissed her again, just as greedily as the first time.

Zora tugged at his shirt, her fingers sliding up his belly to his chest when she had freed the material from the waist of his jeans. Her little nails dug into his chest as if she were clutching at him, needing to hold him as close as he needed her. The little bite of pain was the biggest turn-on Data had ever experienced. It nearly freed the monster inside him clawing to get out and claim its mate.

Eager to see her, he shoved her T-shirt up along with her bra. Her tits were small and firm, the nipples pebble hard. He kneaded one, plucking at the nipple until she closed her eyes and moaned. With one arm still around her, he dipped his head and took one ripe peak between his lips and flicked the little bud.

Zora cried out, her nails biting harder into his chest. She arched her back, offering him more, which he gladly took. Had a woman ever tasted this sweet? Her skin was soft and smooth, erupting in a little sheen of sweat at his touch.

With a grunt, he fumbled with her jeans to unbutton them so he could slide his hand under the waist and between her legs. Her pussy felt like hot, wet silk. And mother fuck if she wasn't *sopping* wet! Her moisture seeped between the two fingers he'd slipped between her lips to glide back and forth over her pussy opening and her slit. He didn't penetrate her, only petted her gently. Even as he did, she squealed once before she widened her stance, her body stiffening and relaxing with each stroke. More and more juice slicked his fingers and her panties.

Off. He needed it all off.

Christ! She was so fucking responsive! Like all this was new to her. He tried to think back to what she'd said about her marriage to Sandlin. Hadn't she indicated that sex hadn't been welcomed? Fuck. And here he was practically forcing himself on her now. She might be in the moment, and he had no doubt she was enjoying herself, but did she really want this?

How could she? Zora was younger than his daughter! The age difference alone was off-putting. At least, it had to be for her.

Reluctantly, Data ended his assault on her. And he truly saw it that way. Was he no better than her father and husband? He knew he wanted her for more than a simple fling, but he couldn't communicate that to her knowing how difficult it would be for her. Gordon Sandlin was a good twenty years older than her -- so was Data. Was he just as bad as Sandlin for taking what he wanted?

God, he needed her! But, fuck! She was too fucking young for this! For him. He wanted to fall to his knees and weep in frustration. If he'd just had a little less of a moral code, he could taste what he knew would be the sweetest pussy in the whole Goddamned world, then give her even more pleasure than she gave him.

"Holy Christ," he bit out, shoving away from her with a hard, jerky movement. "Fuckin' hell."

"What's wrong?" Zora's voice was soft but urgent. He didn't dare look at her.

"This isn't -- I shouldn't have done this."

"But -- but why?"

"Because I just shouldn't have," he bit out. "I have no idea why I brought you here, but it was a mistake."

"I -- shouldn't have brought me…" She looked confused. Dazed. Data knew he sure fucking was. "Oh. I'm sorry." She turned around, to face away from him, fastening her jeans as she did. It took a little more time to straighten her top, but he gave her the time she needed.

When she reached for the door, he got there first, opening it for her. "You're married," he said by way of explaining. "It's not right."

"Oh. Yeah. I filed for divorce, but it won't be finalized for a few more weeks." Then she muttered. "Guess that should have been something I thought of instead of you." She moved into the office and straight to the door. She made it before he did, then out into the hall.

She looked lost. And why wouldn't she be? He hadn't told Angel to get her a room to herself when they'd arrived. They all probably assumed she'd be staying with him. He'd intended for it to be that way, but this had disaster written all over it. Then she took off down the hall. She didn't hurry or run, just put her shoulders back and strolled as if she knew exactly where she was going, and maybe she did. Looking at her now, she was the princess he'd seen in the few photos there were of her and Sandlin together. Yeah. She didn't belong with a roughneck like him. He might be a computer geek, but that was the only civilized part about him. She could do much, much better.

* * *

Zora did what she always did around Gordon when she wanted to cry but refused to. She put on a façade of indifference, shoving her shoulders back. She had absolutely no idea where she was headed, but she wasn't going to ask Data squat. If she could get out of here without being noticed, that was what she was going to do. If not, she'd find a place to curl up for the night. She was pretty sure Shadow would take her in if she went back to him, but she didn't want to do that.

Not because she didn't like the big man -- he seemed like more of a good guy than Data at the moment -- but because she didn't know what his motivations had been in the first damned place, and she was done playing games.

As she turned the corner, she glanced back down the way she'd come. Data wasn't even still in the damned hallway.

God! He confused her so much! Had he truly stopped because she was still married? If he'd dug into her past, surely he'd figured out the only thing between her and Gordon was a piece of paper they'd both signed. Add the fact that he'd forced her into sex anytime it had happened, and she didn't owe Gordon her fidelity. Not only that, but she wouldn't lose a second's sleep over it.

There were several people in the common room when she entered, but she did her best to avoid anyone. She waved and smiled when necessary, but kept moving as if she had a specific destination in mind. Suzie was the hardest to brush off and, when the girl approached her, Zora knew there was no way she could do it. Suzie had joined them in the middle of Angel's tour and had seemed to crawl out of her shell a few minutes later. Zora knew from Angel that the girl took a while to open up to new people. Suzie was so caring, asking after every single woman in their group with a smile and a hug. Girl was definitely a hugger. Angel had whispered to her that Suzie was more insightful than anyone she'd ever met. The girl just didn't seem to realize that sometimes, people wanted to keep secrets.

"Hi!" Suzie called. Her excitement practically bubbled over when she'd seen Zora walking through the room. She was such a conundrum. She acted like a child in so many ways, but Zora knew better. She'd seen firsthand how intelligent and empathetic the girl was earlier that day. As if to prove Zora's point, the second Suzie got close and got a good look at Zora's face, she frowned. Even though Zora had a smile plastered on her face, Suzie saw through it, and Zora knew she was busted. "Are you OK? What's wrong?"

"I'm fine. Where's your boyfriend?" As Zora hoped, that distracted Suzie.

"My what? I don't have a boyfriend."

"The big guy with the glitter in his beard. What's his name?"

"You mean Stunner?" She burst into giggles. "He's not my boyfriend!" She continued to giggle, but there was a becoming blush creeping up her neck. "Besides, he says I'm too young for a boyfriend."

"Oh, he does. You're seventeen. You could have a boyfriend if you want."

"Stunner said he'd have to approve any guy interested in me, and Daniel snorted. He said, 'good luck with that' and walked off." She frowned. "I'm not really sure what that meant. At first, I thought he meant no one would be interested in me, but I don't think Daniel or Cliff either one would say something so mean. Now, if it had been Pig..." She trailed off and ducked her head as if Pig saying it had been exactly what had happened, and her feelings were hurt all over again.

"No, Suzie. Not at all. Everyone here adores you. What he meant was, good luck with Stunner approving any guy who was interested. If you're waiting to have a boyfriend until Stunner says you can? Yeah. You probably won't have a boyfriend. Ever."

Suzie frowned. "Are you saying Stunner doesn't want me to have a someone? I'd be all alone then. All the men are finding girlfriends. Why am I not allowed to have a boyfriend?"

God, she was making an ass of herself. Suzie really was like a child in many ways. They'd said she'd had it rough, but didn't people usually harden up? Grow up quicker than they should? "Honey, what I mean is Stunner is very protective of you. He's not going to want to give up his position as your protector to another man because he wouldn't trust anyone to do it as well as he does."

"You've only met him once. How could you know?" She didn't sound whiny or petulant, only confused. As if, if she didn't know that, how could Zora?

"It only takes once, Suzie. That man adores you. Whether as a guardian or something more, I have no idea. But he cares for you. Deeply." She reached for the other woman, pulling Suzie into her arms. "I didn't mean to upset you. I'm so sorry."

Suzie hugged her back, enthusiastically. Which made Zora wonder how much positive physical affection the girl had had in her life because she it seemed like she was starving for it. Soaking it up like a sponge.

"You didn't upset me." Zora let her go and Suzie continued. "I don't read people very well sometimes. But I love Stunner. I don't know what I'd do without him."

"I don't think there's any need to worry about that." Zora grinned and pointed over Suzie's shoulder. The big man in question was headed their way, a frown on his face.

Again, Suzie giggled. "I might have given him the slip to come see you. But he was drinking a beer with Arkham and Trucker. I didn't want to interrupt."

"Might want to rethink doing that again. He doesn't look happy."

"Yeah. He can be a growly bear sometimes."

Stunner just grunted and held out his hand for Suzie to take it. She did without hesitation, and giggled once again as she waved to Zora.

She let out a sigh of relief. Now. If she could just get outside, she could call an Uber or something and get back home. If Data was right about her being in danger, it was a risk. But she needed some stuff from the house. She had a car. It wasn't untraceable, but she could still use it to get farther away. She'd drive to a larger city -- maybe Lexington or Louisville -- and ditch it. Then she'd take a bus somewhere. Somewhere out of the state. Maybe out west. She'd always wanted to see Kansas and Colorado.

It wasn't all that late, and people were still coming into the clubhouse, so no one was really paying her any attention. She managed to slip past the gate without no one stopping her. Why she expected them to not let her leave was beyond her, but she felt like she was breaking out of jail. Silly.

She walked down the road a few miles before pulling out the phone Stunner had given her and opening the Uber app to request a car. She enjoyed the walk and found a bar where she could order a drink while she waited. The Boneyard. How very family oriented.

"You look lost," the older man behind the bar said. "Need me to call someone for you?"

"No, thanks." She took her phone back out and placed it on the bar. "I'm good. I would like a Captain and Coke, if you have it."

He grinned. "I can do that for you, little lady." A few seconds later, he set her drink in front her. When she put a ten on the bar, he shook his head. "On the house."

"That's very sweet of you," she said. "But I can pay."

"I'm sure you can. But when a lady comes in here, Pops don't take their money." He hiked a thumb at himself, indicating he was the "Pops" in question. "Now. You got a ride home?"

"Yeah. Thanks for asking, though. It's sweet of you."

He chuckled. "I'd do it anyway, but Mama would have my hide if I didn't take care of the young ladies."

Zora turned over her phone and checked the Uber app, seeing if her requested car was close. She thought Pops had moved on to someone else, but when she raised her head, he was giving her a quizzical look.

"Thought you said you had a ride?"

"I do." She picked up her phone and shook it from side to side a couple of times, smiling at him. "Uber. Someone coming to pick me up. Should be here in fifteen minutes. If you'll let me sit here for one more drink, I'll be out of your hair."

"Darlin', you can sit here as long as you want, but I can call one of my boys to take you anywhere you want to go. No need for some stranger takin' you anywhere."

"Well, I wouldn't know your boys, and it would still be a stranger." She grinned. "Besides, I use them all the time. It's perfectly safe."

He scowled at her. "I guess I was just raised in a different time." He took a rag and wiped down the bar in front of her. "Ain't seen you here before. You new in town?"

"Never been here before. But yeah. New, I guess. I'm just here for the weekend." She smiled, crossing her fingers behind her back for lying. She was a horrible liar. Always had been.

"Uh huh," he said, apparently not buying it. "Well. Maybe you'll enjoy your drink here so much you'll stay for a while longer."

"You don't skimp on the Captain, so I'd say that's a definite plus."

"No watered-down booze here, little lady," he replied with a smile. "Where you headed after you leave Somerset?"

Zora started to give some kind of non-answer but didn't want to insult the guy by lying or evading. He was a nice guy. "Home. I have to get my stuff. Then… I'm not sure, really. I thought maybe I'd go out west."

"Everything OK, little lady? My boys can help if you've got trouble." He looked genuinely worried, and it melted Zora's hart just a little.

"Nothing to worry about," she said. "I can lose any trouble I need to. Besides, I've always wanted to see the beauty of the western states. I thought maybe Kansas or Colorado."

His expression hardened. "If you've got trouble, sweetheart, you shouldn't voice your destination out loud." He patted her hand. "Your secret's safe with me, but don't tell no one else. You hear me?"

"I --" she blinked. "You're absolutely right. I never thought of that." Her stomach rolled, and she had to put her clutch her hands below the bar so he didn't see them tremble.

"That's why you need the boys. Let me tell them and they'll protect you."

"I appreciate the offer, but I can't. It's best if I just go." She glanced at her phone when it buzzed. "My ride," she said. "It was good meeting you."

"You too, little lady." He frowned. "Let me walk you out." He hurried around the bar, grabbing a card from the end as he came to her. He handed it to her. "You stay safe. If you have any trouble whatsoever, you hightail it back here or call me. Me and my boys will protect you."

"I'll do that." Zora was surprised to find she really meant it. If she ran into trouble before she got out of town, she'd definitely run in this direction. To her surprise, the old man pulled her into an embrace. He was large and surprisingly strong. Zora was reminded of being wrapped tightly in Data's arms, and the urge to cry was so strong she had to squeeze her eyes shut. When he let her go, she headed out of the bar with a smile.

The Uber was sitting in a parking space next to the door, and she greeted the driver with a wave and a smile. He waved back, unlocking the doors before she climbed into the back seat. Once she was settled, he confirmed the address with her and left. Zora looked back at the bar and saw the old man at the door. He waved to her, but frowned as he did so. She waved back before sitting back and putting on her seatbelt.

Soon, all this would be behind her. It had been a mistake from the start, and she was headed back to the little house she'd bought. It seemed like a step backward, but she was trying to see it as a sidestep instead. She wasn't headed back to Gordon, and she wasn't looking to Data to be her savior. No. She could do this herself. She *would* do it herself. She just had to be careful. Once she got home, she'd put some real effort into falling off the grid permanently. She had the skills. Time to put them to good use. Like she should have done in the first Goddamned place.

Chapter Five

"They're on the move." The call came from the Shadow Demons tech guy, Giovanni. Data was at his computer, assimilating the information Gio was sending his way. "Looks like the lower echelon moving, and Azriel's contact says they didn't give the order."

"So it *is* a setup." Data sat back in his chair, finger curled over his chin as he spoke to the Shadow Demon on speaker phone so Cain, Torpedo, and Bohannon could hear.

"If they didn't have the go ahead from the top, they're definitely doing something not sanctioned. The Brotherhood has people on their way, but you're probably closer. They're pretty far reaching, but Somerset is mighty out of the way."

"No worries there. She's here and locked up tight. They can't get into our compound."

"Well, at least part of that is true." Data turned to see Pops in the doorway to his office, a grim expression on his face. "Your little Zora isn't locked up tight here at the compound."

Data froze. He opened his mouth, but nothing came out. What did he mean she wasn't in the compound?

"If she's not here, where is she?" As enforcer, Bohannon would be the one to take on matters of security. "Wasn't she with you, Data?"

Data swallowed. "She was. Went off on her own a couple of hours ago. I thought she was still in the clubhouse. No one said otherwise."

"Wait," Pops said. "Is this girl… your woman, Data?"

"No," he said, then shook his head. "Yes."

"Well, for fuck's sake, make up your mind, boy!" Pops was obviously not in a congenial mood. "Fortunately for you, I have your back. She has the Boneyard's card with my number on it as well as a tracking device on her."

Bohannon grinned. "And here I thought you didn't know shit about electronics, old man."

"I don't," Pops snapped. "Which is why I gave her the fuckin' card. There's a tracker in her purse, but I have no idea if it's turned on or if she'll still have it tomorrow." He took the five steps across the room separating him and Data. "She's runnin', DHS." Pops only called him that when he was pissed at him. Usually for making him use technical equipment when he was clearly uncomfortable with it. He called him DHS because Data worked for the Department of Homeland Security in cyber security. Pops meant it more as mockery than respect when he used it this way. Normally, Data would take exception and the two would bicker back and forth until one of them got angry enough to stomp away.

Not today. Data deserved anything Pops wanted to dish out.

"Did you drive her away? Because, from all accounts, the two of you seemed to be getting along fine when you picked her up and when you first got here. You've been working with her online for years. Now she runs?"

"I know, Pops. This is my fault. I'll fix it."

Pops pointed his finger at Data, stabbing him in the chest. "You better. She's a sweet girl."

"She's more than a sweet girl," Data muttered. "And she deserves more than anything I'm offering."

"Wait." Cain rubbed his eyes with one hand. "What did you do, Data? Exactly."

He shrugged and sighed. "She's twenty years younger than me, Cain. My daughter is older'n her, for Christ's sake!"

"So? What's that got to do with anything?"

"I kissed her. I nearly fucked her. When I finally came to my senses, I implied I shouldn't have brought her to my room for sex because she was married. I'm sure she took it to mean I looked down on her for that, even though I know she didn't have much of a marriage to begin with and had already filed for divorce. Besides, it was certainly not a marriage she ever wanted. Anyway, she didn't leave in the best of moods."

"Can't imagine why," Torpedo said dryly.

Data gave him a warning look. "We need to find her."

"She said she had stuff to get at home. I'd start there," Pops said before shooting Data a killing look. Then he left. Pops was never a man of many words. Which is why Data always took what he said to heart.

"Fuck," he bit out softly. "This is all my fault."

"Worry about blame later. Right now, she's got some fuckin' dangerous men on her tail. Luckily we know where she's going and we can get there first," Cain said. Then he turned to face the phone and the open line, as if that would help him see the man on the other end. "Right?"

"Depends on where your girl is. Give me the signal specs."

Data was already at work finding the signal for the device Pops had slipped her. Once he found it, he forwarded it to Giovanni. "He's right. She'd headed to the place she rented and had intended on buying. That address is in the message I just sent."

"Got it," Gio confirmed. There was a small silence, probably while the other man did some calculations. "If you leave now, you'll be about twenty-eight minutes ahead of them. I suggest you not fuck around."

"On it," Data said, snagging his jacket. "You keep an open link to me, Gio. I need to know every move she makes."

"There are plenty of men here who know where she lives, Data," Cain said, inserting himself between Data and the door. "You said yourself when you sent Viper after your daughter, you're not a hunter."

"No. But she's wily. She knows she's being hunted. She'll be on her guard. I know where she lives and can get there the quickest. She trusts me."

"Maybe," Shadow said, shouldering his way into the room. "But, apparently, you're not on her list of favorite people right now. Perhaps you need to send someone who's in good with her."

"If you mean you, you smug bastard, the answer is 'no.'" Data growled. "I sent Viper to find my daughter because no one knew where she was. I know where Zora's headed and can take care of her myself. I can get there before she leaves and take her with me into hiding. We'll wait until Gio says the Brotherhood has their end under control. Then I'll bring her back."

"And if she doesn't want to come?" Shadow raised an eyebrow at him as if to say, *Then whatcha gonna do, you motherfucker?*

"She doesn't get a choice."

Shadow looked as if he were about to argue that when Cain raised a hand. "Data will take Bohannon and Shadow with him. The three of you can ensure Zora's safety. But if Zora isn't comfortable with you, Data, Bohannon or Shadow will stay with her and you *will not argue.* You will come back to the club. You don't follow that rule, you're gone."

Like hell he'd leave her. He didn't have to say it to Cain. Cain knew Data would call his hand if Zora protested. No way in fuck he was leaving her again. He didn't care if she wanted him there or not. She'd wanted him before. He could gain her trust again.

Without another word, he left the room, heading for his bike. He didn't wait to see if Bohannon and Shadow followed him. Simply started up his hog and sped off, heedless of the flying gravel. He'd fucked up mightily. It was time to fix what he'd broken.

* * *

The house was just like Zora had left it. Hadn't been that long, though it felt like ages. It was hard to believe only about twelve hours had passed. Hard to believe her prince charming had turned into such an ogre. She'd cried the entire hour-long drive home. As happy as she'd been to see Data when he'd first appeared at her house, she'd been equally devastated to leave him behind and go back. On the ride there, she'd gotten angry as well as hurt and had decided she'd rather face whatever danger she was in by herself than go back to Data. She hadn't asked for his attention, but once she had it, she hadn't wanted to let go. He seemed to know that, and it made the situation that much worse.

Fuck it. Fuck *him*.

The second she stepped inside the house, she knew something wasn't right. The sweet scent of cigar smoke tickled her nose, a scent that shouldn't be there.

"Who's there?" she asked. Why, she had no idea. The smart thing would have been to turn and run. She was in her house, but she'd only been there a few weeks. There were no neighbors. No one to run to. All she had was the hope that no one heard her enter and she could get back to her car and out of there before someone came after her.

"I've been sent to bring you home, Zora." The slightly accented voice was vaguely familiar, but she her mind refused to go there.

"I am home," she said, reaching to flip on the light. Sitting on her sectional was the one man she feared above all others. Drago. Gordon's personal bodyguard. She had never interacted directly with the man, but he'd always intimidated her whenever she'd thought about getting out of line with Gordon. Or refusing his advances. Whenever Gordon had initiated sex with her, Drago had always been nearby. He never interfered, but his presence was enough to render her docile with Gordon. The look in Drago's eyes then had been one of cold heartlessness. Same as it was now. He had a job, and the only thing important to him was getting it done.

"You can come with me easy way, or hard way. Choice is yours."

With more bravado than she felt, Zora lifted her chin. "I'm not going anywhere. You'll have to kill me, because I've let Gordon touch me for the last time. I'm not going back."

"I can assure you, he has no interest in touching you or anything else. He merely needs you back to do a job for him."

"If he thinks I'm doing anything for him ever again, he's delusional." The adrenaline was kicking in now. She had to be very careful with Drago. She'd always got the impression he'd rather kill her than look at her. Like she'd be fun sport. "I know about the embezzlement. I know he's in deep with some really scary people. From what I've heard, I don't think Gordon or my dad realize exactly what they've gotten themselves into."

Drago's head tilted, the only expression she'd ever seen from the man. "Explain."

"They plan to set me up to take the fall because of my computer and network skills. What they don't know is the Brotherhood is on to them. They know it all."

Drago blinked several times, then raised a gun and pulled the trigger.

Zora screamed instinctively, ducking, but there wasn't a loud bang. Instead, there was only a soft click, but something struck her thigh with a heavy, sharp sting. The thick but short shaft of a dart stuck through her jeans about three inches above her knee. Right in the big muscle of her leg. Without thinking, she yanked it out in confusion.

"What the hell?"

"Tranquilizer. Did you really think I'd shoot to kill?"

"Well, yeah," she said. Strangely, she didn't feel any different. Shouldn't she be dizzy or something?

He chuckled. "Little bird, you're not worth killing." She must have given him a funny look because he immediately raised his hands in surrender. "I mean that literally. They're not paying me enough to kill you. Only to bring you back to Gordon."

"It must be pretty important if Gordon let you leave his side to come get me."

"Well, little bird, it is. If he wants to stay alive." Then he shrugged. "If you're right, it won't matter anyway. Brotherhood isn't a group you mess with. Gordon and Frank knew when they started their scheme. Of course, now I know there is mischief going on, I must inform my boss."

"I thought Gordon was your boss." Zora was starting to get dizzy now. The room spun gently, but she knew it was only a matter of time. Apparently the dart was working its magic.

"No, little bird. I work for..." he waved a hand dismissively, "someone more powerful than your husband or your father. Frank was a fool to allow Gordon to take you from him. He wanted money and thought he could handle situation before he was found out, and he might have. If not for you. Your new friends, too." Drago had been glancing at his phone from time to time since he'd shot her. Not once had he reacted to anything he'd seen on the screen. Now, he raised his eyebrows. "New friends who are just as resourceful as you." He turned the screen to face her, as if he were showing her the message. It wasn't like she could see it. Not only was he too far away, but her vision was starting to blur. "They are on way, and I've been recalled."

Recalled? "Whad's dat mean?" Oh, Lord, her words were slurring. She was going to be helpless with this man. He had never done anything to her before, but she wasn't her friend. He would do what he was paid to do.

"It means, little bird," he stood and crossed to her, "That you've been given a stay of execution, so to speak. Lie down and relax. You can't fight the drug. You'll only get sick, and you'll still pass out."

"What're you gonna do?"

He gave her a smile that wasn't unkind, putting a pillow down and urging her to lie on her side. He covered her with one of the throws she had folded on the back of the sectional. "I'm going to try and slip by your friends. If I don't, there may be a small battle, but you won't be hurt."

"Please," she managed, her vision now going black around the edges. "Don't hurt them. They're only here because they're obligated. I ran off, and they probably don't like that I didn't tell them."

He chuckled. "Little bird." She tried to open her eyes, but he placed a gentle hand over them, urging her to keep them shut. "I think you're cared for more than you know. Listen to me carefully before you pass out. Stay with these men. They'll protect you from people like me."

It was the last thing she remembered before the darkness took her.

* * *

Data pulled in front of Zora's house. The big hog he rode would announce his presence like a klaxon, but he couldn't have given two shits. That's what Bohannon was for. He'd have Data's back and kill any motherfucker who came at them. Well, if Data didn't get to them first.

He pulled his gun and chambered a round before calling out. "Zora! Zora, answer me!" Data stormed up the porch steps and burst into the small living room, weapon at the ready.

"Goddamnit, Data," Bohannon bit out from behind him. "Clear the fuckin' place first!"

"You and Shadow clear it," he muttered as he spotted her lying on the couch. He knelt beside her, feeling for a pulse at her neck. She didn't respond, but her heart seemed steady and strong. Then he spotted the tranquilizer dart on the coffee table. "She's been tranked. Someone got here first. Giovanni," he spoke, knowing the other man could hear through the

Bluetooth headset he wore. "What the fuck? That your people?"

"They are *not* my people, Data," Giovanni snapped. "I used to be part of them but managed to leave. It wasn't easy, believe me. My contact says they got a message from a plant sent to keep an eye on Gordon and Frank. Says the man, Drago, was under orders from Gordon to bring her back. Since the Brotherhood believed Zora was involved, the Brotherhood gave the OK for him to leave his charge. He says this Drago knocked her out once he got the information delivered to his sat phone. Satellite service is glacially slow, so he was going on his last set of instructions. Bottom line? He let your girl go when he got the most current information. He couldn't have her following him so…" Data had put him on speaker phone so the others could hear so he didn't have to explain.

"Her husband gonna let her go?"

"Oh, don't think for a second Gordon is going to let her go without a fight. It's his life on the line," Giovanni said. "Drago will either tell him he couldn't find her, or he'll disappear and keep a watch on Gordon from a distance so the Brotherhood has immediate access to Gordon if necessary. But Gordon won't give up, even if he thinks Drago failed. And he knows where to find her now."

"Fine," Data snapped. "We hide her until the Brotherhood takes care of this."

"They'll want to talk with her," Giovanni warned. "Will insist on it."

"Tell them no." No way Data was letting anyone like that near his Zora. "She's innocent in all this. They don't need anything from her."

"They need to know what she found and how she found it. They will want to hear firsthand. Not from you or me or the data she passed on."

"Fuck!" This was getting him nowhere, and Zora might need a doctor. "Tranquilizer darts are hard to control in humans. I need Mama to take a look at her," Data said, getting increasingly worried that Zora hadn't even tried to wake up. "I need to get her back to the club, but, I swear by God and Sunny Jesus I'm not letting any of those bastards near her." He turned to Bohannon. "My instinct is screaming to get her to the mountains. The cabin has all the security we need, and it's easily defended."

"Are you sure you're up to this?" That was Shadow. Until now, the man had been silent. Now, he gave Data his most intimidating stare. "She don't need you being a jackass along with the threats."

"I got this, Shadow," he said, not giving the other man time to say anything else. "She's mine, and I got this."

"Fuck," Giovanni said. Even through the phone, Data could hear the other man's frustration. "Get her to wherever you need to. But do it quickly. You've got maybe ten minutes to get out and away. On the off chance she's gone when they reach her place, there are enough people on the way to follow anyone they come across out of that fucking holler."

"I thought you said the Brotherhood knows what's goin' down," Bohannon bit out. "Can't they call off the dogs now?"

"Can't. Tried. No one's answering. From reviewing everything you've sent me, no way those morons Gordon and Frank did this on their own. I'm willing to bet the bunch on their way to get Zora is in just as deep. Which means it's in their best interest not to answer. The very remoteness of Zora's choice of homes guarantees they have a good reason for not answering their masters."

"We have to go," Data said. "Now. It will take us a good five minutes to get out of this holler, and another fifteen to get off the main road to take the dirt trails to the cabin."

"You'll have to take the rough path," Bohannon said, "if you're gonna get there without being seen."

"Can't exactly take her on the bike," Data mumbled. "Need something off road."

"Trucker is on the way," Giovanni informed them. "We've been keeping the club informed as it all happens, and Cain sent him on with a side-by-side. Figured it might be best to get completely off the grid. It'll take him some time to get to you, but you can take her on the bike to the old strip mines. He'll meet you at the unloading point."

Data nodded slowly, then with more conviction. "Yeah. They might find where we went off road, but they'll never find their way through the maze of trails, especially not to the cabin." He glanced at Bohannon. "I can get her that far on the bike."

Bohannon nodded at Shadow. "Let's go. You'll need as much time as you can get."

"Hope you've got some rope, Bohannon," Data said. "She's completely out of it. No way she stays on unless she's tied to me."

"Rule number one," Bohannon said with a grin.

Shadow tossed something to Data. He caught it in midair. "Always have a knife." He shrugged. "Rope is a close second." Shadow gave Data a grin for the first time since before things all went to hell, and Data settled a little. Finally. *Finally*. He was doing right by his girl.

He picked Zora up and kissed her forehead gently as he cradled her against his chest. She seemed so small there in his arms. All he wanted to do was to lie down with her and hold her while she slept. He wanted to be there to comfort her when she woke. To apologize for the way he'd acted toward her. Then he wanted to explain that she belonged with him. No one else. Well. There'd be time enough for that. Who knew how long they'd need to be hole up in that hunting cabin? He'd explain things to her then.

Data carried Zora outside to his bike. With Shadow's help, he sat her in front, turning her so she faced him. Her legs straddled his hips, and her head rested against his chest. Shadow and Bohannon tied her ankles around his waist and wrapped a length of rope around the two of them so they were tied together at the chest. Data tucked her arms between them before starting his bike. Bohannon helped him drape a soft blanket around her body, and Data tucked it between his chest and her body to secure it. It would be warm, and they could probably use it later. Finally, he shoved a helmet on her head. Shadow secured it and gave him a nod before going to his own bike. Was it the ideal situation? No. But sometimes a man had to improvise.

* * *

The wind was cool in Zora's hair. She wasn't cold, but she was a bit uncomfortable. At least, her hips and legs were. She tried to shift, to move them from the cramped position, but couldn't. She seemed to be tied...

Oh, God! It all came flooding back. She'd been drugged. Gordon had sent his bodyguard after her.

"No!" She tried to cry out, but as her senses came back, she realized she was moving very fast on some sort of open vehicle. A motorcycle? Its engine was loud and vibrated throughout her body. She shivered and struggled, finding her hands weren't tied. But how much did she dare fight while riding a motorcycle? She could get herself killed.

The second the rider became aware of her struggles, he let off the gas and stopped. "Hey, there cutie. It's OK. I've got you."

"D-Data?"

"That's right, honey. You're safe. But we've got to go a little farther. I've got backup coming with a safer and more comfortable ride. We're gonna need it where we're going. Can you hang on like this a little longer?"

"I-I think so."

"Just tuck your arms back between our bodies and relax. I've got everything under control. There. That's it." He praised her. "Let me tuck the blanket back around you. Can you hang on to it and keep your arms tucked in? It will keep the blanket tight so it doesn't flap in the breeze."

"Yeah. I can do that."

"Good. You're doing great. Just relax into me. I won't let anything happen to you."

Once she settled, he took off again. She realized they weren't going very fast. Good thing, too, because the terrain was extremely rough. It wasn't long before they stopped. He cut the engine then pulled off her helmet.

"Hey there," he said, smiling down at her. "Still dizzy?"

"Yeah. Where are we?" Zora had no idea what she was supposed to be feeling, but she was relieved it was Data who had her. When she passed out earlier, she'd just known she'd be back in Gordon's hands when she woke.

"Strip mines. Not too far from your house, just… away from everything and everybody. Especially this time of night."

"Where are we going?"

"Bones has a hunting cabin up here. Cain owns the land. Bought it a few years back when it went up for sale. He built a little place. Not much more than a shack, but it has cover, plumbing, and a propane stove. He keeps it stocked with nonperishables. Usually gets used in the fall by Bones. Can't be sure no one else knows about it, but it's pretty out of the way. Even for the trail riders around here. Put it there on purpose."

Someone untied her ankles and she moved, her legs still draped intimately over Data's. That's when she noticed Shadow and Bohannon.

"Are we all going?"

"Nah, little miss," Shadow said with a smile. "Waitin' on your transportation. Trucker's bringing a ride bit more suited to the landscape."

"It'll be a while," Data said. "Why not just rest your head on my chest and close your eyes. You've got to still be feelin' the effects of that shit."

"I'm sorry," she said, not sure why. He was the one who hurt her feelings. Not the other way around. "I shouldn't have left."

"We'll talk about that later, but none of this was your fault. I was an ass."

"Yeah," she murmured. "You were. Butthead."

His warm chuckle was the last thing she heard before she drifted off again.

* * *

The next time Zora woke, she was being carried. A hushed murmur of voices around her seemed to blend in with the sounds of night bugs and foliage rustling in the breeze. She was shuffled around before she heard the sound of heavy boots on a wood floor. Oh. They must be at the cabin Data talked about. She tried to ask, but nothing came out.

"Shh, cutie. I've got you. You're safe."

Safe. That remained to be seen. While she had no doubt Data would defend her life, it was her heart she was most concerned about.

"Data..." His name came out a breathy whisper. He laid her on a small cot. It was clean, and the linens smelled fresh. "What's going on?"

"Just settling you in for the night. Trucker brought some clean sleeping bags and a few provisions for us. We've got some things here all ready, but this will give us as much time as they need to make sure everything is OK for you to come back."

"So, we're in the middle of nowhere?"

He chuckled. "Oh, yeah, baby. Ain't no one findin' you here. And if they do, I've got an arsenal at my disposal to defend you."

She lay back on the cot and pulled the blanket he'd draped over her closer. "Gordon's not going to let me go, you know. I'm the only thing keeping him alive."

"We're on it, cutie. The Brotherhood is sending people to Gordon as we speak. We just need to keep you safe until word gets out everything is out in the open."

"So, it's not just Gordon who's after me?"

"No, honey." Then he shook his head. "No, that's not exactly right. It is Gordon, but he's got help he wasn't supposed to have. He's made some deals with some very bad people. Unfortunately, you're the collateral damage."

"I already knew he was in over his head. What *don't* I know?"

"That he's managed to score the help of low-levels in a very powerful organization. The upper levels are taking great exception, but they have to reach their underlings before they can stop them. They're after you, and there is little to no cell service out here. Only sat phones can get through with any reliability, but they're not carrying them. You and me are gonna hide out here for a few days. Give everyone time to be on the same page."

"Drago indicated as much. He said he'd been recalled. Do you know what that means?"

"If he works for the Brotherhood, then he's gotten the message that you're not to be harmed or touched. They won't actually protect you, but they are after anyone in their organization not strictly under their control. That Gordon was able to gain even a modicum of cooperation from these guys speaks to how charismatic he is. And how much he believed he could pull this off himself. Anyone associated with these guys knows the penalty for disloyalty is death."

"What?" Zora was stunned. This was fucking serious. She knew she needed to focus on that, but her eyelids were so heavy. How could she be so sleepy when there was so much danger?

"Gordon and your father have both signed their death warrants, along with anyone they had helping them. Since this Drago guy pulled back when he was called off, he's probably not in the same group." Data shrugged. "Don't know. Don't give a flyin' fuck, either."

"So what do we do?"

"We get some sleep. Then we talk. It's gonna be a couple days at least, so we've got plenty of time for both."

She closed her eyes, stifling a yawn. "I guess."

Data sighed. "Scoot over there, cutie."

She did without hesitation, going on blind instinct. "What are you doing?"

Pulling her into his arms, he settled her on top of him, the blanket still securely around her. "Holding you while you rest. No one can get you while you're with me. I'll keep you safe."

"No, you won't," she whispered. "You're the most dangerous person to me in the whole world." Then she drifted off.

Chapter Six

A cool breeze wafted against Zora's face as she slowly woke from what had to be the deepest sleep known to man. She didn't really want to wake up at all, but the breeze beckoned persistently. As did the scent and feel of warm man beneath her.

Data... D. Her D.

She was lying on top of him, sprawled out with her legs on either side of his hips, her head resting on his chest. She was still wrapped in her blanket, but his strong arms were also wrapped around her, securing her in the blanket as his big hand rubbed up and down her back absently. His thick erection pulsed between her legs where she lay against him. It took her a moment to realize what it was, but she gasped softly once she did.

"I'm sorry," he rumbled. Then he stilled. "No. I'm not sorry. You're just going to have to get used to seein' and feelin' what you fuckin' do to me every time I look at you. Or touch you. 'Cause I ain't stoppin', either."

She pushed herself up slightly to look at him. "What?"

"I'm not pretending I don't have a fuckin' hardon the size of Texas for you, cutie." He brushed a curl of hair off her cheek and tucked it behind her ear. "I think I had a thing for you long before we met. One of those stupid Internet things I guess. Before I even knew what you looked like I craved talking to you. That emotional attachment." He cleared his throat, looking uncomfortable. "Definitely thought you were older, but I'm just selfish enough not to fuckin' give a damn."

"You... *want* me?"

"Don't look so shocked, cutie. I know I'm an old man compared to you, but I can still show you a good time if you let me."

She tried to push even farther away, but he held her fast. God, it was such a thrill to know that, if he didn't want her getting away from him, there was no way she could. Not because she liked being helpless, but because she liked being helpless with Data. She had no idea why, but she liked that he didn't let her put distance between them. Physically or emotionally.

"I don't do casual, D. The next man who has my body won't take it unless I want him to, and it won't be something casual. I'll never let a man touch me that I don't trust with my life. And my heart."

"Lucky I'm that man, Zora."

"They why did you push me away before?" No matter how much she tried to hide it, she knew she sounded hurt. She didn't want to show weakness now. Not with Data. He wouldn't ever respect her if she showed how weak she felt near him like this. He could destroy her with one cruel word or gesture because he'd been the only person to help her cling to sanity when she'd been given to Gordon. If it hadn't been for D, for Data, she'd have lost faith. In life. In herself. She had never let him know. Never said anything because she'd known in her heart he'd have come for her, and she never wanted to risk him. To her, D was all that was good and kind in the world. She'd always known there was more to him. That he was probably a hard-ass. But not with her. Never with her.

"Because you deserve better than a man old enough to be your father. Fuck, Zora! You're younger than my own daughter! The last thing I want is for you to be saddled with someone more than twice your age."

It took her a moment to comprehend what he was saying. "You don't think of me as a daughter, do you?"

He barked out a laugh. "Fuck, no! Are you fuckin' kiddin'? Girl, I want you like I've never wanted a woman in my entire life. And I've had a very active sex life." He pulled her closer, so close she could feel his warm breath on her face. "But I've changed my mind."

She blinked several times, unsure if she'd heard him right. Did he bring her here just to torture her? Was he some kind of sadistic asshole bent on breaking her for some unnamed transgression? "Changed your -_"

"Yep. I don't care if being with an old man embarrasses you or not. I'm keeping you. I'll make you happy, and I'll keep you satisfied."

"You're confusing me!" She tried to pull away again, but Data just flipped them over so he lay on top of her, his big body settled between her legs. Without even trying to disguise the movement, he thrust his hips, sliding over her mound. Even though she still had on her clothes, she felt that sensuous, primal movement all the way from her clit to her nipples.

"Then stop thinkin' and kiss me, cutie. Cause if you don't, I'm gonna start kissin' you." When she still hesitated, he chuckled before lowering his mouth to hers.

Bliss…

If she lived to be a hundred, she'd never get over the way she felt when Data kissed her. She'd never liked kissing before. Gordon only did it to assert dominance, and she'd only ever kissed one boy before him. Neither of them had really known what to do, and the boy had been all tongue. Kissing Data was like a dance. Before, he'd been rough, hard. Driving. Now, he was gentle as he coaxed her response. He needn't have bothered. She was all about kissing him. She needed to. Needed this closeness and connection they had together. Nothing in her life had ever been this right. And she wasn't about to let him take it away. Not again.

She cupped his face with her hands, urging him to look at her when all she really wanted to do was to go on kissing him forever. But this had to be done first.

"What is it, cutie? Am I movin' too fast?"

"No," she whispered, trying to find her voice. She cleared her throat. "I just need you to know this is it. You make love to me, you make me yours… I can't go back to being without you, D. Not after having even this short amount of time with you."

He grinned, brushing his nose against hers. "Not happenin', babe. Even if I don't make love to you right now, I'm keepin' you. It'll happen eventually, I'm sure, but you're with me now. And I don't give up easily, nor do I share. You're just gonna have to tell Shadow to fuck off."

She giggled when he smiled warmly at her. "Oh, Data!" She pulled him back to her, kissing him several times. "I…" She cleared her throat again. "I know it's soon, but, well, I love you. I'm learning about the romantic stuff, but *I love you*! The man who's been so kind and patient with me on the Internet. I see that man here too, but more. And I'm learning how much I love the 'more' as well."

"Love you too, cutie. At first, it was just infatuation, but yeah. That shit's grown. I think having the flesh-and-blood woman in front of me did something to me." He licked at her lips teasingly, watching her as he did. "So, we good? I'm yours and you're mine?"

Zora couldn't help the giggle. "Definitely. Except you're gonna have to seal the deal. Right here. Right now."

"That mean you're gonna let me fuck you? 'Cause I can do that."

"Oh, yeah. I'm definitely gonna let you fuck me."

"You know, I ain't got condoms here."

She shrugged. "Are you clean?"

"Absolutely. Mama makes sure we all get tested from time to time 'cause she worries. You?"

"The one thing Gordon did was use a condom. I don't think he wanted any children to complicate matters."

Data snorted. "More likely he thought children could be used against him, and he'd be right."

"It really wouldn't have mattered. Gordon is incapable of caring about anyone but himself."

"Then we start this together. Nothing between us."

She nodded solemnly, getting the double meaning. "Nothing between us, Data."

He sat up on his knees. Zora's legs were draped over his thighs, spread wide for him. Data whipped off his shirt while she wiggled out of hers. He undid her pants and pulled them -- panties and all -- over her hips.

"Take it off," he growled, nodding at her chest.

Zora unhooked her bra and pulled it off. She thought she should probably be self-conscious about him seeing her completely naked, but how could she possibly be when his eyes were drinking her in like he was starving for the sight of her? As he stared, she was very aware of her nipples peaking under his gaze.

He'd shoved his jeans down his legs but sat there staring at her. Since he was looking his fill, Zora figured she might as well do the same. It wasn't like she hadn't been dying to since the first day she'd actually seen him.

God, he was magnificent! Muscles rippled over his chest and abdomen. A light dusting of dark hair sprinkled with gray spread over his chest and down the center of his torso. His cock stood out long, thick, and proud against a nest of dark curls, the tip leaking pre-come as it pulsed.

He gripped her hips and pulled so that her pussy mashed against him. He rocked slightly, his cock pushing through her lips. With every thrust through her folds, his dick rubbed over her clit. After the second or third thrust, she cried out helplessly, unable to fight the pleasure and not wanting to.

"Ah, yeah, baby. That's it," he whispered. He gripped the tops of her thighs, pulling her along his length as he rocked slowly. "Let me hear what you want."

Unabashedly, she rolled her hips, scooting herself as close to him as she could get. When she raised herself up on her elbows, Data pushed her back, shaking his head. The look on his face should have scared her. Instead, she reveled in it. He was nearly as greedy for her as she was him.

"Do that again," he growled. So she did, until he was slick with her moisture. "God, your fuckin' sexy! And you're all mine."

He placed his palm on her lower belly, spreading his fingers wide. His hand nearly spanned the width of her, so big against her small frame. With a gentle but rough slide, he moved his hand up her torso, between her breasts, to rest around her neck. She lifted her chin, giving him as much access to her as he wanted. Using that one big hand around her delicate throat, he held her in place while he guided himself into her with his other hand. Then he shoved himself inside her in one strong, wet glide.

Zora gasped as he filled her. His width stretched and burned, but it also started an ache deep within her that desperately needed to be satisfied. Her whole body was on fire from the inside out. Data's other hand gripped her hip right above her thigh in the crease, holding her to him as he kept himself buried as deeply as he could. She could feel his dick pulsing as her pussy welcomed him.

"Mother fuck! *Goddamn mother fuck!*" Data's face was so strained, an artery pulsed at his temple. "How the fuck are you so fuckin' tight?" Just to be ornery, she clenched her muscles, clamping down on him. His eyes widened, and his hold on both her hip and her throat tightened. "Don't you make me fuckin' come, woman." His voice was a cross between an order and a desperate plea.

"Fuck me," she whispered. She stretched her arms over her head, lifting her chin even more, letting him know she was his to do with as he wanted. She didn't want his hands off her. In fact, she liked the feel of his dominance over her. He squeezed her neck, but didn't constrict her airway. It was just enough for her to realize how easily he could hurt her. Had Gordon ever had her in this position with this particular look on his face, Zora would have been terrified for her life, fighting to be free. But with Data, she just smiled up at him. Or, rather, she tried to. She was almost certain she looked as lost in pleasure as he did.

"Zora! Fuck!" Sweat erupted over Data's body, and he trembled. Zora watched in fascination as his muscles quivered and he shook with the effort to hold himself back.

"Do it," she hissed. "Come in me, Data!"

Abruptly, he let go of her neck, snatching his hand back. Then his thumb was on her clit, rubbing in fast circles. "Take it from me if you want it."

"Fine!" Two seconds later, Zora felt the spasm start at her clit. Another second and her lower body clenched, followed rapidly by the rest of her. She screamed as she let the pleasure overtake her. It was the first time she'd ever come with another person. And it was *amazing*!

Now, he just knelt there, still inside her, a stunned expression on his face. His come was warm where it trickled from her body. She let out a little gasp as her body finally settled, the spasms relaxing to a pleasant, lingering tingle.

"Goddamn." Data let go a full-bodied chuckle. It actually vibrated through her so that her clit tingled in protest at the added overstimulation. "What the fuck was that?"

"The best orgasm I've ever had," Zora answered, stretching. She also wiggled and clenched her pussy around him. Data groaned, and his cock gave a small pulse inside her. "I suppose that's it for a while." She tried her best not to look disappointed, but she wanted more. Then she felt him twitch inside her. And again.

"Oh, baby," he grinned, laying his weight on top of her. He kissed her thoroughly, lapping at her tongue and coaxing her tongue inside his mouth. Before he stopped, she was panting and whimpering, rocking her hips to get him moving again. Then he grinned down at her. "I'm just getting warmed up."

* * *

Falling off the grid was never something Data thought he'd do willingly. He couldn't fathom being away from a computer or cell phone or anything to do with the Internet. But he honestly didn't want to go back. Having Zora here, in this primitive cabin... Nothing could ever be better. He'd just finished heating up lunch when she came in with a huge grin on her face.

"I found the most amazing place! Right beside the creek where water comes from a cave. On the other side? I saw the ferns moving, and there was a huge rush of cold air! I think it's where the stream rushes through the cave, but it's like a natural refrigerator! We could totally put beer at the entrance and have a cold one in the morning."

God, he loved her! She was so full of life, lost in the wonder of little things like this. To Data, it was like a second chance at his entire life. Only this time, he got to spend it with her.

"Yeah, cutie. Around here, we call it a blow hole."

She jumped into his arms and wrapped her legs around his waist, peppering kisses all over his face. "That sounds so naughty." She giggled.

"I guess it does." He kissed her, thrusting his tongue deep before retreating and licking her lips gently. "You could blow me. I could fill your hole."

Her giggle was delightful. "That's so corny!"

"Corny? Why, you little imp!"

He dug his fingers into her ribs, tickling her without mercy. She shrieked and laughed, giving him her most glorious smile. The second he eased up on the tickling, she slid down his body, her fingers catching on the waist of his jeans. Before he realized what she was doing, she had unfastened them and pulled his cock free.

"Well, you've got it out. Whatcha gonna do with it, huh?"

She gave him a wicked grin before slowly sinking her mouth down on him. When she did, his world turned upside down and inside out. The heat of her mouth was a brand on him, one he was only too happy to accept. She slid back up until only the head of his cock was in his mouth before sinking back down on him as far as she could go. Over and over she did this, humming occasionally and pumping the length she couldn't swallow. With the other hand, she kneaded his balls gently, caressing him until Data thought he'd go mad with the exquisite pleasure of it.

"Fuck." His voice came out a breathy whisper. His fingers tunneled through her silky hair, and he guided her faster. She eagerly took his direction, relaxing her throat to take him deeper. Several times he had to stop after only a few seconds in her mouth, about to come down her throat. But he didn't want that. Not yet. He wanted inside her pussy for that.

With a growl, Data pulled Zora to her feet and unfastened her jeans. He spun her around against the rough, wooden counter before shoving the material down her legs. His fingers found her pussy wet and slick for him, and he groaned.

"God, I love fucking you. I could do this every single day for the rest of my fuckin' life, Zora."

"Me too," she answered, sticking her ass out in invitation. "Fuck me now, Data."

Who was he to argue?

Data guided his cock to her entrance, shoving home. The second he did, his body relaxed. Well, as much as he could relax in the given situation. It just felt right somehow. Like this was exactly where he belonged. Inside Zora. Their bodies one.

He pulled her upright, his hands going under her shirt to find her bare breasts. Her nipples were hard little peaks he immediately pinched and tugged until she groaned. The second she did, Data moved inside her. Shallow snaps of his hips sent waves of sensation coursing through him. His cock was so heavy and hot, he knew he'd never last. But then he seemed to always have to fight the immediate urge to come the second he entered her.

She tried to bend forward, to use her arms to push herself back onto him, but he was having none of it. He held her against his chest while he found her clit and began a steady stroke. One thing he promised himself was that she'd always come before he did. No matter what. She'd had so little pleasure and comfort in her life, he was going to do his damnedest to make up for it.

"D! Oh, God, D!"

"You like that, baby? Like me pinnin' you against me while I fuck you?"

"Yes!" She'd bent her elbows so she could hang on to his arms. Her little nails dug in. One of these days, she was going to draw blood, but he was good with that. Just meant she was caught in the moment. Data loved it.

"Good. Gonna come soon. You ready?"

"Yessssss!"

Zora's little pussy clamped down on him as she came. Her screams echoed in the distance along with his own hoarse shout. Again, he filled her pussy, his seed trickling back down his cock and her thighs to pool on the floor beneath them. He loved coming inside her, too. Was there anything about her he didn't love? Nope. He couldn't think of one single thing.

She sagged against him, her legs giving out. He knew the feeling, but he kept himself upright for her. Hell, he wanted to pound his chest but was afraid even that movement would send him tumbling to the floor. He'd always been a sexual person, but this was on a whole other level. *And she was his. Forever.*

They stood there, catching their breath for a moment or two. Zora giggled as she pulled away from him and cleaned herself before pulling up her jeans. A knock at the door had Data growling.

"Hey, lover boy." That was Torpedo's voice. "You OK in there? 'Cause I can totally send for Mama if you strained something."

"Imma beat the fuckin' shit outta you, Torpedo."

"No you're not. 'Cause I brought reinforcements."

"Fuck," Data swore under his breath. He looked at Zora. Her eyes were wide, her hand over her mouth as if that could keep back the screams she'd let loose earlier. Which only made Data smile. No way he could play indignant when his brothers hearing them make love was just one more way he'd tied her to him. "If you want me to kill them, I will, cutie."

Finally, she let out a giggle. "I doubt you can kill them all. Besides, maybe they'll tell your little tart at the clubhouse you're taken."

"Only if they tell Shadow you're taken," he muttered.

"Already know, brother. Now open the fuckin' door before I break it down."

"Jesus Christ, Shadow! Keep your fuckin' pants on." He winked at Zora, who blushed, but giggled just the same.

"I ain't the one with his pants down. Open the fuckin' door. We got shit goin' on."

Data knew his brothers. If it there was an immediate threat, they'd have come on in no matter what was going on inside. All the same, it must be serious for more than one of them to come all the way out here, especially the vice president. Bohannon and Shadow had come with Data, so they weren't unexpected.

When he opened the door, a procession of bikers stormed inside. "What the fuck, Bohannon?" The man should have warned him they were having company. Of more than one sort, apparently. "How many fuckers did you invite to the fuckin' party?"

In the tiny cabin that had been cozy for him and Zora stood six big men. Two of them were Azriel Ivanovich and Alexei Petrov from the billionaire playboy club, Shadow Demons. Ok, so they weren't exactly a playboy club. Hell, they weren't even a club. The Shadow Demons were vigilantes. The people in the underbelly of the city of Rockwell had given them the name Shadow Demons and it had stuck. Though some, like Alex's adopted daughter, had tried to call them Shadow Angels. Even though they were just as deadly as any member of Bones or Salvation's Bane, Bones's sister club, it was hard for Data to see them as equals. The third member of Shadow Demons was Giovanni, who was likely back in Rockwell in his own command center that probably made Data's look like some patched-together setup in his mother's basement. Just another reason for Data to hate them. But they came in handy from time to time. And they had more tech gadgets than a small country. Came with the territory since they owned Argent Tech, one of the largest technology companies in the fucking world.

Bohannon shrugged. "They just showed up. What was I supposed to do?"

"You coulda shot 'em," Data grumbled. "This better be important." He knew it was, otherwise he'd still be playing with Zora and his brothers would be a decent distance away.

"They came for her last night," Alex said softly. He didn't look at Zora and even tried to keep his voice soft as if hoping she wouldn't hear. But the cabin was too small, and Zora was right beside him, his arms firmly around her. Her swift intake of air and the way her body stiffened told Data she knew exactly what Alexei was talking about. "We were on the way when Giovanni gave us the word." He glanced at Bohannon. "Also, you should know that El Diablo and three of his inner circle at Black Reign are in Tennessee." He nodded at Zora. "I think he made your woman a widow and an orphan."

"What?" Data tightened his hold on Zora, trying his best to comfort her. "Shh, cutie. I'm so sorry."

She pushed back against him so she could look up at him. "Just hang on a second." She took several deep breaths, turning her head to look over her shoulder at Alexei. "Are you sure?"

The man didn't hesitate. "That you're a widow? Yes." He shook his head. "I can't confirm that your father is dead, but Giovanni says El Diablo had orders to kill them both. With a man like El Diablo, that's enough."

"Wait," Bohannon pinched the bridge of his nose, squeezing his eyes shut a moment before shaking his head slightly. "I thought El Diablo left the Brotherhood."

"As far as we knew, he did." Azriel leaned against the door frame, crossing his arms over his chest. "There's a reason. Could be money. Could be he worked out some kind of deal to keep his club -- or his daughter -- safe. Who knows? Giovanni can't find anything on the downlow, and my contact in the Brotherhood isn't talking."

"Why the Goddamned fuck is it always something to do with either El Diablo or these Brotherhood fuckers?" Data wanted to smash something. Enough was enough. This shit had to stop. One way or the other. "If El Diablo has somehow put the Brotherhood on our tail, then we need to teach that motherfucker a lesson. I'm fuckin' tired of them constantly throwing shit at us and harassing our women!"

Torpedo just leaned against the rough, wooden counter and nodded to Azriel. "Ask him. He's the man with the fuzzy balls."

"Just relax," Azriel said, obviously trying to soothe Data. Well, Data didn't want to be soothed. He wanted blood. "It's not El Diablo, or the Brotherhood. At least, not directly." He scrubbed a hand over his face, something Data had rarely seen the other man do. Azriel was a billionaire and always conducted himself as such. Even dressed in jeans and a T-shirt he didn't look like anything other than a rich tech mogul.

"Here's what you've got to understand," he said, looking at all of them in turn as if he was trying to figure out how best to explain something that was complicated yet simple at the same time, and didn't quite know how to get his point across without oversimplifying it. "Organized crime is everywhere. Literally. You know this part. What you may not understand, at least to the extreme extent, is that all of it -- every single peon out there in a gang trying to sell smack or MC laundering money or Joe Blow moving sex slaves -- answers to someone. He may not realize he does, he may be stupid enough to think that he won't have a price to pay if he doesn't deliver on something, even something he manufactures himself. Even the little shit heads growing and selling their own pot have to answer to someone. Maybe it's the person who moves it for them. Or maybe it's the person that person uses to move it. Whoever it is, there is always someone above them. In a chain that literally has thousands and thousands of links, at the very top is the Brotherhood."

Azriel glanced around the small room to include the whole group. "The Brotherhood controls it all. At the very top there are five. No one knows who they are but the men or women immediately below them. Same with the next ranking. And so on. The Brotherhood are so entrenched and pervasive, they control governments at the highest level in every country on Earth. You ever wonder how a certain person in a mid-level election wins when no one knows who they are? That's the Brotherhood. And it goes all the way to the top of every place on Earth. The Brotherhood controls... *everything*. Honestly, there's no way they can know every single one of the millions of people or organizations intimately, so they're not targeting Bones or Salvation's Bane or even Shadow Demons specifically. And they know I'm with Shadow Demons."

"So, why do we keep getting messed up with them?" Data asked?

"And when are we actually gonna catch their notice?" Leave it to Cain to cut to the chase.

"That's what you don't get. Or at least the main part of it. They know you. They just don't care about you. More importantly, they know that, even though you're cunning, determined, and resourceful, you're no threat to them. At least, not at present. They don't go looking for trouble because they have enough to deal with. You're not cutting into their interests or trying to take down someone they are using for whatever thing they have going on that involves, say, Gordon Sandlin. He's involved, but whatever he's doing is maybe thirty moves ahead of the real end game they're playing. If he can't be replaced, he'll be guarded until he's served his purpose. Which it looked like they were doing." He nodded at Zora. "Until your little girl here came along. They thought she was going to sabotage the greater plan. Wittingly or not. So they came after her. In the process, the data she uncovered not only proved her innocence, but the guilt of so many people the Brotherhood had no choice but to put everything on hold and clean house."

"What does that mean?" Zora asked, looking up at Data. "What's happening?"

"I think what he's saying," Data said, "is that Frank and Gordon are only two players in this. Maybe not pawns in this particular game, but replaceable after the current game. They might think there are only two or three others they recruited, but in order to get those two or three, several other people had to agree and expected a cut. It constituted a mutiny in the ranks." He looked at Azriel. "Right?"

"Exactly. And they deal with disloyalty harshly. There will be a massacre. Most will be guilty. Some not as much, but if the Brotherhood finds out even a whisper that someone knew something and didn't report it, they will die. Horribly."

Zora looked horrified. And scared. "You sound like you know this firsthand. Are they coming after me, too?"

"You're safe, Zora," Azriel said immediately. "After reviewing what I sent them, even knowing it came from you, they believe your complete innocence in this. As to knowing firsthand... I do," Azriel said softly. "I was part of them when I was younger. No one leaves them. Only two people, that I'm aware of, ever did and managed to live. Myself. And El Diablo."

"So how does he fit into all this?" Torpedo crossed his arms over his chest. Data knew his friend, and right now, the vice president of Bones was weighing his options. Deciding how best to deal with what could be a threat in the future.

"You know he was a high-level enforcer for some shady people. What he didn't tell you -- and rightly so -- is that he was *the* enforcer for the Brotherhood. And when I say *the* enforcer, I mean literally that. All sanctioned kills were handed down to him. Every single one. The small-time stuff he handed off to one of his men capable of handling it. Anything questionable or difficult, he handled himself. There was only one shot given. If someone failed to take out his or her target, the assassin was executed and El Diablo severely punished. Except, I never heard of any target being missed during his tenure. He was the best of the best, and he recruited and trained the best."

"If they're so fuckin' big, so all encompassing, how come we've only recently heard about them? I mean, I can see how it all leads back to them, but why now?"

"Because of your connection to Alexei." Azriel was referring to the leader of Shadow Demons. He and Cain had known each other for many years. In fact, Alex often hired Cain's men through ExFil, Cain's paramilitary organization. "You introduced Data to us, who made nice with Giovanni. If you and your sister club, Salvation's Bane, didn't have that connection with us, you'd never know the Brotherhood. You'd just wonder why El Diablo kept turning up on your door, and only because he announced his presence to you, preferring to take on any problems with you himself. And to answer your question, no, El Diablo isn't still working for the Brotherhood, he's just trying to stay out of their way. Yes, he probably sends questionable things your way more than he should, but it's to keep his nose clean. One of his many talents is knowing how to read individuals and the groups they form. He will never send you something you can't handle with a minimum of fuss, but he won't hesitate to deflect anything he can to your clubs in order to keep himself and his inner circle away from the Brotherhood."

"Fucker," Data muttered. "Why us?"

"Because Sword has his daughter." Alexei said simply.

"Wouldn't he want to keep danger *away* from her?" Torpedo asked with a raised eyebrow. "Seems kinda risky to me."

"Perhaps, but he's testing Sword. Also, he could be convinced the man and your club are completely capable, so he knows that as long as Magenta is with Sword, the man will kill anyone who puts her in danger. Probably why he hasn't visited like he promised he'd do."

Data looked at Zora, who was wide-eyed and more than a little scared. "Sounds pretty Goddamned fucked up to me."

Azriel gave a snort and a wry grin. "El Diablo isn't what one would call a normal individual with a stable way of looking at the world."

"So what do we need to do? I want Zora protected. If we know where all the players are and which side everyone is on, we need to remove some threats." Data was *so* done with this. He wanted the motherfuckers dead. Now.

"That's why we're here, brother," Torpedo said. "They came for her last night but hesitated to enter her house. They're currently surrounding it, hiding out in the woods until they get further instructions."

Data looked at Torpedo. "So, what are we gonna do?"

Torpedo stared at Data a long time. Data wanted blood. Torpedo, as vice president of the club, had to look out for the greater good. He figured Torpedo would warn him to back off, but the man just stared at him. Data wasn't about to lower his gaze. He needed to send a message, but what would be the repercussions if they killed men they had little to no information on? If those men went farther up the food chain than they all thought, Bones could end up in a war they'd never win.

Finally, Torpedo seemed to come to a decision. "We have a chat with 'em. They don't let up on Zora, we eliminate the fuckin' threat."

Chapter Seven

The upcoming fight with trained assassins didn't worry Data nearly as much as the fight getting Zora to go with Stunner and Trucker back to the clubhouse without him. He'd cajoled, rationalized, and pleaded with her. Finally, he'd taken her back inside the little cabin and spanked her bare ass. Then he'd fucked her. And she'd finally, *finally*, agreed. But only because he'd threatened to spank her again. In front of everyone. She'd been angry, but there was no way in hell Data was letting her stay anywhere near what could turn into a bloodbath if the men the Brotherhood had sent refused to give up on finding her and either taking her with them or killing her.

As they stood outside, Data took her in his arms and kissed her gently. "Don't worry, cutie. I'll be back before you know it."

She sniffed, tears glistening in her eyes. "You better." Stunner placed a big hand on her shoulder and met Data's eyes. The younger man nodded solemnly, aware of the trust Data was placing in him to keep Zora safe and to get her back to the clubhouse. Then he urged Zora to climb into the side-by-side the group had brought with them and fastened her seatbelt. Trucker jumped into another one, and the three of them sped off into the woods.

"All right, men. Let's get to work." Torpedo took immediate charge, laying out the plan he and Alex had put together. It was solid, assuming Giovanni had the correct numbers. He'd said his contact assured him they were spot on, but the men were ordered there by Frank and Gordon's sect. Data knew there was no guarantee of a correct head count.

"We're expecting no more than five. And really, that's overkill for one small, unarmed woman."

"Probably someone trained by El Diablo," Azriel mused. "Habit of overkill to keep from failing."

"Should we be worried?" Torpedo raised an eyebrow but otherwise looked unconcerned.

"Just don't underestimate them. They'll be well trained and fearless."

The group of five Bones and two Shadow Demons set off in their own side-by-sides and four-wheelers, the only reliable means of traveling so deep into the wooded territory. It took them the better part of an hour for all their vehicles to cross the area before stashing them to walk the rest of the way. No sense giving away their presence when they didn't have to.

"Your five o'clock, Torpedo," came Deadeye's voice over the earpieces they all wore. "Two set up for the long haul. I'm guessing they know she's not home and are expecting her back."

Torpedo was too close to the guy to acknowledge verbally, but he stuck his right arm out to the side and bent it at the elbow up twice to indicate he'd seen the contact on his right.

"Two more directly in front of you, Data." There was no missing the two. Data had already caught sight of them and was just about to signal he'd spotted them. He did so now, pointing his rifle at the duo while using his non-firing hand to point with his index finger at them, thumb down and the rest of his fingers closed.

"Last guy to left of Shadow. Eight o'clock." Shadow acknowledged his target by holding out his left hand and waving it up and down twice like Torpedo had.

"Giving the area one last scout," Deadeye said. He was their sniper, at seventy-five meters out in a tree watching over them. It was closer than he normally liked because of the lay of the house and surrounding area, but the man had made absolutely no noise when gaining his position. Hell, Data had no clue where he was exactly. "Azriel. Alex. There's a sleeper in the back. West corner of the house. Only one that I see, but assume there's a second."

Alex acknowledged their visual, and the team went to work.

Data had two men in his sights. Orders were to wait for backup. In this case it would be Shadow, once the big man had taken care of his target. There wasn't so much as a twig snapping to indicate anyone had moved. Shadow took Data by surprise when he tapped his shoulder to let Data know he was with him. Data nodded, the only other communication. Seconds later, they both had their targets in choke holds before delivering a fast-acting tranquilizer to the thigh with an auto injector. Then all they had to do was hold on until it took effect. Which didn't take long.

"Shit, that was fast," Shadow said, amazed at how quickly the medicine put the men down. "My other target took even less time. What the fuck'd you put in those things, Azriel?"

"Just a little cocktail of a modified tranquilizer introduced with an auto injector. Even if the subject is too big for a standard dose, it will be enough for officers to subdue him. If it's too much for a smaller guy, there is another auto injector filled with a counteracting drug to neutralize the first drug's effects. We're hoping to get it approved for military use as a fast track for usage in the federal penal system."

"Well the shit works faster than anything I've ever seen."

"Of course it does. Argent Tech doesn't create products that don't work." Azriel's superior tone grated on Data's nerves, and he could see it did Shadow's as well.

"Sanctimonious asshole," Shadow muttered.

"If you want a supply for Bones, you'll watch your tone," Alex warned. There was no real heat in his voice. More like he was enjoying the battlefield camaraderie.

"Get them inside. Once they're awake we'll question them," Torpedo instructed. "How long will that shit last, anyway?"

"Not long," Azriel said. "Maybe another fifteen minutes. Less on the biggest guy. It's quick to act, but quick to metabolize as well."

By the time they got all six into Zora's garage, the biggest was coming around. He groaned once before opening his eyes. They were glazed, but aware.

"Where'm I?" His words were slurred, but he was making an effort to get his wits about him.

"Right where you were ten minutes ago," Torpedo said, squatting down to get face to face with the guy. "You're in the garage with your buddies." He let the guy fully absorb his situation.

"You gonna kill us?"

"That depends on why you're here."

"You know I'm not tellin' you anything about our objective. Same as you guys wouldn't if the situation were reversed."

"Fair enough." Torpedo nodded, a grudging respect for the guy showing on his face. The kid was respectful, but Data could see from the look in his eyes he wouldn't budge on this. Torpedo did too. "How about I give you some information, and you can decide what to tell me afterward." The guy opened his mouth, but Torpedo plowed on, not letting him speak. "Your boss is from one of two factions. The young woman who lives here is the only truly innocent one in either of those two groups. So, you've been sent her to kill her by one of the two groups. One side tried to set her up to take the fall. The other side recently got some information supplied by our girl. Now, she only had part of it. The rest was up to the group to dig into. Which they did. She's innocent. That innocence is her only crime."

The kid looked wary now. "We got a garbled transmission on the sat radio about thirty minutes before we arrived here. Radio got wet and couldn't give us a good signal." He shrugged. "Boss didn't contact us via sat phone, so we were going with our last confirmed order, but the chick ain't here."

"Why not try to contact your boss instead of waiting around for him to get around to calling you?" Data asked. "Especially if the radio was FUBAR."

"Orders. Sat phone is for them to call us. Not the other way around."

"Fair enough," Torpedo said. "Now that you know there could be an order hangin' out there you need to look into, you can call."

The kid shook his head. "Not my call. It's more than I should say, but all of us were for breakin' protocol and checkin' in."

"They why didn't you do it?" Data bit out the question, wanting to pull his hair out in frustration. These men were about to terminate a young woman. Didn't they want clarification on a garbled transmission on a satellite radio? It wasn't like they could get bleed-over from just anyone, or that anyone could hack their signal. This was a highly secured signal from fucking space. They had to know it came from their bosses.

"Like I said. Wasn't my call, and this ain't a democracy." He looked to Torpedo, obviously knowing he was in charge. Kid might be young, but he'd been around the military long enough to recognize the boss. "I will say that killing anyone without one last check-in doesn't sit well with me. We were supposed to have one last radio check before executing our orders."

Torpedo looked at Data with a raised eyebrow. "Not satisfied," Data grumbled. "But that will do for now."

Shadow squatted down and held a water bottle to the kid's mouth. "What's your name, boy?" he asked gruffly.

"Chase," he said.

"Last name?" Shadow raised an eyebrow.

Chase grinned. "Sorry, man. Chase's all you get."

Shadow chuckled, clapping Chase on the shoulder. "I like this one. Honorable. Loyal. Yeah. I like him."

It wasn't long after that the others started to wake. Three of the biggest first, then the last two, leaner and slighter built men.

"Wha' da fuck?" One of the smaller men groaned as he tried to move his bound hands. Didn't work out so well.

"Your target isn't here," Torpedo said. "And I think you have a garbled transmission you need to clarify."

The older man's gaze snapped to Chase, as if he knew exactly who had leaked that little bit of information. "When we get out of this, I'm gonna kill you, kid."

Chase just shrugged, not concerned in the least.

"You got more to worry about than anything Chase said to us," Torpedo said. The man rolled his eyes and looked back at Torpedo. He looked for all the world like Torpedo was an irritating fly buzzing around his head instead of a two-hundred-and-fifty-pound, pissed-off soldier.

Data added his weight to the menace. "This goes one of two ways. You back off and leave the girl alone, or you continue and you all die right here."

The man snorted. "So the boss was right. Bitch left to get some strange." He looked Data up and down. "Gotta say, had I known the girl was into roughnecks, I'd'a fucked her myself." That got the man a solid backhand from Data. Blood and spit went flying. The man gave one harsh grunt. He shook himself, opening his eyes wide as if trying to clear his vision.

He tilted his head and looked up at Data. "You don't scare me none, boy."

"Then you're a complete dumbass," Shadow said. The man was in full intimidation mode. His arms were crossed over his chest, and he stood tall with his shoulders back.

"I was told to kill the bitch. That's what I'm doin'."

"We have a protocol we follow," one of the other guys offered. He still sounded groggy but was obviously aware of what was going on. "We have to get a final go ahead before we execute an order like this. Don't know why you're resistin', but it's wrong."

Chase spoke up. "Never liked the order to kill a woman. But I was willin' to follow 'em because I have respect for the group and the chain of command." He shook his head. "This ain't somethin' they'd like."

"You complete the job or you die," Azriel said. "Isn't that the rule?"

A guy who'd been silent until now looked at him with suspicion, but nodded his head. "It is. But Chase is right. Besides, the penalty is worse if you kill the wrong person, or don't follow protocol and kill an innocent." He shook his head. "El Diablo might not be in charge anymore, but he still carries out punishment. At least, that's what we've all been told."

Azriel knelt in front of Chase. "Where's the phone?"

He nodded to a pack on the floor. "There. Beside Stone. Number is programmed."

"Gonna fuckin' kill you, Chase, you fuckin' little bastard!" Absurd since Chase looked to have at least seventy or eighty pounds on the other man.

"We ain't worried about you, Bill." This came from Stone. "You think you're the shit since you're in charge, but everyone knew you were gonna fuck up. Well, this was it. It was our bad luck we drew your team this rotation. If I'm dyin', it ain't gonna be hard. I can handle torture to save my team. I've done it. But it ain't worth it to save your sorry hide."

"You his second?" Torpedo asked Stone.

Stone nodded. "Yeah."

Torpedo nodded to Shadow, who cut the zip tie holding Stone's arms. His feet were still tied. Torpedo tossed him the sat phone. "Make the call."

"With fuckin' pleasure," Stone muttered, stabbing a couple of buttons and putting the phone to his ear. "Yeah. Radio's toast. Lost Angel Leader." There was a brief pause. Then, "Dunno. Maybe a bear? He'd gone ahead of us to scout and never came back." Stone glared at Bill. The man opened his mouth, but Sword immediately shoved a rag inside and held it there. The man thrashed and squirmed but was no match for Sword's raw strength. All the while, Stone continued to speak calmly. "All I know is he was pretty torn up, sir. Pretty messy." There was another pause while Stone received instructions. The man's expression didn't change. "Understood, sir. We'll pull out immediately. What do you want us to do with Angel Leader?" Another pause. "Not sure, sir. If we follow the exfiltration route, the woods will make it hard going to carry him out. We could do it, but it will take time." Another pause. Finally, Stone's face relaxed into a menacing smile. "Understood sir. I'll get the team out without detection." More silence. "Yes, sir. If the bears don't finish him, the coyotes will." He disconnected the phone and looked at Torpedo. "We clean up our own mess."

"Up to you, hoss," Torpedo said. "You already declared him dead. Ain't like he can just magically come back if you want to live. You know that, right?"

"Like I said. We clean up our own messes." He jerked his head at Bill. "He's a mess that shoulda been cleaned up long before now. I think the bosses knew, too. They didn't sound surprised." He shrugged. "It was only a matter of time."

One of the other team members snorted. "And a matter of who had the bigger balls."

"You also understand that we can't just trust you'll do it," Torpedo said carefully. "We have to make sure it's done. He'll come after Zora, and we can't have that."

"Oh, I understand perfectly," Chase said. "I also know that I can't shoot him." Chase studied Bill like he was trying to puzzle out a problem. Bill just looked angry. Sword pulled the cloth from his mouth and stepped away, also eyeing the man critically. "I'll probably have to cut his throat. Then slash him several times. Serrated blade should work to tear the flesh. We put him in the path of those coyotes, nature should make it impossible to determine much. As long as I use slashing motions and not stabbing."

Torpedo glanced as Sword. "What do you think, Sword?"

"Should work. I ain't as good a tracker as Viper, but I should be able to help you put him in the animals' path."

"You pussies ain't gonna do nothin'," Bill sneered, gesturing at Chase. "I know for a fact he ain't got the nuts for it. Little pussy whined all the way here about killin' a woman. He ain't gonna kill no man in cold blood."

"Normally, I'd agree with you, Bill," Chase said pleasantly. "The mere fact you did everything you could to force this team into allowing you to kill a *woman* in cold blood makes this a whole fuckin' lot easier for me. My only dilemma is whether to tear you up before or after I kill you. Thinkin' 'before' would be way more satisfying."

There must have been something in the look Chase gave the other man, because Bill sucked in a breath, paling under their gaze. Then he chuckled. It was one of those sounds people make when they think there's no way for anything bad to happen but then suddenly realize it's really happening. Right before their eyes. Could have been because Chase pulled out a big-ass Rambo knife.

"We need to get him away from the house," Chase said. "The rest of the team can stay here, tied. Where you can keep an eye 'em."

"No way, mate." This guy spoke with an Australian accent. "You're not goin' alone."

"Sword can take whoever he needs to with him. I'll go and do the actual killin'. I'll be the only one stepping around Bill. If anyone gets this laid on 'em, it's gonna be me, Keith. Ain't draggin' the rest of the team down with me."

"No one's gonna know any different," Torpedo said confidently. "The coyotes got him. Besides. No one's gonna know you're even here. Data. Sword. Shadow. Want you guys stickin' together on this. See it done. Bring Chase back here."

"Not a problem, Torpedo," Shadow said, clapping Data on the back. "No problem at all."

"You can't fuckin' do this! I'll kill all you motherfuckers!"

"No," Chase said as he hefted the man up and over his shoulders in a fireman's carry. "You won't."

It took them the better part of an hour to find an acceptable spot to kill the man. When they did, Chase seemed to take great delight in telling Bill in great, graphic detail what was going to happen. In the end, though, Chase took the man unawares while he was spewing threats at the three Bones members. He cut one side of his jugular, then the other. One cut vertical, the other horizonal. Both slightly off angle. If he was found before the wild animals could do much damage to him, there was hope the man's death could be ruled an accident.

Because of the nature of their assignment, there were no identifying markings or personal effects on any of them. Chase took his guns, including the holdout he wasn't supposed to have, and three knives they found on him. Again, something the man wasn't supposed to have.

"If command knew about the unsanctioned weapons the guy carried, they'd have done worse to him." Despite the earlier cruelty, Chase searched the body respectfully, almost reverently. The man didn't take death as callously as he'd appeared. "The man was an idiot, but I hate that he wasn't home. Don't know if he had a family or not, but I hate the thought of them not knowing what happened to him. Having his body to bury or whatever. Some people need it to have that closure, you know?"

"Yeah. I know," Data said quietly. "You understand why this had to happen. Right? None of this was your fault."

"Yeah. It had to be done. No question. I just wish it could have been someone above me doin' the killin'." He picked up his knife and cleaned it on Bill's clothes as best he could. "Let's get back to the garage and get the fuck outta this place."

Data couldn't agree more.

* * *

Zora couldn't remember ever crying so much. After she'd gone back with Trucker and Stunner, she had gone to Data's room and locked herself in. Not because she was antisocial or didn't like the people she was forced to be around. She just didn't want any of them to hear her crying. OK, so, crying was too insipid a term for what she was doing. Sobbing her heart out like a small child who'd just lost her kitten? Yeah. That *might* touch it.

Several times one of the ol' ladies had come by and tried to get her to open up, but she'd refused. No, didn't need anything. Yes, she was perfectly fine. It wasn't until Suzie knocked that she finally relented and opened the door.

The young woman took one look at her and gently forced her way inside. Stunner gave them a dark look before turning his back and placing himself solidly in front of the door so no one could get past him.

Once the door was firmly shut, Suzie put her slim arms around Zora, and Zora dissolved once more into tears.

"Everything will be all right," Suzie said. "He'll be back soon. You'll see. Not a scratch on him."

"You can't know that. If what Azriel said is true, those men they're facing are highly trained killers! They could all be dead!" Zora knew she sounded as panicked as she felt, but she couldn't stop the outpouring of tears.

"You know Stunner wouldn't have left his brothers if he thought they couldn't handle the threat."

"How do you know he wouldn't? Especially if he thought he needed to protect you if those guys made it through the line of defense."

When Suzie didn't immediately speak, Zora pulled back slightly. She really needed to see the other woman's expression. Instead of scoffing at her or telling Zora she had no idea what she was talking about, Suzie was really thinking about her question.

"No. Stunner would stay with his brothers. He'd take the fight where he thought it needed to be taken most." Zora was struck at the abrupt change in Suzie. She'd gone from childlike before to having a very good insight on Stunner, the person she was closest to. "He knows every single patched member of Bones, and every single prospect here would defend the clubhouse and everyone inside with their dying breath. That includes me and you. He'd fight with his brothers no matter what." She grinned. "And before you argue that he'd follow Torpedo or Cain's orders, let me assure you. If Stunner doesn't want to do something no one can make him do it." She shrugged. "He's stubborn like that." The girl was a conundrum, unique in many ways. Zora thought she might be trying to reclaim a little piece of her childhood at times. Others, like now, she was all too grown up.

Zora sighed. "I'm sorry, Suzie. I'm sure you've got other places you'd rather be than here babysitting me."

"Nah, I'm good. I love it here, but you're the only woman my age at the clubhouse. Angel is so wonderful but she's more of a mother figure. I'm glad you're here. You'll be my best friend."

"She absolutely will," came a deep voice from the door. Zora gasped, whipping around to see Data standing there with a smile on his face. Giving a glad cry, Zora launched herself at Data, wrapping her arms and legs around him tightly.

"I was so scared!" She pulled back, taking his hands in her face and raining kisses all over him. He chuckled and she cried. "Are you OK? Were you hurt?"

"No, cutie. I wasn't hurt. I'm perfectly fine."

"What about..." She stumbled over the words. "You know. Am I in danger?"

"Not at all. I wouldn't be here if you were. I'd be out there eliminating any threat to you."

"So, that team you went to find. They weren't there to kill me?" She hated how hopeful she sounded, but she didn't want Data to kill anyone on her behalf.

Data winced. "That's complicated, cutie. Short of it is they had a shit commander who needed to die, and he did. The others were good men following the orders in their chain of command. Just like we all follow Cain's orders when we work for ExFil while he's getting instructions from our employer. Same with

Bones. We follow Cain. He does whatever he committed us to do. Once they were in contact with their boss, he confirmed the order was rescinded, and that you were to be left alone. All of them agreed but one, and he was overruled." He cleared his throat, looking a little embarrassed. "Forcibly."

"So what happens now?"

He grinned. "Now, I get to come home to my sweet cutie. And you, sweet cutie, get to pamper me and indulge me with sex."

Zora burst out laughing. "Is that so?"

"Oh, definitely."

"But, I've got company, and you can't be rude to my best friend." Zora turned to indicate Suzie, but the other woman wasn't there. "Where'd she go?"

"You two kids have fun," Suzie said from the door as she backed out, closing it as she went. "We'll talk later, Zora." She giggled as the door clicked shut.

"Now look what you did, you sex-starved maniac," she said through her giggles. "You ran off my friend."

"I have a feeling she's OK with it. Now, you gonna let me fuck you or what?"

In answer, Zora hurriedly stripped off her clothing and took great delight in helping Data with his when he didn't get them off fast enough. He was still sweaty from the trip and, though she really just wanted to eat him up, she wrinkled her nose. "Someone needs a shower," she said. "Come on. I'll help you get all the tricky parts."

"I think I like this side of you, cutie," he laughed as he allowed her to take his hand and lead him to the bathroom and the oversized shower.

She adjusted the water for them and stepped in ahead of him, pulling him with her. Zora couldn't bear to let him go. Not yet. She needed him even if he didn't need her. "I was so scared," she said as she let him pull her into his arms. All playfulness was gone, her fear and insecurities surging forward with alarming speed.

"Nothin' to be scared of, cutie. I will always come back to you. Always."

She gasped when his hand went between her legs to her pussy. His fingers slid through her folds. Zora knew she was hot and slick for him, needing him inside her as much as she needed him to hold her.

Once he'd tested her readiness, Data urged one leg up around his hip. Then he guided himself inside her and slid home. She wrapped the other leg around him and gasped when he moved her. Zora soon picked up his rhythm and moved on her own, sliding up and down his length over and over again.

"So fuckin' good, baby," Data bit out. "So fuckin' good."

"I love you," she gasped out. "I really love you, D!"

"I love you, too, cutie. So fuckin' much."

For long moments, they moved like that, taking what they needed from each other. Finally, when it wasn't enough for either of them, Data set her away and turned her around.

"Hands on the bench." When she complied, bending over and presenting her ass, he growled possessively. "Spread those lovely legs, baby. I'm gonna fuck you from behind until I come. You ready for that?"

"Yes! Please!"

He did. Data gripped her hips, and Zora thought she'd die from the pleasure. As good as it had been before, this was even better. Maybe it was the added sensation of the water running over her body. Maybe it was knowing she was finally safe, and it was because of this man. All she knew was that she was about to come apart at the seams. The pleasure was that intense.

Then he slid his hand down to her clit, flicking it several times. It was over.

Zora screamed, throwing her head back in abandon. Her legs were rubbery, the pleasure shooting up through her body like a firework on the Fourth of July.

Data gave a couple more powerful thrusts then bellowed, "I'm coming!" and emptied himself inside her, his big body shuddering at her back.

"Fuuuuuck," he chuckled, kissing her shoulder. "You're so fuckin' hot, baby. So fuckin' beautiful. God! I love you!"

"I love you, too," she panted, still trying to catch her breath.

Data turned off the water and snagged a towel, drying them both before carrying her to the bed. He laid her down, lay beside her, then pulled her close.

"I'll never get tired of that," he mused, kissing her shoulder once more. "Never in a million years."

"Me neither," she said, the stress of the day and the explosive sex finally getting the better of her. "But I'm not sure I can stay awake."

"Don't. Sleep." He sounded just as sleepy as she did. "Love you, cutie."

"Love you, too."

Much as she wanted to just sleep, to forget the horrible evening she'd had, she couldn't. She gripped the arm around her, holding her so close to him. How things had changed for her in such a short period of time. *Days*! She had to wonder at the swiftness of her relationship with Data.

"Don't like you thinkin' so much, cutie. It leads to all sorts of bad things." His words were soft with sleep. She should have known Data would know she was fretting over something. Even when they communicated over the Internet, him not seeing her face or hearing her voice, he'd always seemed to know what she was thinking or feeling.

"I'm just reflecting on everything that's happened," she said.

Data chuckled. "No, you're frettin' about us."

"Does anyone say fretting anymore? You're showing your age, honey."

His arms tightened around her slightly as he continued to chuckle. "I'd ask if me being as old as Father Time bothered you, but I think I told you before, I don't care anymore. You can deal with it. And I'll have you with me always."

That settled something inside her. Maybe not completely, maybe not forever, but it was a start. "I guess I'm just afraid it's not real. We're burning so hot, we're bound to burn out."

"Honey, I doubt Holy Water could douse this fire I have for you. You, my sweet cutie, are everything to me."

"But your daughter --"

"Will love you as much as I do when she gets to know you. She's not put off by our age difference at all. Hell, she and Viper have nearly as big an age gap as we do. You're worrying for nothing."

"But you don't know me... Oh!"

Data was done with this shit. Zora was a wonderful, intelligent woman, but she'd not had much in the way of permanent relationships in her life. Her father hadn't cared for anything but what she could get him. Her ex husband had been even worse. Data had no idea exactly what her mother was to Zora, but she obviously didn't care for her either or she'd have intervened long before now.

So he did the only thing he could to distract her and prove his point all at the same time. He aimed his cock and thrust inside her in one swift slide.

"It's true I don't know what the future holds for us," he said as he gripped her hips and pulled her back against him. "But I know one thing with absolute certainty. I. Love. You. *You*, Zora." He moved back and forth, thrusting inside her, doing his best to give her as much pleasure as he could. "I love your sass. I love your intelligence and your cunning. I love this hot little body and how it's greedy for me." He reached around and flicked her clit with his finger, giving her body a little push of pleasure just to prove his point. She cried out sharply when he did. "That's right, baby. I love you. And I'm not going anywhere."

She reached back to curl her arm around his neck and turned her head to kiss him. When their lips met, Data thrust his tongue inside her mouth, and she opened willingly, moaning into the kiss. Nothing had ever felt so right. Data's life hadn't been tame by any means, but he'd never felt for any woman what he felt for Zora right from the start. He knew she was the woman for him. Would always be the woman for him.

He hooked her leg over his arm and settled in to fuck her. The hard, driving rhythm satisfied him, as did her little cries and the sharp bite of her nails at the back of his neck.

"So fuckin' sweet, Zora," he whispered into her mouth. "Never get enough of you. Never!'

"Come inside me, D. Make me come, then come inside me with your hot seed."

He gave a harsh growl before speeding up his movements, surging into her with ever-increasing speed. When she gave a sharp exhale followed by a shuddering scream, Data smiled, letting himself go. Not long after, he gave his own brutal yell and did exactly what she'd demanded. He emptied himself inside her with spurt after spurt of his come. Satisfaction beyond measure filled him, and he knew it always would. Every time he made love to her, every time she came apart in his arms. Nothing would ever surpass this feeling of bliss and utter contentment.

For long moments, he couldn't seem to catch his breath. Couldn't move. Then he chuckled and kissed her neck. "You're everything, Zora. You've given me back something I hadn't realized I lost."

"What's that?"

"Peace, cutie. You give me peace."

He got up to get a wet washcloth and cleaned them both before pulling her back into his arms. Then, with her head resting on his chest, her little fingers curled into his muscles, Data drifted off into a contented, peaceful sleep.

Thorn (Salvation's Bane MC 3)

Marteeka Karland

Mariana -- If it weren't for bad luck... Yeah. That's me. I found myself stranded on the side of the road after my boyfriend threw me out. My mother, bless her heart, thinks I'm dragging her to the pits of hell because I got myself knocked up.

All of which I could deal with. What nearly put me in a panic was the big, muscle-bound, tattooed biker who pulled up behind me, ordering me to "pop the hood." I was scared, but, God, the man was smoking hot! Had I not been hot, tired, and pregnant, I might have gotten on my knees and begged him to take me. Instead, I kept that part of myself tightly under control. Sort of.

Thorn -- Ana isn't like anyone I've ever come across. If there's a woman in this world who needs pampering, it's her. She's half starved, on the verge of heat stroke, and I steamrolled my way into her life.

But I wasn't prepared for the call I got from the hospital or the sight of her broken body. I'm all about vengeance, and someone is going to pay for this. Dearly. And my little Ana is going to have to learn to take on a man like me. Because somewhere around the very first time I saw her, I might have gone and fallen in love with her.

Chapter One

"Come on... Come on..." Mariana Everly cranked the engine of her little Chevy Cavalier. The poor thing had been on its last legs for a while, but she'd hoped she could coax it along for a few more months until after the baby was born and she was back to work full time. As she turned the key for the sixth time, that hope dwindled. "Just a little longer," she crooned as she patted the dashboard. "Just a little longer and you can rest."

It didn't help.

The hot August Florida sun beat down unmercifully on her, the interior of the car so hot she could barely breathe. No way she could sit there like this. She had to have the vent blowing or something. She reached across the console to roll the passenger side window down before doing the same with the driver's side. Then she sat there, trying to figure out what to do.

She'd pulled off the road because her phone had rung. When she'd tried to answer it, she'd dropped it between the console and the seat. Normally, she'd have just gone on and worried about the damned thing later, but she'd been waiting on a call about work and hadn't wanted to miss it. The second she'd put the car in park, she'd turned off the ignition. Force of habit and fatigue, she supposed. Anyway, she'd retrieved her phone only to find it had been a spam call, then her car had refused to start.

This was just her luck. She had no one to call. No one. Jason had broken up with her. Her mother had kicked her out of the house when Mariana had told her she was pregnant. Jason had run off any friends she might have had early in their relationship -- which should have been a clue he was no good for her. Compound that with the fact that Jason had controlled all their money, and she was well and truly screwed.

Thank God she'd gotten her job's human resources department to issue her a paper check for the current pay period, or it would have gone straight to Jason's bank account. Just like it had since they'd been together. Stupidity on her part, but there it was. Unfortunately, that paycheck wouldn't come for another eight days.

Seeing no other option, she called Jason. Surprisingly, he answered on the second ring. "What do you want, Mari?"

"My car broke down. I can't get it to start."

"And?" God, the man was an ass! What had she ever seen in him?

"And you get my paycheck deposited to your account, so you know I don't have any money. You kicked me out without a dime to my name. I need a tow and money for a rental until it's fixed so I can get to work."

"Nothing doing, sweetheart. I got my own shit to think about."

"You can't leave me here like this! I need your help this one time. Once I get paid, you'll never hear from me again!" Mariana hated begging. Especially begging him. He relished it and loved making her grovel for him. It was so humiliating! She'd promised herself when he kicked her out two days ago she'd never beg him again. Yet here she was.

"One more time turns into another and another. I've got my girlfriend to think about. How do you think she'd feel if I dropped everything and came to bail you out? And all that money? I should be spending it on her instead of my ex."

That hurt. Badly. "You just broke up with me two days ago, Jason! How could you possibly have met another woman that quickly?" She didn't mention the baby because she was really hoping he'd forget about the child she was carrying. She didn't want anything from him because to insist on child support meant giving him access to her child, and that wasn't happening.

"What can I say? I'm a hot commodity."

"Yeah. Apparently." Her sarcasm was probably lost on the dolt.

He chuckled. "I'm surprised you're not using the old 'think of the baby' line."

"This is about you and me, Jason. The baby has nothing to do with it." She wanted to tell him the baby was none of his business anymore, but didn't dare. If he thought it mattered to her that he was out of her life for good, he'd do everything in his power to get joint custody. Right. She'd move to Canada first.

"Sorry, Mari. I can't help you."

Mariana hated when he shortened her name. He knew it, too.

"Look, Jason. I've never asked you for anything since we've been together. I need this one thing. This is an emergency. It's a hundred and three out, and I'm stuck on the side of the road. I need help."

"I'd suggest you call 911. It's what people usually do in an emergency."

Mariana heard a female giggle, and her face flamed. She guessed he was serious about the new girlfriend. Just as well. If she never saw the guy again, it would be too soon. Right now, though, she needed his help.

"Jason --" Before she could say anything else, he hung up on her.

Realizing she couldn't stay in the car without roasting, even with the windows down, she got out of the car and moved toward the rear passenger's side door, out of the direct sunlight. The sun was still high, but at enough of an angle that there was shade on that side of the car if she sat down. Which she did, gratefully. Normally the heat didn't bother her too much unless it was extremely humid, but, with her advancing pregnancy, she found even simple things she'd always taken for granted sometimes took a toll on her.

As she sat, the baby gave a little kick in her side. She was just past twenty weeks. A little more than halfway through, things were starting to be uncomfortable. Slight as she was, Mariana was already showing prominently. Also, the cute little maternity dress she'd worn wasn't very comfortable for sitting on the ground. The only fortunate thing about this whole situation was that she'd been on a back road. Pulling to the shoulder meant she could sit in the grass so she wasn't too uncomfortable.

She put a hand on her rounded pooch, trying to soothe the little one inside her. "We're gonna be OK, sweetie," she murmured. "I'll figure out a way out of this."

The only other option open to her was to call her mother. Much as she hated to, even though she knew the answer already, she had to. Not for herself. For the little life growing inside her.

"Mom?"

"I have no daughter. Who is this?"

Great. This wasn't going to go well. Still, Mariana plowed on. "I'm in trouble and I need help. My car broke down and I'm stranded."

"If I had a daughter, I'd tell her she should call the bum who got her pregnant in the first place. If she thought so much of him as to throw away her only family, it should have been her first call."

"He broke up with me, Mom. I did call him, but he won't help me." No way she was telling her mother he was with someone else. That would be too humiliating. As she spoke with her mother, she heard the rumble of a motorcycle in the distance. Sure enough, one rounded the curve the way she'd come and, to her surprise, seemed to be slowing. Her heart sped up. This could be bad. Really bad.

"Well, perhaps you should have chosen a better man. I'm sorry. But I can't help you."

"Mom! Please!" As she continued to speak, the bike pulled behind her car, and the man riding it shut the thing down. He pulled off his helmet and Mariana's breath caught. This had to be the scariest man she'd ever seen. Full beard, tattoos creeping up his neck. Piercing blue eyes. The harshest scowl she'd ever seen on a human being. "I just need someone to pick me up. I'll figure out how to rent a car on my own. Just, please don't leave me here!" No doubt the man could hear the conversation once the bike was off. She stood now. Readying herself to run for it. "Mom, there's a man who pulled up behind me on a bike. I need help!"

"Perhaps you should have thought about that when you took up with the first unsavory young man you met and got yourself pregnant out of wedlock. Once you do that, men like him can smell you out. I'm sorry. But, like I said, I have no daughter anymore. She's dead." The line disconnected.

Mariana let out a sob, putting the back of her hand to her mouth in an effort to contain her hysteria.

"Don't come any closer!" She needed to call 911 but was so scared the signal couldn't get from her brain to her fingers.

"Calm the fuck down, will ya?" The man strode past her to the front of the car. He reached in through the open window and popped the hood latch. Moving to the front of the car to examine under the hood, he asked, "What's it doin'?"

Mariana stayed on the other side of the car, clutching her phone, afraid to say or do much. When she didn't answer he stopped looking at the car and turned his gaze on her. "Well?" He barked the question sharply, as if she were wasting his time.

"I-it turns over, but won't start."

"Got gas?"

"Yes. Uh, h-half a tank."

He pulled something out of the guts of the car, looked at it, then put it back and shut the hood. "Your ignition module's fucked."

She waited for more. When none was forthcoming she asked, "What does that mean?"

"Means you're not getting fire to your spark plugs, which means your car won't start. You got someone comin' to help you?"

"Sure," she squeaked, but he just gave her a look. "That is, uh, I will. I-I just gotta call, uh, my, uh, ex-boyfriend."

"Ex-boyfriend, huh?"

"Yes. I'm sure he'll help me out."

The guy waved at her phone. "Call him. Not leavin' 'til I know someone's comin' for ya." He put his hands on his hips, his feet planted shoulder-width apart.

This was a no-win situation. If she called Jason, he'd make her beg. It was likely what he was waiting for, because that's what he did. Denied her something she desperately needed until she groveled enough to satisfy him. Once was never enough. It usually took three or four tries before he actually did what she needed. Always, there was a steep price to pay. Besides all the begging, that was. Anything she said to Jason, she'd have to say in front of this guy. If she refused, or if he decided not to help her, this guy would know. Then what would he do? What would she do?

She studied him and found nothing yielding about him. He was made of steel, as far as she could tell. He'd do exactly what he said he'd do. If that meant he didn't leave until she had someone coming to help her, then he'd stay.

With a defeated sigh, she dialed Jason's number again. This time, he waited until the fourth ring. "I told you, Mari --" There was a pause as something that sounded suspiciously like a kiss sounded next to the phone. "I can't help you."

"Put it on speaker," the biker demanded.

She tried to turn away, but he simply snagged her phone and put it on speaker himself.

To her horror, Jason continued, the intimate noises of sex going on in the background. "I'm currently busy getting a blow job, so you'll just have to find another sucker to help you. I'm done."

"Jason, please," she pleaded, unable to look at the biker witnessing her humiliation. "Just put enough money in my checking account to pay for a tow and I'll never bother you again."

"Damn straight you won't bother me again. I've had enough of your constant whining and pretending to be sick. Being pregnant doesn't cause that much of a fucking mess. Besides, I'm sure you tried to trap me into marriage, but I got news for you, bitch. Ain't no woman who can tie me down." There was a moaning sound followed by a gasp and a slurp. "I'm tired of not being able to get a fucking blow job when I want it. Fix your damned piece-of-shit car yourself." Then he ended the call.

Mariana turned her back to the biker, her emotions getting the better of her. She shook with both her humiliated sobs and the effort to hold them back.

But that wasn't the end of it. The biker handed her phone back as he pulled out his own from his back pocket, scrolled through it until he found a number, then put the phone to his ear.

"Grease. Need a roll back. Have Ripper ping my cell. Got a car needs some work." There was a pause. "Yeah. Take it to Grease. Blue eighties model Cavalier Z24. Headed west on 80. I'll meet you there soon as I can."

He put a surprisingly gentle hand on Mariana's shoulder. "Come on, little lady. Let's get you something to drink and this car taken care of."

When she turned around, the biker put his helmet on her head before taking her hand and leading her toward his bike. He threw one thick leg over the seat and started it up. When she just stood there, he pulled her toward him.

"Get on."

"I can't ride that thing!" She had to yell to be heard over the motor. "My dress --"

"Just tuck it under your ass. You'll be fine. Watch the pipes and put your feet on the pegs." Seeing little alternative, she did. Once seated, he snagged her arms and brought them around him and pulled her closer so she was mashed tightly against him. "Hang on, sugar." Then they were off.

* * *

How the fuck did Thorn manage to get himself into these fucking situations? The girl he'd picked up on the side of the road was not someone he needed to mess with. She was too fucking young, for one thing. For another, she was pregnant. While he had nothing against young or pregnant women, he had a tendency to be a little overprotective. Especially when, out there somewhere, a man was responsible for her, and he was doing a piss-poor job of taking care of her. Women and children needed men like him to protect them, and he took the mandate more seriously than most.

This particular woman, though...

Yeah. She just screamed "battered woman." Might be mental abuse, but she had it coming at her from all sides. Shame, too, because she was insanely lovely. Slight of build, she had dark, chestnut-colored hair, dark brows, hazel eyes, and that adorable little baby pooch swelling under her little maternity dress. How any man could be mean to her, let alone leave her in the middle of the road in this fucking heat, was beyond him. And to do it while fucking another woman? Little asshole was getting a visit later.

Thorn pulled them into the parking lot of a local diner, one he and his brothers in Salvation's Bane frequented. It was cool inside, the food was good, and she could wait with him in a public place and be fairly comfortable doing it.

She slid off the bike gingerly, a little unsteady on her feet. He took her arm as gently as he could to steady her, and she peeked under her lashes at him, not pulling away but obviously not comfortable with his touch either. Understandable.

"I thought we were going to the garage to wait on my car."

"No sense in that when you could get a bite to eat and wait in the air conditioning. By the time we're done, Red will have it fixed and you can be on your way."

When she hesitated, he put his hand at the small of her back and urged her inside the diner. He was greeted heartily by Tito when they walked in.

"Thorn!" The rotund man's face split in a genuine smile in greeting. "'Bout time you brought a woman in here! Ready to settle down, eh?"

The girl seemed to shrink in on herself, her shoulders hunching. "Unfortunately, she won't have me, Tito. Perhaps Elena could help with that?"

"She'll be happy to sing your praises. I've resigned myself to losing her to one of you boys someday." The man sounded dejected, but winked at his young charge. "If my Elena likes someone, young lady, you can bet they're a good person. And she loves your Thorn there." He pointed his spatula at Thorn before turning back to his grill.

Thorn ushered her to a booth and slid in across from her. Leaning his forearms on the table, he looked at her until she met his gaze. "What's your name, girl?" He tried to keep his voice soft. He didn't want to frighten her any more than she already was, with a big, rough biker swooping her up like he had.

"Mariana Everly," she murmured before looking away.

With a sigh, Thorn picked up a menu and opened it for her. "I can recommend the burgers and the pancakes."

She picked up the menu, showing obvious interest, then winced slightly and put it down when Marge approached.

"What'll it be, sugar?" She grinned at Thorn before turning to Mariana.

"Um, just a glass of water. We really don't have that much time."

Thorn snagged the menu from her with more abruptness than he should have, but really. It was obvious she was hungry and thirsty. "She'll have a house burger and fries. Bring her water now, and she can decide what she wants to drink while we're waiting. I'll have the same and a beer."

Marge grinned at him. "Now and later, sugar?"

"You know it."

"Comin' right up." She eyed Mariana speculatively. "I think I know what the young lady would like. You leave it to Aunt Marge, honey. I'll put a smile on that pretty face." Marge had worked at the diner as long as Tito had owned it. She knew everyone in town and never failed to peg her customers' wants. It was the reason Thorn had brought her here. Good food and caring service.

She looked up at him with hurt in her eyes. "I can't pay for this," she said bluntly.

"No one said you were payin'." When she just ducked her head, he said. "My name is Colin McGregor, but everyone calls me Thorn."

"Thanks for helping me out, Mr. McGregor. I'm not sure what I would have done if you hadn't come along." She was silent for long moments before finally sighing. "I suppose you deserve to know what's going on."

He shrugged. "None of my business. Not a requirement for me helping you, either. You want to tell me, I'll see if there's anything I can do to better the situation."

She gave him a look like she didn't quite believe him, but she didn't offer more, either. Just laced her fingers together nervously and stared at them.

Thorn sat back, sprawling as much as his large frame would allow. One arm draped lazily over the back of the booth as he studied the young woman in front of him. She was pale. Too much so. Probably hadn't had a good night's sleep in a while. From the parts of the conversation he'd overheard, it sounded like the pregnancy was hard on her. The heat couldn't be helping, he was sure. He was just about to do exactly what he'd said he wouldn't and pry into her personal problems when Marge returned.

The older woman reminded him of a character from a seventies sitcom. Flo from Mel's Diner in the flesh. Slim, flaming red hair, and gum she smacked constantly. "Here you go, sugar," she said, setting the beer down in front of Thorn and the ice water in front of Mariana. "And here's the Marge special for any woman brave enough to enter this place with Thorn." She gave Mariana a smile as she sat down a huge chocolate malt with whipped cream, a cherry, and chocolate sprinkles in front of her.

Mariana's eyes widened and her hands reached for it immediately before she curled her fingers into fists and put them under the table. "Thanks, but I can't --"

"Can and will, honey." Then she frowned. "Unless you're allergic." Marge turned to Thorn. "She allergic?"

Thorn shrugged. "Don't know."

"It's not that," Mariana said. She took a deep breath. "I just... I can't... pay for all this."

Immediately Marge relaxed. "You don't worry 'bout the malt none. That's on the house." She waved a hand at Thorn. "And this one here don't pay for your food, he'll answer to Elena." She patted Mariana on the shoulder. "I bet you could use a man like this one in your life. Bit on the wild side, but then, don't all women like to live dangerously once in a while?" With a wink, Marge went back to her other customers.

Mariana eyed the malt longingly but didn't reach for it. So Thorn picked up the straw Marge had left, took the wrapper off it, and stuffed it into the frozen concoction.

"Here," he said, sliding it closer. "Drink."

She still hesitated, but finally curled her hands around the glass and lifted it. When she drew on the straw, her eyes slid closed and she let out a soft moan of pleasure.

And just like that, Thorn was hard as a fucking pole.

"Oh, God," she said around a mouthful of ice cream. "This is the most amazing thing I've ever tasted in my life."

How pathetic was it that just this girl's smile made Thorn feel lighter? He absently rubbed his chest, the feeling there uncomfortable. Fuck. This was bad. "Marge knows her customers. She can peg just about anyone."

"Well, she certainly got me," she said.

At that moment, Marge appeared with their order. "There you go, sugar. You eat up." She looked at Mariana with a critical eye. "Need to feed that little one and build yourself up. You got a long road ahead of you, sweetie. Good thing you got a man here who can see you through it."

"He's not my man," Mariana said, the joyful smile fading from her face.

Marge just laughed. "Oh, sweetie. That's rich." The feisty waitress patted Thorn on the shoulder. He raised an eyebrow at her. She only winked, as if it were all an inside joke only the two of them were a party to.

Mariana eyed her burger, then glanced up at Thorn. He met her gaze steadily, not backing down. So help him, he wasn't letting her leave here until she'd eaten that fucking burger. The girl needed it. The greasy meat might not be great nutrition-wise, but it was high in calories, and she looked like she desperately needed energy.

Finally, with a halfhearted sigh, she picked up the burger and took a bite. As she chewed, her eyes seemed to glaze over and she chewed faster. Again, those moans of pleasure came as she took one bite after another. The mixture of arousal and amusement in Thorn was a heady combination. When the girl finally dropped her inhibitions, she had the burger in one hand, the shake in the other and was eyeing his burger as she took another bite.

Thorn picked up the squeeze bottle of ketchup and squirted a generous dollop onto her plate next to the crinkle-cut fries. It was the only encouragement she needed. Reluctantly, she let go of the shake and snagged a fry, dragging it through the ketchup before popping it into her mouth. The bliss on her face was mesmerizing. When she let out a little burp, Thorn had to bite his lip to keep from laughing. He had the feeling she wouldn't appreciate it, and he'd happily cut off his right arm if she'd just keep eating.

When her fries were nearly gone, he waited until she got distracted by a noise. The second she glanced away, he put a handful of his own fries in her plate. Girl didn't miss a beat, continuing to eat until everything on her plate was gone. Not long after, the malt was gone as well.

She set the glass down and picked up her napkin, eyes scanning the plate. Probably to make sure she hadn't missed anything. Then, as if coming out of a trance, she blinked. Her eyes went wide before she glanced up at him. Thorn was pretty sure he didn't manage to wipe the grin off his face before she saw him.

"Oh, God," she whispered.

"Nope. Not God," he said, taking a bite of his own burger. "That's all Tito. Well, the shake is Marge, but you get the idea."

Almost in a panic, she grabbed her napkin and frantically wiped her face, letting out a little sigh of relief when it came back with only a small dab of mustard from the corner of her lips. Good thing, too, because Thorn had been giving considerable thought to cleaning it for her. With his tongue.

"I'm so sorry," she whispered. "I must look like a maniac."

"You look like a pregnant woman craving a good, hot meal and a delicious milkshake. Happens to most pregnant women. Nothing to be sorry 'bout."

Marge appeared again, a huge smile on her face. "Good! Bet you feel better now, doncha, sugar?" She scooped up their plates before asking, "Dessert?"

Thorn held up a hand. "I'm good."

"How 'bout you, sugar? Elena makes a mean apple pie. Just took one out of the oven. Big ol' scoop of vanilla ice cream on hot pie makes everything better."

"No, thanks," she said, rubbing her belly. "I'm not sure anything else will fit."

Marge chuckled. "You get a pass this time, honey. Next time, though, I'll expect you to save room for dessert." She glanced at Thorn. "I'll add this to your tab. You get this little lady home so she can rest. Looks better, but still a little pale."

"Marge, we're not, you know, really together," Mariana said. "He was kind and helped me when my car broke down."

Marge just grinned. "Whatever, sugar. You still have to eat dessert next time he brings you here."

Thorn checked his watch. "Should still be a while before your car's done. We've got time to kill." He nodded to the back corner down dimly lit hallway. "Bathroom's down there if you need to freshen up. I can also take you anywhere else you need to go if you need supplies or something."

"I'm good, thanks. Just let me wash my hands, and I'll be ready." As she headed off to the bathroom, Thorn couldn't help but watch that sweet ass of hers. From the back, he would have had no clue she was expecting. The dress she wore was knee length and swished delicately around her legs. It didn't cling, but he suspected her body was tight and compact. He tilted his head, mesmerized as she walked away.

"Someone's got it bad," Marge said from the counter. She had her hip cocked with a hand resting on it. "Where'd you find that little innocent thing?"

"Broke down on the side of the road."

"You keepin' her?"

"Marge, at some point you really need to learn to mind your own business."

The older woman wasn't deterred. In fact, her grin widened. "Now, what fun would that be? Besides, you'll need all the help you can get with that one. Got a feelin' she has some things goin' on." Marge glanced in the direction of the restroom where Mariana had disappeared. "I know her mother. Go to church with the ol' hag. You know, that woman tells everyone her only daughter is dead? Can you believe that?"

Thorn's senses went on high alert. "That so?"

"Yep. Started about the time she found out little Mariana there was pregnant. Woman don't live in the twenty-first century. Would rather everyone think the girl was dead than that she got pregnant without being married. Probably giving the girl hell if she speaks to her at all."

"She was talkin' to her mom earlier, when I found her. Couldn't hear the other side of the conversation, but from what I could hear, it sounded like she was willin' to leave the girl where she was rather than help."

Marge shook her head, anger and frustration on her wrinkled face. "I've never wanted to give a person a piece of my mind more than I do Adelaide Everly. Woman never deserved to have a child in the first place. Drove her husband into an early grave, now she's about killing her daughter."

Great. Another person he needed to have a talk with. "You know anything about the boyfriend?"

"Hmm. Not sure about that one. But I can find out. Think his name is Harrison or something. Parents are Catholic, so they attend church across town. Don't think he's much account, though." She patted Thorn's shoulder again. "You keep a watch on that one. She's a good girl. Works hard."

"If you knew her, why didn't you say something when we first came in?"

Marge shrugged. "Knew the situation with her mother. Figured she'd be more comfortable if she thought I didn't know anything about it."

"If you weren't already married, Marge, I'd propose."

She slapped at him playfully, her cheeks blushing slightly. "Now, you know I'd never be caught dead ridin' behind someone on a Harley."

Thorn barked a laugh. "Yeah. You don't ride bitch."

"Exactly."

Mariana walked back out, and Thorn rose. "You stay out of trouble, Marge." He raised his voice, calling out to Tito. "Give Elena my love."

"No way, Thorn," Tito said with a grin. "I do that, she might take off with you. Then where would I be?"

Thorn chuckled as he took Mariana's hand and escorted her out the door. "Careful of the pipes when you get on. They'll still be hot." He helped her on, handed her the helmet, then climbed on himself. Once she had the helmet secured, he started up the big hog and pulled out of the diner.

Chapter Two

No matter how much she knew she should be on her guard, Mariana found herself casting caution away as Thorn sped down the road. Wind in her hair, a powerful man insisting she hang on to him, the freedom of something like flying -- all of it was like a balm to every single hurt she'd experienced in the past five months. She laughed as she tipped her face up to the sun and the breeze. After they passed the same grocery store the third time, she suspected Thorn had driven around the outskirts of Palm Beach because she was enjoying herself so much. Any trepidation she might have held for the biker vanished with that realization. He might look tough, but he was a good man. One who would take care of his woman and their child, not leave them stranded on the side of the road while he got a blow job. The memory of that stupid phone call with Jason finally sobered her.

When her laughter died, Thorn gave a heavy sigh. Mariana didn't miss that he glanced over her shoulder at her. Five minutes later, they pulled into Red's Garage. To her surprise, her car was in the bay, a mechanic bending over it. Another surprise came after Thorn helped her from the bike. As she turned back to the garage, she caught sight of two men arguing just outside the first big bay area. Was that... Jason? Arguing with Red?

Jason seemed to be in a heated debate with the big mechanic, gesturing to her car more than once as he did. Red looked like he couldn't give two shits and seemed to be only half listening. He stabbed at his cell phone while Jason yelled at him. Any time she'd needed someone to look at her old car, she'd always gone to Red. They knew her car better than she did.

Surely Jason wasn't trying to sabotage her being able to get her car fixed. That was just her being paranoid. Wasn't it?

"She can't even pay you, Red!" Jason was yelling, nearly pulling at his hair in frustration. "That piece-of-shit car isn't even worth fixing! Just tell her to fuck off!"

Red said nothing, just kept tapping on his phone. When he tucked the thing into his shirt pocket, Thorn's phone pinged. Red crossed his arms over his chest and said something to Jason she couldn't hear, but it seemed to infuriate her ex. He let out a string of expletives, moving threateningly toward Red. The bigger man didn't budge. In fact, he uncrossed his arms and leaned forward subtly. That small move made Jason halt abruptly, or he'd have run into his adversary.

Thorn stopped, placing a gentle hand on Mariana's shoulder to stop her as well. He pulled out his phone and read the text message. Apparently, Red was reaching out to Thorn. She wondered why as Thorn looked at his phone for several seconds. It was hard to read his expression. He kept glancing sharply at the two men until he finally put the phone away and just stared. The look on his face made Mariana cringe. She took an unconscious step away from Thorn, and his focus instantly landed on her. The second his gaze met hers, Mariana froze. Thorn took back the step she'd put between them and took her hand.

"That your baby's daddy?"

Mortified, Mariana closed her eyes and nodded. This was beyond embarrassing. It was one thing for Thorn to have heard the earlier conversation, but for him to actually witness firsthand how Jason treated her? She'd never live this down. Never be able to look at him again. Which was just as well. The second she left -- hopefully in her car -- she was sure Thorn would never lay eyes on her again. Which suited her just fine. Didn't it?

"Eyes up," he snapped softly. Instinctively, she brought her gaze back to Thorn. "If you can't look at him, look at me. Do not lower your gaze to him. Don't let that bastard think he's better'n you. Got me?"

"I -- yes. I'll try."

"No. You won't try. You'll do what I fuckin' tell you to or there will be consequences." OK, she didn't want to know what consequences he was referring to. At. All. When she gave a faint nod he asked, "Do you shorten your name?"

"Jason does. He calls me Mari, but I don't like it."

"You prefer your whole name, then?"

She thought about it. "When I was little, my dad used to call me Ana. He was so different from my mom. She hated it when she heard him shorten my name, but I always liked it. No one else ever called me Ana."

"Good," he said, then cupped her cheek gently and bent his head to brush his lips over hers. It wasn't any more than a quick, tender movement, but it was enough for Jason to see them. Which was probably what Thorn had intended. Didn't mean she didn't enjoy it. Her stomach fluttered, and she knew she whimpered a little. When he pulled back, he gave her a slight smile. "That'll do." His grin widened. "For now." The clasped her hand tighter and urged her forward toward Red and her car. "Red!" He called. "How's the car goin'?"

"I think she's ready now." Red hiked his thumb at the man putting down the hood and wiping down the edges. "Tinker's just putting the finishing touches on her. Should purr like a kitten now."

"I can't thank you enough, Red," she said softly. "You guys always do a wonderful job on such an old car. It's because of you it keeps running."

"You take good care of her, Mariana. Always bring her in for oil changes and tune ups on time. You're one of my best customers."

Jason snorted. "Just 'cause she has a piece-of-shit car you have to continually repair. Hell, she probably keeps you in business." He crossed his arms over his chest. "If she can't pay you, she fuckin' you for payment? 'Cause I'd totally pay to see Little Miss Prim and Proper get fucked by a grease monkey."

Thorn subtly moved Mariana behind him as he stepped in front of Jason. "You need to learn some respect, you punk-ass cunt."

Jason blanched, but one look in Mariana's direction was all it took for him to stiffen his spine. "Look, man. I've had the bitch. She ain't much to write home about. All I meant was that fuckin' a roughneck might loosen her up a little. Get her to do something more than just fuckin' lay there."

Thorn looked over his shoulder at Mariana. She wanted to sink into the ground, but she didn't dare look down. "He not make it good enough for you to want to move on him? Seriously?"

Mariana had no idea what to say, so she just shrugged, her gaze glued to his. Those consequences he'd spoken of earlier hovered in her imagination, taking all kinds of unpleasant shapes.

Thorn chuckled at her before he looked back at Jason. There was an amused look on his face. "Man, if she didn't move when you fucked her, that's on you. I can't get her to stay still. She wiggles on my dick like she's never had cock before. Best pussy I've ever had the pleasure of fuckin'."

Yeah. She wanted to die. Right there. Then Jason's face turned every shade of red she could imagine, from a light pink to, finally, a deep purple.

"You fucking slut!" He made a grab at her, but Thorn backhanded him, then stepped into him and grabbed him by the throat, slamming him against the wall.

Just like that, Thorn's face was a mask of rage. Mariana had never seen a man so scary looking. She actually whimpered, taking a step back, but then Tinker was at her side, a hand at the small of her back. "Shh, there, girl. Just watch and listen." He stepped a little farther away from her, but stayed close while Thorn dealt with Jason.

Thorn was up in Jason's face, his hand still firmly around Jason's throat. Jason was up on his tiptoes against the wall, his face growing more and more mottled by the second. "This is your only warning, so I suggest you listen good, you little fucker. You so much as breathe in her general direction again, I'll tear your fuckin' head off. You say nothing about her. You don't get near her. You don't even fuckin' think about her. Get me?"

There was no way Jason could move his head. He opened his mouth to say something, but nothing came out. He tried again, and, this time, managed to force out a "Yes." Thorn held him there a few more seconds. Jason began to claw at his wrist, and Thorn just squeezed tighter. She knew because Mariana could see the tendons working in those massive forearms of his.

Finally, he gave a little shove and let Jason go. The smaller man crumbled to the ground, gasping for breath.

"Red, if you don't mind, escort Ana wherever she needs to go. Me and this little motherfucker are gonna have a talk."

"No!" Jason scooted away on his ass, a hand raised defensively. "I understand! I'll leave her alone! I won't talk about her!"

"Good. Now that we all understand each other, I suggest you go change your fuckin' pants. Looks like you made a mess."

Mariana glanced down at Jason. Sure enough, her ex-lover had wet himself. There would likely be hell to pay later, but maybe Thorn had scared him enough Jason would just leave her alone. She doubted it, but a girl could hope.

Thorn walked over to her and pulled her into his arms. He rested a hand on her rounded tummy and the baby kicked. A tiny movement, but definitely there. He gave her a little grin. "Looks like Bruno there's wantin' to join the fight. Don't like anyone talkin' bad 'bout his mama."

Before Mariana could say anything, Thorn kissed her again. This one lingered just a little, but was no less chaste. She'd give it to him -- he played the part well without freaking her out. Had he discussed it with her beforehand, she'd have said absolutely not, but the look on Jason's face was worth it. He was equal parts disbelieving and angry-jealous. While she didn't really want him jealous, it felt good to know she'd finally shocked him. Mariana wasn't a fool. He didn't want her any more now than he had an hour ago. But she represented something he'd thought of as his. Now, another man had what had been his. And Thorn had proven he didn't care that she'd been Jason's before.

She was Thorn's now. And he was keeping her.

Except that was a fantasy.

Before she could protest, Thorn ended the kiss, rubbing her baby bump tenderly. She almost hoped he'd continue with his plan to send her along with Red as her escort because she didn't want to embarrass herself when they were alone. Right this second, she was feeling a little possessive her own damned self. Even as the thought entered her mind, she knew that wasn't going to happen. Thorn would be her escort. Then he'd have to know she had no place to live yet.

Yeah. This was going to be humiliating.

* * *

Thorn followed Mariana to the Motel 6 she was staying at. He wanted to toss her on the back of his bike again and take her to the clubhouse, but there was no way she'd go for that. He didn't like her staying here, though. Didn't sit well with him. When they pulled into the parking lot near her room, he pulled up beside her and climbed off his bike. Opening the door for her, he frowned down at her.

"You're staying here?"

"It's temporary. I'm supposed to look at apartments once I get my paycheck." She didn't quite meet his gaze.

"When's that?"

She shrugged. "A few days."

"Come on," he said, urging her away from the car as he shut the door. "I'll walk you to your room."

"I'm good. Really."

Thorn studied her. She wouldn't meet his gaze, looking down at her shoes where she toyed with a pebble on the asphalt. "You know I'm not gonna hurt you. Right?"

"Yeah. I just don't like strangers knowing where I'm staying. I'm sure you understand."

He did, actually. Didn't mean he liked it, though. "Give me your phone," he said, holding his hand out. She hesitated, but handed it over without a word. He sent himself a text from her number, then handed it back to her. Once his phone pinged with the message, he sent her a message that included the Salvation's Bane clubhouse number.

"Add both of those to your contact list. The number I sent you as well. That's the clubhouse. You need anything, you text me. I don't answer immediately, you call me. You still can't get ahold of me, call the fuckin' clubhouse. Ask for Thorn. Get me?"

She nodded. "I understand. What I don't understand is -- why?"

"'Cause you need someone lookin' after you, and I got a bad feelin' about that motherfucker Jason. You keep your doors locked. Don't let him in, no matter what."

"Hadn't planned on it," she muttered.

He was silent for a long time, staring at her. She was uncomfortable with his gaze, he could tell, but he had to offer her more. "There's a place you could stay in the clubhouse until you get your shit together. No rent. All you gotta do is help with the chores."

"Thank you, but no. I'll be fine. Once I get my next paycheck, I'll have a start on the next couple months' finances. It's all about priorities and management." She sounded confident. Like the very thought was appealing to her. Hell, he couldn't blame her. If she'd lived with that son of a bitch for any length of time, she probably felt like she'd been freed from an interminable prison sentence.

"Fine. Just keep the offer in mind. If you get into trouble, don't let your pride keep you from what you know your baby needs." It was a low blow, but he had to throw that in there. If it took guilting her into looking out for her safety, Thorn wasn't above it. She gasped a little and looked away, but nodded her head, her hand going to her belly in a gentle caress. "Good. Use all the locks on your door. Don't go out after dark."

"Are you always so bossy?" The little thing looked equal parts annoyed and embarrassed she'd asked the question, but didn't back down.

"No. I'm usually worse." He tried his best to keep his lips from twitching, but it was nearly impossible. So he got on his bike as if to leave, hoping she'd take the hint and get her pretty little ass inside.

"Don't forget to add that fuckin' contact to your phone," he called out as she ascended the outside stairs. She clutched the phone to her chest and nodded once before continuing on. She waited at the top of the landing, apparently wanting him to move before she went inside her room.

He took off, headed to the clubhouse, which was about fifteen minutes away. It wasn't long before he felt his phone vibrate in his back pocket. When he stopped at a stop light, he checked it. Sure enough, she'd followed his instructions and sent a text. He grinned. Thorn honestly hadn't expected Ana to obey, but then she had been pretty shaken up.

A few minutes later, he pulled into his clubhouse, parking the bike just outside the entrance to the common room. He went straight to Ripper's office. Ripper was their intel man. He could sometimes work miracles with his computers. Thorn didn't necessarily want a miracle. He was just hoping he could keep an eye on one feisty little brunette.

* * *

The room Mariana had rented for the week wasn't anything fancy, but it was clean. Just not in the best part of town. Thorn wasn't wrong to warn her to use all the locks on her door and to not be out after dark. So, when the knock came just after dark a couple of days later, when the whole block was still going strong outside with a weekend party, she ignored it.

"Mari! Open up! It's me, Jason!"

"Shit," she muttered. Jason was the absolute last person she wanted to see. When she didn't answer right away, he continued to pound on the door.

"I know you're in there, Mari! I'm just gonna keep knocking until you answer. It'll make a lot of noise. Might even get you kicked out!"

She sighed. Was it his mission in life to make her miserable? "Go away, Jason. I think you said all there was to say when you left me stranded on the side of the road."

"I just came to apologize."

"Fine. You've apologized. Accepted. Now leave."

"I'm not leaving until I talk to you, Mari."

She stood up from her chair by the window in a huff. "Don't call me Mari!" She undid the deadbolt. Then the chain. "Say what you've got to say then leave." She finished speaking, and finally got the door opened. Just as it cleared a couple inches, Jason shoved his way inside, knocking her back. She stumbled and fell to the floor on her ass.

"What the hell, Jason?"

He shut the door, then he was on her. The first blow took her in the temple as she attempted to stand, knocking her silly. She couldn't even get out a cry of pain, the beating was so intense and sudden. And he continued to punch her. Over and over. Then to kick. He didn't say a word. Just beat the living shit out of her.

When she rolled over and protected her head, he kicked her back and stomach. Jason seemed to target her abdomen -- and the baby -- but the second she balled herself up and covered her unborn child with her arms, he moved to her head. Each blow landed like a hammer on an anvil until she once again covered her head with one arm, still desperately trying to protect her unborn child with the other arm. The coppery taste of blood was heavy, so heavy she thought she might choke as she tried to suck in a lungful of air.

Finally, there was one solid kick to her abdomen and the huge pressure in her stomach suddenly gave way with a gush of fluid between her legs. She tried to scream, but nothing emerged. She needed to breathe, but when she tried to gasp for air, the pain in her side was so intense she could barely take a shallow breath. Nothing in her life so far had prepared her for this kind of pain. Every part of her body was battered and bruised. Mariana had no idea if any of her injuries were life threatening, but she had the feeling this was how she ended. She knew her baby was dead, and that was even worse. She knew in her heart that, if Jason didn't stop immediately, she was going to die here. Might still die even if he stopped. But she couldn't take anymore. Finally, she just gave up. There was no way to win against Jason, and maybe she didn't really want to. Maybe dying was just easier. Dying meant she didn't have to face the reality of what had just happened.

Dying also meant that bastard had beaten her.

"Filthy little whore!" he spat at her. "Where's your needle-dick biker now! See? He doesn't want you any more than I ever did. No one wants you, you little cunt! You're not good enough to have my baby! Fucking whore! Probably wasn't even mine." Jason gave a harsh laugh then. "Not that it matters much now. Bet I killed the little shit. Oughtta kill you too, but you're just not worth it. Good luck, Mari." He spat the shortened version of her name at her. Probably because he knew how much she hated it. "Hope you rot in hell!"

* * *

"Hey, Thorn. Got a minute?"

Ripper didn't usually venture out of his cave this time of day. If he needed anything, he generally sent a text. Thorn hated texts, but he recognized it was the medium Ripper was most comfortable with for delivering news. The fact that he'd sought Thorn out said this was important.

"What's up?"

The other man hesitated. "It's your girl. She's on the move and I'm... concerned."

Instantly Thorn focused fully on the other man. "Explain," he barked.

"I think she's in trouble."

"Where?"

Again, Ripper hesitated. "She's on her way to JFK Memorial Hospital. I hacked into 911 and it sounds bad, Thorn."

Thorn swore as he bolted from his chair. "Get a team. Include Beast and Blood. We go with a show of force. I leave in five. Anyone not ready follows as soon as they are."

He'd just straddled his bike and reached up to start it when his phone buzzed. Normally, he'd have ignored it, but with Mariana having his number, he still held hope she'd call him. When he pulled out his phone and glanced at the screen his heart accelerated.

"Ana?"

"Uh, no. This is Miles from JFK Memorial Hospital Emergency Room. There's a woman here with your number on her phone. We were hoping you might help us."

"I'm on my way."

"Sir!" The man had been pretty calm and neutral until this point. He obviously didn't want Thorn to hang up. "Is her name Ana?"

"You don't know her name?" Thorn asked the question with a harsh, growled snap.

"Uh, no, sir." There was a voice in the background Thorn thought he recognized. "Put Doc on."

"I'm sorry?"

Thorn had to rein in his patience. "Put Dr. Collins on the fuckin' phone."

The people Doc worked with didn't necessarily know he was a member of an MC, but Thorn was past caring if he stepped on toes at this point. Logically, he knew the man was only doing his job, but there was an urgency inside him Thorn had never felt before. Not even during his time in the service. A knot in his gut that was busy tightening with every breath he took, making it harder and harder to think rationally. He needed to get to the hospital and actually lay eyes on Mariana. Ludicrous since he'd only just met her, but she needed him. He knew it in his heart.

A moment later, Doc's voice came over the phone. "Dr. Collins."

"Doc, it's Thorn. What the fuck's goin' on?"

"Gonna have to give me a point of reference, Thorn." Doc was unruffled as always.

"I didn't call you. You fuckin' called me. Through your flunky."

Thorn could hear Doc give an exasperated sigh. "You know, I ain't the only fuckin' doc around here, Thorn. What the fuck're you talkin' about?"

There were giggles in the background and a mumbled apology by Doc. "Mariana Everly. Pregnant girl. She's apparently there and unable to give anyone any information. They found my number in her phone and called. Ring a fuckin' bell?"

There was silence then, "I'll call you back."

"Don't bother. I'm on my way now. I'll be there in ten. Meet me in the ambulance bay."

He didn't wait for the other man to answer. Seconds later, he was on the road with Beast and Blood flanking him. He knew that all he had to do was give the word and his brothers would unleash hell on anyone he told them to.

The entire eight-minute ride to JFK Memorial was an exercise in control. Control his brothers. Control the bike. Control his fucking emotions. It didn't help that, all the way to the hospital, Ripper kept feeding him a running commentary of what he could pick up between EMS and the hospital. Mariana was hurt. Badly.

And she hadn't called him. He shouldn't have been surprised. She didn't know him. Still, he'd have thought he treated her better than that fucker, Jason. Maybe he'd overdone it. Not that he could have helped it. Thorn wasn't a guy who could watch women being hurt. Sure, he'd killed his share when it was necessary, but he'd always made sure it was a clean kill. Women as sweet as Mariana turned him into mush. Not a good thing for an MC president.

The second he pulled into the wide alley designated "Ambulance Entrance Only," Thorn saw Doc leaning against the building. He straightened and hurried over. Thorn parked his bike next to Doc's in the physician's parking spot.

"Now, tell me what the fuck's goin' on." Thorn pinned the other man with his most lethal stare. He couldn't help it. All he wanted to do was to find Mariana and fix whatever had happened. If that meant he killed someone, so be it.

"She just got out of surgery. She'll be in recovery for a while, and you can't go in until you calm the fuck down anyway," Doc said softly. "We've got time. How well do you know this girl?"

"Not well. What happened?"

"She was attacked. Lucky she was able to get to her phone at all. EMS said she basically dialed 911 and just whimpered. They found her by her phone's GPS."

"Yeah. Ripper said as much. Now, tell me what exactly happened. Ripper told me some, but he's getting clinical information from the radio reports. I need the actual rundown."

"Bottom line?" When Thorn nodded, Doc continued. "She's been beat to shit. Was pregnant, but lost the baby. Miscarried before they got to the hospital. That's what they're fixing now. She was pretty torn up inside. They cleaned out her uterus -- it's called a D&C -- to try to control the hemorrhaging. She should recover, but the OB guys don't know if she'll be able to have kids in the future. Whoever did this did a number on her."

"She tell you anything?"

Doc shook his head. "She was in and out of consciousness when she got here."

"Take me to her."

Doc nodded and led the way inside. After a phone call, he led Doc upstairs to a hospital room. There, in pristine white of the bed clothes, lay Mariana. Thorn could still see the lovely women he'd bullied into eating at the diner, but…

One side of her face was bruised and swollen, that eye shut. A cut marred the perfection of her lower lip, and blood oozed from a small piece of gauze laid over a cut just under her eye. The other side of her face was relatively unharmed. Probably because she'd been lying on that side. The ground would have protected her unless she'd rolled. One arm was in a cast -- the same side as her battered face. She lay still as death, but was breathing on her own. No ventilator.

"She should be fine, once she rests and heals. Do me a favor and don't scare the poor child to death. She's been through enough." Doc clapped him on the shoulder and turned to go.

"Hey," Thorn said. "Thanks. Tell the others to make themselves comfortable on hospital grounds. I'll text when I need them."

Doc nodded, then left.

Chapter Three

Mariana floated in and out of consciousness. There was pain, but it was muted. She knew that if she tried too hard to wake up the pain would engulf her, so she just let herself drift. In the back of her mind, she knew she needed to see what was going on, but if it kept away the agony she'd experienced before, fuck it. She'd deal with it later.

It wasn't until she heard the familiar male voice in the background that she had something to focus on. Her mind wouldn't find that calm, tranquil sedation and go blissfully numb. It latched on to that voice. It was scary, but familiar in a comfortable way. It felt safe. She gravitated to it until there was no choice but to open her eyes.

She turned her head slightly and the movement sent shards of glass stabbing through her brain. She cried out, but that only made the pain worse, so she immediately shut her mouth. Eventually the pain ebbed, and she realized someone was holding her hand, stroking the back of it gently.

"Hey there, honey." The man continued to rub her hand, his voice low and pleasant. It was hard to read his emotions. His face seemed relaxed, but his eyes were flat. Cold.

"Thorn? What are you doing here?" Her voice was rough and her throat scratchy. "Is there water?"

"I came when I realized you were in trouble."

"I would have called you," she said quickly, not wanting him angry with her. "I just couldn't talk."

"I know. Doc gave me a rundown of your injuries. Said you'd called 911 and just left the line open. They have to investigate those calls, so they came right to you. Good thinking on your part."

That shocked her. She'd half expected Thorn to berate her for not doing as he'd told her. Instead, he just seemed happy she'd gotten the help she'd needed. He sat up and poured her a cup of water from the pitcher a nurse had left. He set the straw in the cup and held it to her lips. She took a sip gratefully. Then another. Water had never tasted so good. He must have only poured a small amount because it was gone quickly. When she looked back at the pitcher, he shook his head.

"Give it a second to settle on your stomach. The nurse said you might get sick if you drank too much too fast."

She sighed, but relaxed against the pillow. "How long have you been here?"

"A while."

"I appreciate you watching over me, but you don't have to stay."

He said nothing, looked at her so long she finally did what she knew she needed to do. She used her free hand to touch her face gingerly. It seemed to be grotesquely swollen on one side. One eye was swollen shut, but she'd known something was wrong there. What else? She remembered a horrible pressure...

"Oh, God," she whimpered, her hands flying to her belly.

Thorn grabbed her wrists gently, leaning over her and kissing the delicate skin of each wrist. "Shh, shh. I know. Just breathe through it. I'll help you get through this."

Mariana tried to do what Thorn instructed, but instead of taking deep, calming breaths, she ended up taking in great gulps of air, hyperventilating instead. "No!" The sob sounded broken, even to herself. *I lost the baby.*

She remembered, during the attack, realizing the baby was beyond her help. Knowing that and facing the reality were two different things. "I tried to protect the baby," she sobbed out. "I tried, but he seemed to be targeting my belly as much as my head. When I started gushing fluid, that was when he stopped. Oh, God! Oh, God!"

"Who was it, Ana?" Thorn asked. His voice might have sounded gentle, but there was nothing gentle in his eyes. This was a man out for blood.

There was a long pause while Mariana stared at Thorn. If she gave this man Jason's name, if she named him as her attacker, Thorn would kill the man. She knew it as well as she knew her own name. It was there in his eyes. "What are you going to do?" Even knowing the answer she had to ask.

"You know what I'm doing. Now tell me who did this."

She looked at him a long time, trying to decide what to do. Blurting out Jason's name was what her heart wanted most. Not for herself, but for her baby. It'd never had a chance. One look into Thorn's eyes and she knew he'd kill Jason and not even bother to dust his hands off.

It was a horrible thing to know you held a person's life in your hands. Mariana had never expected to have that kind of responsibility. Even though there was a part of her who knew Jason deserved everything this man chose to dish out to him, she wasn't sure her soul could stand the stain. In her heart, she'd already killed him. If she whispered his name, Thorn would make Jason's death as brutal as her child's had been. But she also felt that, by doing so, not only would she condemn her own soul to hell -- which she could take -- but she'd be condemning Thorn to the same fate. That, she couldn't live with, no matter how much better she thought it would make her feel.

"I'm not telling you, Thorn. Not because I want to protect the miserable bastard, but because you don't need that. This is my fight. I'll take care of it."

He looked at her for a long time. So long Mariana had to look away. They sat in silence then. The pump that delivered her pain medicine at regular intervals had shot her full of whatever was in the thing, and she started to get fuzzy headed. Just as she was about to doze off, Thorn leaned close.

"I'll get this from you, Ana. Then I'll do what's necessary. We both know it was Jason. I've only got to get the confirmation from you, and it's done."

"No, Thorn." Her tongue felt thick and unmanageable. Her words slurred despite her best efforts. "I can't be responsible for this."

"You won't be, honey. Just… let it go. Tell me. Was it Jason?"

As darkness closed in around her, to her complete and utter horror, Mariana heard herself whisper, "Yes…"

* * *

He needed to go. To get this done. But Thorn couldn't bring himself to leave Mariana's side. When the police showed up, he was sure they'd try to arrest him, thinking he'd had a hand in beating the young woman senseless, but it turned out the men were two he knew, and they didn't give him trouble.

"Let us handle this, Mr. McGregor. If you go all Batman on the situation, you'll only hurt our case against her attacker or end up in jail yourself. We'll be in touch with Mariana when she's awake."

"Then you find the little motherfucker and put his ass in jail before I find him." He shrugged. "Not so hard, is it?" Thorn meant it, too. The second he saw Jason Harrison's face would be the second that fucker died. Now, if he could just manage to leave Mariana's side long enough to take action.

The doctors kept Mariana sedated with pain medicine for the better part of the week, letting her body heal. Thorn hadn't left for longer than it took for him to shower, and he did that in her hospital room bathroom. There was something in the way she'd told him that said she wasn't trying to protect her ex, but was trying to protect him. Thorn. What could she possibly mean by that? Thorn had killed more times than he cared to admit. He knew dangerous men. Jason Harrison was only dangerous to people smaller and physically weaker than he was. Even if he came at Thorn armed to the teeth, Jason wouldn't be a danger to him.

Finally, five-and-a-half days after she'd been beaten so badly, Mariana had stayed awake more than a few minutes at a time. They'd gotten her up and made her walk. Brought her unappetizing meals that she'd refused to eat until Thorn had coaxed her into it. That was when she finally gave him the look he'd been dreading. The one with suspicion and fear in it.

"Say what's on your mind, girl."

"Why are you here?"

He shrugged. "Someone's gotta look out for you."

"No, they don't." Her reply was soft but unmistakable. "I've been looking out for myself for a long time."

"And look where it got you." He almost wished he could take the words back, but if it bullied her into accepting his help it was worth it to see that crestfallen look on her face. At least, that's what he told himself. "Until that son of a bitch is out of the picture, you're stuck with me. Get used to it."

Her hand slipped up to her belly. She sat up in the bed, the sheet and blanket over her lap. Her eyes misted over, and she blinked rapidly. "Of course. I'm grateful for any help you're willing to give."

Thorn let out a long breath. "I'm sorry you're going through this. It's partly my fault. I thought I was helping by letting him think you had a strong protector. I should have followed through with my statement. Made you come to the clubhouse with me."

"I wouldn't have," she said softly. "Besides, I never thought he'd do something like this. He's the one who dumped me. Even had another girlfriend. I never thought he'd react so… violently."

"Well, we both know now," Thorn said. Carefully, so he didn't startle her, he placed his big hand over hers, completely swallowing it. "I'll help you through this."

When she looked up at him, those luminous eyes of hers seemed to swallow him, making him drown. She looked lost. If ever there was a female in need of saving it was this one. Not that Thorn blamed her. It seemed she'd lost everything. Her father. Her mother. The father of her child. The baby. She was beaten down, but he knew there was fire in her. She just needed to lick her wounds a little. Regroup.

Tentatively, she picked up her other hand and, looking up at him through those long lashes of hers, placed her hand over his so that his hand was sandwiched between hers. Thorn placed his other hand over the stack and squeezed.

"Together?"

"'Til the very end, little darlin'."

After that, she'd slept some more. Thorn called to check in with Havoc.

"Any word on that little bastard?"

"He knows he fucked up," Havoc said. "Found some guys from the garage who led me to the guy's buddy. Says he's hidin' out from the law." Havoc snorted like that was the height of absurdity. "Unfortunately for him, his buddy thinks he's just as much a dickwad as we do. He'll keep an eye out and let us know if he hears anything."

"You believe him?"

"About ninety percent. If Harrison were to pay him he might keep his mouth shut, but I doubt that happens. Guy says Harrison is with this new girl 'cause her daddy's loaded. He's looking to cash in. Apparently he thinks she'll be his sugar mama. Ain't smart enough to figure out she don't control her old man's money."

"They're talkin' 'bout lettin' Ana go home tomorrow if she has a good night. I'll talk to Doc, but I want more for her."

"You know, we could ask Bones for help. Mama and Pops would be perfect for this."

Thorn thought for a minute. The couple weren't exactly a couple, and no one knew their past or even their real names. Except Thorn. He knew them all too well. He might not know exactly what they were to each other or what they'd done in the service, but he knew them. They were good people, and he trusted them to take care of Mariana, but he also knew Mama had never liked him and probably never would. Old wounds always left a scar. But there was no denying the skill and patience either of them had with treating the club members at Bones. While Thorn wasn't ready to say he trusted the couple, the Bones president, Cain, certainly did. Cain was a close personal friend of Thorn as well as his boss. Salvation's Bane and Bones were sister clubs as well as home to many of the men and women who worked at Cain's private contracting company, ExFil. If Cain trusted Mama and Pops, Thorn would reserve judgment. Besides, he needed their help for Ana.

"Do it. Reach out and see if they're willing to come down for a week or so. We'll compensate them however they see fit."

"On it, boss."

Mariana was, indeed, released the next day. She'd tried to insist on walking to the car Red had brought. Thankfully he'd thought to pick something ordinary. The late-model Taurus was nauseatingly normal, but putting Mariana on the back of his bike back to the clubhouse wasn't happening. The nurses, however, had insisted she ride in the wheelchair. When she argued, Thorn had simply scooped her up and carried her himself as a nurse escorted them to the car. Thorn was surprised at how his chest swelled when she wrapped those slender arms around him when they stepped into the elevator and sighed as she laid her head on his shoulder. He'd absently kissed her forehead before realizing what he'd done. Red snickered, earning the mechanic a glare, which the big man just shrugged at.

Once they were in the car, Thorn looked over at Ana. "I know you don't trust me yet. Just give it a few days. If you still have reservations, we'll talk about them, but I want you to stay at the clubhouse until this is done. No matter what, I swear to you that man will never touch you again."

"Honestly?" Ana raised her eyebrows at him, waiting for him to respond. When he nodded for her to continue she said, "I do trust you. You've given me no reason not to. From the moment I met you, you've done nothing but help me." Then she blushed. "Well, you did take some kisses I didn't give you permission for, but I won't hold that against you."

Thorn smiled when he really wanted to groan, take her in his arms, and repeat the experience. "Good, then. I'll make sure to ask next time."

On the way to the clubhouse, he noticed her wince from time to time, holding her ribs. Though the doctors had assured her they weren't broken -- a miracle in itself -- the bruising would be sore for a few more days. Other than that, the only pain she had was from her abdomen. The pain there, both mental and physical, would be longer in healing. Thorn vowed to himself he'd see to both injuries.

Once at the clubhouse, they were met by Lucy and Fleur, Vicious and Beast's ol' ladies. "We've got a place set up for her," Lucy said. "It's got the most beautiful view of the ocean in the morning. The sunrise is absolutely gorgeous."

"No," Thorn said, gruffly. "Puttin' her in my room." He strode up the stairs.

"I'll be fine by myself," Mariana said softly. "I don't want to put you out."

"Ain't puttin' me out. I'm stayin' with you."

The girls giggled, and Mariana turned beet red. "I'm not sure that's appropriate," she said with a glare.

Thorn went down the hallway straight to his bedroom. "Do I look like I give a fuck about what's appropriate? This is my fuckin' club. I'll do what the fuck I want." He carried her inside and set her gently on the bed. As he stood, Thorn looked down at the small woman in the middle of his big bed. The sight was at once heartwarming and heartbreaking.

Her face wasn't as bruised and swollen as it had been, but there were greenish yellow splotches where the bruises were healing. Her eye was still swollen and the white still had blood, but it was in the last stages of healing. Because she'd had such a difficult time eating due to the swelling, she'd lost weight she couldn't afford to lose, making her cheeks stand out sharply. Dark circles still colored the delicate skin under her eyes as well. Even though the evidence of why she was with him was a stark reminder of her ordeal, he wasn't sorry she was with him now. He'd keep her safe.

"Honey," Lucy said. "Take my advice. Don't argue with them. You'll rarely win, and they enjoy it." She smiled warmly at Mariana. "The stuff from your apartment is downstairs. We'll bring it up tomorrow. For now, just do whatever Thorn tells you to. Welcome to Salvation's Bane."

Thorn picked up a couple of fluffy pillows from a nearby chair and propped them up behind her at the head of the bed. "I'll get you some water," Thorn said gruffly.

"Thorn," she called out as he neared the door. When he paused, looking back over his shoulder, she said, "Thanks. Thanks for coming for me."

Thorn nodded once, then closed the door.

He was so fucked. Because the girls were wrong. He'd never win an argument with Mariana, because he'd move heaven and Earth to give the little female anything she wanted.

* * *

It was another two weeks before Mariana could move without wincing. A couple from Kentucky had come to help her with a kind of rehabilitation. Mama, the woman said her name was, and Pops. Mama and Pops were a Godsend. Not only did Mama see she was healing properly, but helped with what Mariana had come to think of as her rehab. Though, amazingly, she didn't have any broken bones, the pain from her bruised ribs and the trauma to the rest of her body was nearly unbearable at times. Mama had taught her how to move without straining her muscles too much. All in all, Mariana suppose she had it easier than it could have been. Through it all, Thorn hadn't much more than let her lift a finger if he was around. Finally, she had to put her foot down.

"I'm going outside. You can come with me if you want, but I'm going to sit in the sun for a while."

"Well, at least take some sunblock," Thorn grumbled at her.

Marinara couldn't help herself. She let out a giggle. When he gave her a dark look, she clapped her hand over her mouth, but the giggles persisted. "You, the big tough biker, actually said the word 'sunblock.'"

"Yeah, well, don't tell anyone."

He put a hand at the small of her back and escorted her outside. The day was hot and humid, but Mariana soaked it up. She was used to being outside. Working. Playing. The lack of physical activity was starting to wear on her. Mama and Pops were wonderful and encouraged her in everything she did, but even they said it was time for her to get out and back to life.

"Tomorrow, I want to go to the beach," she told him. "I want to swim."

"Christ, Ana," he swore.

"Please, Thorn. I'm going crazy cooped up here. Your friends are all wonderful, but I can't lay in bed all day and expect everyone to wait on me hand and foot. Mama and Pops are the only ones who let me do anything, and I suspect you've been growling at them. I need to get out. Get my strength back. I've got to be ready to get on with my life."

"How about we compromise? Baby steps," he said. "I'll take you back to the diner. We'll do a little shopping for you."

"I have to be careful with my money --"

He cut her off with a wave of his hand. "Stop. Don't start that nonsense again."

Money had been a point of contention between them. Mariana had insisted she pay her way, while Thorn hadn't allowed her to spend one dime. Anything she wanted or needed just magically appeared, and it was getting old.

"You stop. I'm perfectly capable of taking care of myself. I know you don't think much of me right now, but once I'm back at work, I'll be on better footing. I'll be out of your hair."

"Who the fuck said you were in my hair?" Thorn looked thunderous. Like whoever had put that idea in her head was going to pay and pay hard. "Haven't you figured out yet I want you here?"

"Thorn!" A young man hurried into the common room where they currently stood. His eyes were wide, and he looked excited. "Ripper needs you. He's found something."

Thorn growled, pulling Mariana into an embrace. He rested his chin on her head. The gesture took Mariana by surprise. Though he was constantly by her side, Thorn hadn't shown anything more than mildly affectionate gestures. A hand at her back. Tucking the occasional escaping curl behind her ear. He hadn't hugged or kissed her since before the attack. It was one of the reasons Mariana was growing increasingly uncomfortable. She had no idea where their strange relationship was going, and she was afraid she was coming to rely on him too much.

"Give me a minute, Skip." Thorn said over her head. "Tell Ripper I'll be right there."

When the prospect left the room, Thorn pulled back to look down at Mariana. He tilted her chin up gently so she had to meet his gaze. "Listen to me, Ana. I'm not letting you go anywhere I don't follow. We're in this together."

What did that mean? She was so confused, but the biggest part of her was so hopeful she couldn't stand it. Over the weeks she'd been here, she'd watched Thorn closely. He was exactly the kind of man she wanted in her life. Thorn would be the protector she wanted and needed. Not a man like Jason. A man who'd beat a woman carrying his child with the intention of making her lose it. Hastily, she shut the door on that line of thought. If she let it out, it would plague her the entire day.

"Do you trust me, Ana?" Thorn's gruff voice brought her back to the present.

"Yes," she said without hesitation.

"Then rest in here for a while. I'll go see what Ripper wants, then we'll go upstairs and talk. After that, I'll take you out to eat, and we'll go for a walk on the beach. Will that be good?"

He was so patient with her, never raising his voice. Even when he sounded put out or grumpy, she knew it was to make her laugh. His brothers had commented on it too, ragging him mercilessly. Thorn just flipped them off and put his arm around her and they went about their business.

"All right," she said softly. "I'll wait here."

Then he did something unexpected. Thorn bent his head and kissed her gently, cupping her face in his hands as he did. When he straightened, he held her gaze for several seconds, searching her face for something. When he found what he was looking for, he nodded once, then turned and left.

* * *

"Tell me you found that little fuck." Thorn knew he was in a foul mood, but he had to get this taken care of so he could work on helping Ana heal -- and more. He desperately needed to get on with the business of making her his.

"He's in Flat Springs," Ripper said. "About thirty minutes from here, give or take. Little shithole apartment in town above one of the local businesses. According to his landlord, he hasn't come out since he rented the place. Got buddies bringing him food, but once we knew where to look it was easy. The more time passes without anyone looking for Mariana or her attacker, the braver he's getting. I'd say he'll split before paying next month's rent. Which leaves you about a week to decide our next move."

"My move," Thorn corrected in a steely voice. "I'll use Bane to find him, but I'm dealing with him myself."

"Like fuck," Havoc growled. "We're in this to-fucking-gether."

Thorn looked his vice president in the eyes, not blinking. "I intend to kill the fucker. No need for anyone else to get his hands dirty. This isn't for the club. This is for me."

"The club is about all of us, Thorn," Vicious said softly. "She belongs to you. You belong to us, which means she belongs to us. Don't start fuckin' things up now just 'cause you're trying to be noble or some shit. We take care of this together."

"I said no," Thorn snapped. "This is going to be messy."

"All the more reason for a full crew," Havoc said, not in the least intimidated. "You're not going alone, so bite my head off if you want. It's still not happening."

"I've already got a plan going," Red, the road captain offered. "Little fucker won't know what hit him. Until you're done playing."

The four other men in the room looked at Thorn with steady expressions. None of them was backing down. In fact, they were ignoring his assertion in the first damned place.

"She's a good girl, Thorn," Beast said softly. "She deserves justice."

Thorn snapped his gaze to Beast's. "She doesn't find out about it. That one has a tender heart, and it's been trampled on again and again. She's not going to get in her head she's the reason that fucker died. She's not. I am."

"Fine. Still a simple matter," Red said, distracting Thorn from Beast's line of thought. "Knock him out. Take him to the swamp. Beat the living fuck outta him like he did your woman, then, when you're ready, he dies. Like Mariana's child. We can take him anywhere you want. I have a number of places marked for just such occasions."

Thorn gave each man a hard look. He needed to know if there was any give in even one of them. If there was, he'd exploit that weakness and continue on his own like he wanted to. There was no give. No weakness. Each man was with him to the death. Literally.

"Fine. Set it up for someplace that has absolutely no ties to Mariana. I won't have the police looking at her for longer than it takes them to establish she was nowhere near him and has moved on. If it comes back to me, I can take it. But she's not to be touched."

"Won't come back to nobody," Red said, confidently. "I'll get Blood to help with the clean-up at the site and the apartment. When we're done, it will look like he up and vanished like a fuckin' fart in the wind."

Chapter Four

Gaining entrance to the old building from the back side, away from the streetlights in the middle of town, was a piece of cake. What was hard was getting there in the first fucking place. The street was wide, a crossroads of sorts in the middle of downtown Flat Springs. The city boasted a little over three thousand residents, the majority of which were within a half mile of where the Salvation's Bane crew stood now. The building was old, and the second story run-down while the first story was used as a business. Most of the buildings along Main Street were just like it, but the building across the road was adjacent to one of the oldest banks in town. Which meant security cameras. Bikes were too loud, so Red had furnished them with a truck pulling a small enclosed trailer. The dark Ford F-150 was in good shape and nondescript. Nothing stood out about it, and there were probably a hundred other vehicles just like it in town. A quick change of the license plate, and it now belonged to someone other than any member of Salvation's Bane.

They parked a couple blocks away, out of the street lighting, taking different routes to the target building so they had it covered from every angle. Thorn was still annoyed Beast had overruled him and gotten others in the club involved, but it also made him smile. These men were his brothers. They had each other's backs. He'd do the same for any one of them. Had done it, helping both Vicious and Beast secure their women.

As he waited, a pair of binoculars to his eyes, he thought about Mariana and his gut tightened. Her body was healing. After he'd met with his brothers, she'd talked him into letting her go swimming. When he and the boys had left the clubhouse, she was happily splashing around the pool with the other ol' ladies. Lucy, Vicious's woman, had urged Mariana and Fleur into the water with her and then it was on. They had races, water fights, and were in the middle of a water volleyball game with three of the younger prospects when he'd left them to it. Mama and Pops had been sitting under a large umbrella, watching the activities with a smile, obviously approving of the activity. Mama had promised Thorn not to let her overdo it, but had stressed to Thorn that Mariana needed to get back to normal. She had more than physical wounds to heal.

"Heads up." Beast's voice was a growl through the earpiece Thorn wore. "One target approaching from the north side of the building. Looks like he's headed to the stairs. That our guy?"

Thorn looked. Really looked. At first, he thought it was. Jason was a little skinny fucker with a mullet he had shaved on the sides of his head. But this guy had tattoos peeking from under his shirt sleeve and the collar, and his hair wasn't hardly long enough.

"Negative. But I'm bettin' this guy knows somethin'. They look too much alike for him not to."

"You think they're settin' you up?" Beast, ever the protector, sounded ready to take matters into his own hands.

"I doubt it. More likely, this Jason punk set up some putz to take the fall in case someone was lookin' for him." He flipped a switch on his radio. "Ripper. How sure are you about this local? Guy here ain't the target."

"Had eyes on him yesterday. Hacked into the city's security feeds and made a positive ID from his driver's license."

"It possible this guy has a brother?" Thorn was starting to feel the sting of disappointment. He wanted this done, Goddamn it! The silence while Ripper checked his information wasn't long, but it seemed to Thorn like it lasted a fucking year.

"No. But he has a first cousin who is nearly identical."

"Is it possible you mistook one for the other?"

Another silence. Then a sigh. "Maybe." Another beat. "Yeah. It's possible. I'm sorry, Thorn."

He wanted to rail at his brother, but it wasn't the other man's fault. He'd pushed, and Ripper had gotten him what he wanted. "Might not be a bust," Thorn said. "Beast, can you get inside and question the guy?"

"He'll likely go straight to his cousin."

"Probably," Thorn agreed. "Bettin' you can persuade him to keep his fuckin' mouth shut."

"I'll lay it out for him, then help him decide." Havoc sounded like he was looking forward to the helping.

"You've got ten minutes," Thorn said. He wanted to go himself but knew that, one, Beast would never let him put himself in a questionable situation, and, two, it was better that someone with a clear head talk to the innocent bystander. The way he was feeling now, Thorn thought he might take out his frustration on the wrong person.

Havoc left the comm open so his brothers could hear, and Thorn was glad of it. He took out some of Thorn's frustration on the cousin but didn't injure the man too badly. In the end, it had taken a small amount of blood and the threat of losing more, but Thorn had been certain the man had given him the correct location of Jason Harrison and wouldn't tip off his cousin they were after him. He called Havoc off, but his vice president had stayed a few minutes longer. Taking a little more blood and making his point very clear. Only then did he back off. It was probably more a show for Thorn than it had been for the other man. A message that Havoc would do whatever he had to do in order to get the job done, whether Thorn liked it or not.

Under normal circumstances, Thorn would have called Havoc out on it. He didn't tolerate insubordination. But in this case, he could see the other man's point. Thorn had tried to do this himself when he'd never allow any of his brothers to go it alone in a similar situation. Havoc was letting him know none of them would allow Thorn in this by himself either.

"I hear you, Havoc," Thorn said by way of acknowledgement. "Let's go."

"Good," the other man replied. "Just so we understand each other."

"We do." Once back in the truck, Thorn laid out his instructions as they headed back down the road to Palm Springs. The night was hot and humid, the darkness providing little relief to the oppressive heat this time of year. "When we get back to the clubhouse, get a team together. I want a working plan in a week. If this guy's scared enough, Harrison won't be expecting us and won't be on his guard. Even so, I'm sure he's looking for word on Mariana. He may be actively hunting for her."

"That'll make our job easier," Carnage offered. "My only concern is that he'll follow her out of the clubhouse. You ain't exactly got her locked down."

"She won't leave on her own," Thorn said, confident he'd made an impression on Ana that evening. Except, he'd kinda bailed on her to come here. He'd been supposed to take her for a walk on the beach, wine and dine her, then talk about their future. Instead, he'd gone off to kill her ex. Which hadn't turned out the way he'd wanted. Which irritated the fuck out of him.

"I hope not. I have a bad feeling."

Thorn's gaze snapped to his road captain. Any time any of them got a feeling, they all listened to it.

"I'll make sure of it," he said.

* * *

It was full night. Probably close to midnight if Mariana had to guess. The half moon shone bright in the sky reflecting off the water of the pool inside the Salvation's Bane compound. She had been lazily swimming laps while Mama and Pops looked on for a couple of hours now. The other women had gone back inside, and the club girls had come out to take over the pool until one of the prospects had waved them off. They'd given her dirty looks, but Mariana was too deep in thought to worry overmuch about it.

After he'd left her, promising to talk to her tonight, Thorn's meeting had turned into a full on "run," as the club had called it. He'd kissed her lightly, promising he'd be back soon, then had left abruptly. He hadn't looked back once. Yeah. She was definitely in over her head with this whole situation.

On the plus side, she was feeling much better. Her body was still sore, but not nearly as much as it had been. Today, the swimming taxed her muscles, but in a good way. She'd been at it for a couple of hours after the others had left and, for the first time since Jason's attack, she'd started to feel like herself. Well, minus the pregnancy. Which she was trying very hard not to think about.

She was slowing down, swimming for the shallow end when an arm snaked around her waist, stopping her dead in the water. Mariana screamed and thrashed about. For the briefest moment, she just knew Jason had found her again.

"Get off me! Get off me, you bastard!"

"Jesus, Ana! Stop!"

Thorn.

Her fear turned to anger in a second. "Motherfucker!" She screamed at him, turning in the water to slap at him. She even threw a punch, which he caught with little effort. "Don't you ever do that again, you prick!"

"I'm sorry, baby," he soothed, pulling her in closer. At first she resisted, too angry and afraid and embarrassed by her reaction to allow him to comfort her. He just ignored her protests, tightening his arms around her in the pool, their wet bodies sliding against each other. He alternatively rubbed and patted her back as if reassuring a child, repeating, "It's just me. I've got you," over and over until she stopped trembling.

When she had control of herself, Thorn tilted her chin up to look at him. "You OK? I didn't mean to scare you, honey."

"I'm fine," she snapped. Mariana tried to put heat in her response, but the truth was, she was fine. The longer Thorn held her, the more secure she felt. It was crazy how at ease she was with him. In fact, no one had ever been as considerate and caring toward her as Thorn had. Right from the beginning.

"Mama said you've been at it a while. Thought the activity was doin' you good. You tired or do you need more?" He looked down at her. Probably judging her response.

Finally, she just relaxed into his embrace. "No. I'm good. I need a shower, though."

"Good," he said curtly, swinging her up into his arms as he made his way to the steps at the shallow end of the pool. "We'll shower together."

* * *

Only an idiot wouldn't know where this was headed. Mariana fought her instincts to just let nature take its course. Setting herself up with the wrong guy was what had gotten her into this mess to begin with. But hadn't she just realized how safe Thorn made her feel? She didn't have many absolutes in her life, but she knew with no doubt at all that Thorn was the one man she'd ever met who could and would keep her safe. He'd fight her demons whether she wanted him to or not. Besides, she wanted this. Wanted Thorn. It might be the only time he allowed this, but, if he wanted her, she was willing to give herself to him. Whatever happened afterward, she'd deal with.

He adjusted the water temperature in the shower adjacent to his room before turning to face her. "We need to talk," he said, stalking toward her. Why did he have to be so... over-the-top dominant? Why did she have to respond to him?

"No good conversation ever started out that way." She crossed her hands over her breasts. The wet bathing suit was starting to make her chilly in the air-conditioned room.

"It will in this case. At least, we'll both know where we stand with one another."

She sighed. "Yeah, I guess this needs to happen. We gonna do it before or after we get out of the shower?"

His lips twitched. "No reason we can't wash and talk at the same time. I mean, unless you've got other ideas."

She was self-conscious about sex with him. Jason had been her only lover, and she hadn't really learned much from him. He hadn't been lying when he'd said she just lay under him. Still, she could muddle through that, she thought. After all, enthusiasm trumped experience in this case. Right? What she was unsure about was his desire to have sex with her in the first place. He was much older than her. What if the idea creeped him out?

"Well, I had an idea. I mean, showering together means we'll have to be naked." She shrugged. "Figured one thing would lead to another." Mariana tried to hide how much she wanted this. Tried to be cavalier about it. Like she could take it or leave it. Truth was, she thought she might want this more than anything in the world at that moment.

Thorn studied her for a long moment. Any amusement he'd shown was completely gone. "Be very sure what you're asking for, Ana." His voice was like honey over gravel. It was a weapon he used shamelessly. Even if she hadn't been sure, that voice would have made her drop her panties at a hundred paces.

"I think you know I'm sure. You don't get to be your age in this kind of lifestyle without knowing what a woman wants," she said softly.

"Then we definitely need to talk first. Because you get one shot at this. One, Ana. You decide you're letting me have you, that's it. It's not over until I decide. When I decide I'm done, I'll tell you in no uncertain terms. There will be absolutely no misunderstandings along those lines. Do you understand me?"

She didn't, but wasn't sure how to express herself. Apparently, he was adept at reading her expression because he let out a frustrated growl.

"Fuck," he swore softly. "What were you expecting?"

She swallowed. Obviously, he was displeased. "I don't expect anything from you, Thorn. You wanna fuck, I'm down with that. Hell." She gave him her best cocky grin. "I think it would be the best time I've ever had. I won't betray you or your club, and I won't be clingy."

He jerked his head back like she'd taken a swing at him, then his features shut down. "We definitely need to talk about this. For now, all you need to know is that, while you're with me, you're only with me. Clear?"

Mariana nodded.

"Words, Ana."

"We're clear," she squeaked.

Again, he studied her before nodding once. "Strip," he said. It was a command, and simple. Before she realized it, she'd peeled down the shoulder straps of her bathing suit. His gaze was hot and intent, staring at her tits. Naturally, they peaked hard and pointed through her suit top under his scrutiny.

"Didn't say stop, honey."

"What about you?" She was trying to postpone this to gather her courage.

"You can strip me when you're done."

OK, that sent a shiver through her. Would he really let her strip him? If so, would he let her explore his body? Lord knew she wanted to.

He didn't rush her, just let her gather herself, making up her mind. That alone was enough for Mariana. This truly was her choice. Taking a deep breath, she wriggled out of the bathing suit and kicked the wet fabric away.

Thorn took a step toward her, resting his hands on her hips, his nostrils flaring. Mariana looked up into his eyes, recognizing the hunger there. Strangely, it gave her courage to keep going. No man had ever looked at her like that. Like she was desirable. Like he wanted her.

Thorn slid one big hand up to cup the slight weight of her breast. He kneaded gently, finding the nipple with his fingers and tugging. Mariana had to bite back a whimper, not wanting to look like too much of an innocent.

"God fucking damn it," he whispered. "Never seen such perfect tits." He lowered his head and took the other breast in his mouth and sucked. Mariana did cry out then, unable to stop herself. Her hands went to his head, threading through his hair as he sucked and licked at her breast. Jason had never played with her like this. Her experience with sex consisted of literally lying under Jason. He'd never given her pleasure. Certainly hadn't played with her body. Now, here came Thorn. In three or four seconds he'd given her more pleasure than she'd experienced in her adult life, and he hadn't even made her come yet. But, oh, when he did, she had no doubt it would be life altering.

"Easy," he murmured around her nipple. "Let me taste you a while." He moved to the other breast, and her legs did give out then. Thorn just wrapped his arms around her back and opened his mouth to take in as much of her breast as he could. His arms were strong and warm, giving her the illusion of safety when she knew she was anything but safe. At least, where her heart was concerned. This was just sex to him. He might be possessive and want her all to himself, but eventually he'd either grow tired of her inexperience or simply lose interest in her. When he moved on to someone new, Mariana knew her heart would break. Thorn had been the one to pick her up when she fell. He was the one who'd been with her during all the trauma of the past few weeks. How could she possibly give him up after this?

She could feel his raging erection through his jeans and desperately wanted to get to it. She just wasn't sure if she should without permission.

"Get in the fuckin' shower," he growled. She thought he was impatient to get in with her, but he kept hold of her arm until she was safely inside. "Sit." It was nothing less than an order. Thankfully, she had the presence of mind to spot the small shelf molded into the shower and took a seat as he commanded. Once she sat, Thorn stripped and climbed in with her.

God, the man was glorious! Wide shoulders, tattooed skin, heavy muscles over his chest, arms, and thighs, all made for a treat she wanted to lick up. Rigid abs seemed to dance with his every movement. Everywhere she looked she found raw brawn and masculinity. Scars mingled with the tattoos along his body, and Mariana ached to trace every single one of them with her tongue.

She must have been licking her lips, because Thorn smirked at her. "Like what you see, honey?"

Unable to form words, she just nodded, still looking her fill. Without thought, she reached out for his cock. It stood up hard and proud from a neat patch of dark hair. The thing was intimidating but, in that moment, Mariana knew she'd do anything to have it.

She needed to touch and taste it. To fill her mouth with it. Her pussy.

Her ass?

Hell, she'd do anything he wanted. No question. Even if what he wanted might be uncomfortable for her, she'd try it, not doubting he could make it pleasurable for her.

"You wantin' to suck me, baby?" Again, she nodded, her gaze never leaving his cock. "Then, what're you waitin' for? Suck it."

She did. Mariana lapped at the head of his cock once before groaning and engulfing him. He tasted salty and wild, pulsing inside her as if he appreciated what she was doing.

"That's it. Take me deep as you can."

It was difficult because he stretched her lips wide, but Mariana did as he ordered. She loved the velvety feel of his skin in her mouth, the veins and ridges prominent. She'd never done this before. Jason had never seemed to want her to touch him at all. In high school, her girlfriends had laughed about giving head. Some of them liked it, others hated it. All of them were in agreement that men adored it. She'd thought maybe it was her, that she just didn't look like the kind of girl who'd enjoy that sort of thing, because none of the boys she'd dated had even hinted they'd want her to suck them. Judging by Thorn's reaction, she wasn't doing half bad.

"Fuck! Ah, fuck!" He gripped her hair, moving her as he needed her. Sometimes, he held her still and fucked her mouth like he might fuck her pussy, though his thrusts were always measured. He didn't hurt her or make her gag, but he seemed to skirt the edge of discomfort. Just one more thing to suggest Thorn was very experienced indeed.

Finally, he pulled out and pulled her to her feet. "Put your hands on the wall and spread your legs," he commanded.

Mariana obeyed without thought. She heard something tear, then glanced over her shoulder to watch him rolling a condom over his cock.

"I'd rather take you bare, but we've not discussed that." He gripped her hips and aimed his cock at her entrance, tucking it so the head pressed against her but didn't penetrate her. "Last chance, baby. You sure this is what you want?"

How could he possibly ask her this now? "Oh, God! Yes, Thorn," she whimpered. "Plea -- AH!" Mariana screamed as he pulled her hips to him, entering her fully. Her head thrashed as the burn overtook her, the pleasure mingling with pain.

"Shh, shh," he said, pulling her back against him so his arms were wrapped tightly around her and her back was to his chest. His lips grazed her ear, and he snagged her lobe between his teeth, biting down gently. Again, she got the sense he gauged her reaction. She reached out blindly and found his thigh, gripping it with her hand. "You good? Hurt?"

"No," she gasped. "Yes!" She shook her head, trying to clear it of the haze of pleasure. "No, I'm not hurting. Yes. I'm good. Please don't stop." That last was almost sobbed out. Nothing had ever felt this... desperate in her whole life. It was like if he didn't finish this, she'd die. And she might. The unfulfilled pleasure was steadily chipping away at her sanity. He'd barely touched her, played with her tits for a few seconds, and this was what he'd brought her to. She was so fucked.

"Good," he rumbled, sliding out and urging her to turn in his arms so she faced him. "I'm going to hold you tight, but feel free to move as much as you need to. I won't hurt you or let you fall. When you feel the need to come, tell me."

Gasping for air, she nodded.

Her body wasn't her own. She knew that the second his mouth closed over her nipple. Now, as he thrust in and out of her pussy, Mariana knew this was meant for her. Because no way Thorn was getting as much pleasure from this as she was. If he was getting any pleasure at all from her body, he was still managing to keep tight control over his reactions. His focus was on her. She knew it like it was her own thought.

When she shivered, he dropped one hand to her clit...

And it was over.

"Coming!" The word was more a gasp than anything else. She sucked in a breath to scream, but the spasm of her body was so hard, she couldn't let it out. Her muscles seized, and her whole body shivered with tension. Finally, she was able to let go her breath, the scream erupting from her like the most violent volcano. Thorn stiffened, his thrusts going deep once, not retreating. His arms tightened around her, his fingers at her pussy gripping her instead of stroking. Then his bellow mingled with her screams.

* * *

Thorn looked down at the woman sleeping so trustingly in his arms. After having sex in the shower, Thorn had carried her to bed -- his bed -- and crawled in with her. He'd pulled her into his arms and wrapped her up tight, her head resting on his chest. She'd been stiff for a few seconds, then her delicate fingers had curled against his chest muscles as if clutching him to her. Then she relaxed into him, her body molding itself to his like she belonged there.

Did she? Thorn wasn't sure. He knew he wanted her there. But first, he had someone to kill. The little bastard had fooled them once. Wouldn't happen again. Next time he unleashed his team, no one would find the fucking body.

She shifted her position, then gave a small moan like she was still a little sore. He'd have to question her thoroughly about that when she woke. Last thing he wanted to do was cause her more pain. Lord knew she'd had enough in her life without him causing more.

There was a soft knock at the door before it opened slightly and Red poked his head in.

"You decent?"

Mariana sat up, her eyes wide, voice slurred with sleep. "Wha -- Whosdare?"

"Shh, baby. It's just Red. Lay back down and rest." Surprisingly, she did, only murmuring softly something incoherent. Thorn gently tucked the covers around her naked body as he sat up. He placed a soft kiss on her lips before walking to the door. He was still naked.

Red opened his mouth to speak, but Thorn gave him a hard look, shaking his head once before slipping out into the hallway and closing the door carefully behind him.

"This better be good." Thorn normally wasn't grouchy or minded when he was called out late into the night. Red raised his eyebrows but didn't mention his bad mood.

"You wanna put on some fuckin' pants?"

"Not really. Didn't plan on being out here that fuckin' long. Now what the fuck is it?"

Red stared at him hard for a moment, then delivered his message. "Little fucker's been askin' around about you."

"Good. Make sure he knows where to find me." He turned to go, but Red continued.

"I don't think that's a good idea, Thorn. He's not stable."

"Well aware of that. Man who could beat the woman carryin' his baby until she lost it ain't fuckin' stable."

Red grabbed his arm as Thorn turned to go back to Mariana. "I'm serious, brother. You need to prepare for this. Got no doubt you can take care of yourself and your woman. But you've got more here to worry about than the two of you. Kid's gettin' some buddies together who think they're tough. They ain't, but the guns they have are."

"Fuck!" Thorn swore softly. "Don't fuckin' need this." He thought for a moment. While he had every confidence in his brothers' abilities to protect the clubhouse and everyone in it, he didn't believe in borrowing trouble. "Inform Beast and Vicious. I want a meeting in fifteen minutes with every member here. Restrict the club girls from going in or out. They leave the premises, they're on their own. Put out the call to everyone. They ain't at the clubhouse in two hours, they need to shelter on their own. No one gets in or out without my say."

"On it, boss."

"And Red?" The other man raised an eyebrow. "Anyone who sees that fucker anywhere other than at the fuckin' front door and makes a positive ID, they're to take the son of a bitch out. We'll deal with the fallout."

Red nodded once then headed off to do as Thorn instructed.

Fuck. He didn't need this. He needed to take the hunt to the little motherfucker. Not wait around until he came after Mariana.

Front fucking door…

Then he paused.

If he let Jason Harrison and his buddies inside the clubhouse, then… Sure, it would put Mariana in more danger than he liked, but it would also give him the greatest advantage. With absolutely no chance of an innocent getting hurt.

"Red!" Thorn called out, hurrying down the hall and to the stairs. "Change of plans."

Chapter Five

Church was full. Every member of Salvation's Bane had made it to the meeting, even those not at the clubhouse. All of them were stoic and focused on the orders Thorn was handing down. "Harrison will show up. When he does…"

"We invite him into the lions' den." Ripper finished. "We killin' all of 'em?"

"Not if we don't have to. Jason Harrison, though, does not leave this place alive."

"Gonna be witnesses," Ripper said. "I can fuck with any city cameras pointed in this general area, but there's bound to be someone who sees them heading this way. Ain't exactly rural."

"Blood?" Thorn turned to the man they depended on to take care of any mess that might lead back to the club. The man was ruthless and, more than once, had been called on to silence wayward tongues.

"Kill those who need killin'," he said softly. "I'll make sure the rest are appropriately ignorant should they be asked."

If Blood said he'd take care of it, it was as good as done. His methods might be questionable, but Thorn had learned that, in most cases, it was best not to question his cleaner much. Or at all, really. Done was done.

"Good. Work with Beast if necessary," Thorn said.

Blood shook his head. "No. This is on me."

Thorn raised an eyebrow. That meant Blood anticipated trouble. Which meant any "convincing" he had to do in order to keep quiet any buddies Harrison brought with him, wouldn't be pretty. Or gentle.

"Ripper, you hear anything on them?"

"Yeah. Our boy's inquiring about a gun. Wantin' something unregistered. Inquiring in all the wrong fucking places, though."

"Assume he's able to pull it off," Thorn said. "Prepare for an armed enemy. We'll welcome him until he proves what he's after. Then we'll finish it." He rapped his knuckles on the table, their signal church was adjourned, and everyone got up.

After everyone left, Beast hung back. "You sure 'bout this, Thorn? I mean, I'm behind you a hundred percent, and Jason Harrison deserves to die hard. But are you sure about his buddies?"

"They come here to harm my woman, then yes. I'll kill the little bastards and won't lose a second's sleep."

"You sure 'bout her?" Beast held Thorn's gaze steadily. Thorn understood. Beast needed to know where Thorn's head was. He couldn't blame his brother. If they were going to kill, it needed to be worth the cost.

"I'm sure. She's mine."

Beast snorted. "She know that?"

Thorn shrugged. "Mostly. She'll understand soon enough. I've been trying to take it easy on her. She's been through a hell of a time."

"Mama and Pops both say she's recovering nicely, though Pops says he worries she's not fully acknowledged the loss of her child. Could be an issue for you down the road."

"Yeah. I'm aware. I'll help her work through it."

"You sound awfully confident. She opening up to you?"

Thorn hesitated. "No. But she will."

Beast just shook his head, offering a derisive snort. "Yeah. She knows she's yours, all right. Might want to clear that up first. Then worry about this other shit."

"She knows we're in an exclusive relationship. That's enough for now."

"Do you know anything about women?"

"Know enough."

"Right. Keep telling yourself that." Beast clapped Thorn on the back. "Good luck. Sounds like you're gonna need it."

Thorn sighed. "After this, I'm gonna need something else worse." When Beast's brows knit together, but the man remained silent, Thorn continued. "We'll need a new clubhouse. Once I've killed here, we'll need to relocate."

"You want to stay in Palm Beach?"

"Maybe farther out of the city. More isolated."

Beast nodded. "I'll get with Ripper. Something comes to mind, though we'll have to do some modifications."

"Just be ready. We may need to move quickly. I won't jeopardize anyone in the club. Not even to save myself."

"So I'm back to my original question. You sure about her? Because, if you are, every man in this club will fight to the death to protect her. Everything else be damned. Our women, our ol' ladies, will be protected at all costs. Even our freedom, to our very lives." Beast's words were like a balm to Thorn. He was hesitant to have his club help if they all felt like it was for him. But if they saw it as helping his woman, then all was well. Same end, but they were fighting for his woman. Not for Thorn. He would never ask them to do anything so drastic for himself. For Mariana, he'd ask anything, but would never sacrifice less than his brothers would.

"She's my one and only, Beast. Ain't quite sure how it fuckin' happened, but she's the woman I want."

"Brother, ain't none of us sure how it happens. They're sneaky. Catch you when you ain't lookin'." They both had a small chuckle at that. "We got your back. To the death, brother."

"That's what I'm afraid of," Thorn answered. "That's what I'm fuckin' afraid of."

* * *

Mariana was restless. Thorn had barely let her out of the clubhouse all week. Had insisted she stay inside as much as possible. The only time he let her out was at night, and only at the pool. The only lights allowed on were the pool's underwater lights. They gave off a soft glow that gave the patio a romantic feel, but Thorn's tension ruined any romantic interlude they might have shared. Oh, he'd fucked her plenty of times, but it was always a frantic, hard ride. Like he was doing it for the last time. The thought disturbed Mariana in more ways than she cared to admit.

In the short time she'd known Thorn, she'd come to rely on him for nearly everything. Especially when the not-so-distant past tried to creep in on her. She could go to him, seduce him, and he quickly made all her troubles go away.

"You know, you can't fuck your past away forever." That was Mama. The woman was a conundrum. Her touch was gentle, but her words weren't always kind. She could strip it naked and lay it all out there in such a blunt way, Mariana actually felt like the woman had taken a sledgehammer to her insides.

"What makes you think that's what I'm doing? I like sex. Thorn's readily available." She shrugged, trying to make light of the situation when she really wanted to wince. Her relationship with Thorn wasn't like that. At least, not to her. For him? Who knew? He wasn't a man to talk about his feelings much. When he did, he was like Mama in that he just laid it bare.

"Pfft! You're hiding. The past hurts in so many ways, and you're avoiding it by losing yourself in Thorn's body." Mama stood at the edge of the pool, hands on her hips. It was hard to tell how old she was, but Mariana guessed late sixties. Mama's hair was long but steel gray, and she kept it in intricate braids wound around her head most of the time. She was slender and fit, but her skin had some age on it. Mama didn't seem to care and neither did Pops, though Mariana wasn't sure if they were an actual couple or just very close friends.

"Tell me you wouldn't enjoy the same thing, and I'll call you a hypocrite."

"Ain't sayin' I wouldn't enjoy that man. Any woman would. You need more than sexual gratification. You need a man to have your back. To stand with you and in front of you when necessary. Thorn's that man. By compartmentalizing him into a sex object, you're doing you both a disservice."

"I don't know what you're talking about. He said we're together, so we're together. I'm just not getting my hopes up for a happy ever after. Men like him aren't built for that."

"And your other man was?" By the low tone of Mama's voice, the older woman knew that would be a crippling blow. Mariana felt it so hard through her body, she pulled her knees up, buffering herself from a truth she didn't want to face.

"Well," Mariana said, swallowing a small sob. "That stung."

"Meant it to. He ain't mine, but he's Cain's. When Cain sent me here to help, I came for Cain's people. You were not my first priority, no matter what Thorn thought. You still ain't. But I think you and Thorn could both benefit from this relationship if you give it more than just your body."

"Mama, I do that and Thorn will eat me alive," she said starkly. "I'm not just being dramatic, either. I thought I loved Jason, no matter his tendency to be an asshole. If I give Thorn more than my body, he'll crush my heart. I... I can't do that, Mama."

"Have you talked to him about more than sex? What about what you want out of your relationship?"

"What relationship? We have sex." Did she sound bitter?

Mama scowled. "Girl, you need to sit and have a talk with your man. He's putting his club on the line. For you. Even he sees it. He's letting his brothers convince him they're doing it for him, but they're getting ready to kill. For you. The least you can do is throw all in. Give him the benefit of the doubt."

"And if you're wrong? If this is just what he said it is? Then I'm the one with a bleeding heart and permanent wounds." Mariana was as close to tears as she'd been since the attack. Which she would not think about. Not now. Not ever. "He feels bad for me. Sorry that I made shit decisions with my life and willing to help me turn myself around."

"You already got permanent wounds, girl," Mama snapped. For a supposed doctor, the woman had a horrible bedside manner. "And that man feels every single fuckin' one of 'em! Why do you think he's willin' to let his club get involved with this? If he just felt bad for you, if you were just a pity fuck, don't you think he'd just beat the fuck outta your baby daddy and go on with himself? Thorn is readying his club for battle. And they're bringing it here. To his house! Their house! They're doin' it because they can control every aspect of the situation from here and keep your enemies here as long as they need to before they die. They're gonna die hard and mean, and Thorn's gonna enjoy every fuckin' second of it."

Mariana let out a little sob. "I don't want that for him. None of them. I didn't ask for this! Why are you even telling me?"

"Because you need to know the lengths Thorn is goin' through to keep you safe and avenge your child. He wouldn't do that for just anyone. Not his problem. The club is treating you like one of their own. That means Thorn has given them reason to. He's claimed you, and you're either too fuckin' blind to see or too stupid to care!" By the time Mama had finished dressing her down, Mariana was sobbing openly, clinging to the edge of the pool, and Pops was trying desperately to calm Mama down. He was shushing her and looking around like he expected trouble. Man even had a wicked-looking knife out, as if readying himself for a fight.

"Shut up, woman," he hissed. "You'll bring the whole place down on us!" Pops continued to scan the area. A burst of lightning lit up the sky, evidence of an approaching tropical storm forecast for the area. In the background, a tall, hulking shadow was lit briefly, making Mariana catch her breath.

Thorn stood tall and proud, his shoulders back. His eyes glinted in the scant light, his gaze firmly fixed on Mama. "You done?"

"I didn't say nearly enough, boy." The older woman really was pissed off. "This is as much your fault as it is hers. You're so consumed by your lifestyle you can't conceive of actually committing to a woman. You think all these club girls will satisfy you?"

"They never have. Why would I think that would change?"

"Then get off your ass and tell that girl how you feel. I'm tired of babysitting the two of you. You've fucked her. Now put a fuckin' ring on it."

Thorn's voice never changed inflection. "Intend to." He took a step forward, and Pops pushed Mama firmly behind him. The older woman hissed out a warning, drawing her own wicked-looking knife. Neither of the pair backed down an inch from the much larger, stronger, and younger threat. When Thorn spoke again, his tone held that same calm demeanor, but there was an underlying threat of retaliation if they fucked with him. "I appreciate your help with Mariana. While Doc is wonderful, he doesn't have quite the… feminine touch you were reputed to have, Mama. Please tell Cain I appreciate the gesture, but I think it's time you and Pops head back to Kentucky. Red is waiting to take you to the airport. Your flight leaves in a couple of hours."

Pops nodded, then skirted around Thorn, not turning his back to the larger man. Pops didn't look scared, more like wary. Like a man might move around a snake coiled and ready to strike. He kept Mama firmly at his side, not letting her far enough away to get away from him and possibly attack Thorn, as she looked on the verge of doing. "I think that's a good idea," Pops muttered.

"Thank God," Mama snapped. "Ain't never met a more unworthy president in my years." She stabbed a finger at Thorn. "A president puts his club at risk for something, he tells them straight out why. You drug your men into a hunt letting them think it was for you when, in reality, it was for her."

"Not your business, Mama," Thorn snapped right back at her. "I have my reasons for everything I do. My brothers know the score. And they know me as well as I know them."

The older woman bared her teeth at Thorn. "Good riddance, Thorn."

"Goodbye... Aunt Josephine."

* * *

Mariana stayed very still in the pool, unsure of her footing. How much had Thorn heard, and what had he taken exception to? Because he'd obviously taken exception to something.

"Out with you, girl," he ordered. He didn't sound angry, but just like he expected her obedience. Which kind of rankled. While she wasn't pissed at him, she knew she had to assert her independence or risk losing herself.

"I'm not done swimming. You've hardly let me out of the clubhouse all week. I'm enjoying the fresh air."

"Ana," he said, his voice caressing her name. "Please. We need to talk."

"Uh oh. There's that phrase again." She sank to her neck in the cool water, a subtle retreat.

He looked at her for long moment. When she made no move to obey him, he sighed and scrubbed a hand over his face. "Fine." He sounded more resigned than grumpy. To her complete shock, he started stripping. Everything.

If she lived to be a hundred, she could look at his body twenty-four hours a day, seven days a week and never get tired of it. He was covered in a myriad of tattoos and more than a few scars. And muscle. Lots of muscle. His cock was semi-erect but growing as he approached her. As he moved from the steps into the pool, he seemed to stalk through the water to her. Like a shark on the hunt. Perhaps that's exactly what he was.

"What are you doing?" Her question came out a squeak, and she had to stop herself from moving away from him into deeper water. He'd taken her in the pool more than once, but this was different somehow.

"You ain't comin' to me? I'll come to you."

"Thorn," she said, using her best no-nonsense voice. "Be reasonable. The sex is great, but I've got too much baggage for you to fool with. I'd leave now if I thought I had a chance in hell of escaping Jason. I'd be gone. Not too ashamed to admit I'm afraid of him." She shivered before she could stop herself, a wave of fear and revulsion going through her. To think she'd given that bastard her body. Had tried to please him. To take care of him outside the bedroom.

"Ana! Focus on me!"

Her gaze snapped back to Thorn, who was now inches from her. He reached out and cupped her cheek gently. The gesture seemed more intimate than any other time he'd touched her. And it was only his hand touching her face. Not that gloriously naked body of his. She wanted to reach out and run her hands over his chest and shoulders, but didn't dare. Not in her present mood. Or his.

"Mama's right." With those words he pulled her closer, wrapping those strong arms around her. "We both have things we need to have a serious discussion about."

Mariana stiffened. "With all due respect, it's none of her business."

"No. But she reminded me I need to make it mine."

"Look, Thorn. I appreciate what you've done, but you really don't have to do anything more. Just let me ride it out here for a while. That's all I'm asking. You don't have to do anything about Jason. I'll just leave, and he'll forget me soon enough. Hell, he already has another girlfriend." She had to look away then, the pain still sharp if she dwelled on it. Not because she'd loved Jason so much as because Jason obviously loathed her enough to beat her until she miscarried. "Just let me have another couple of weeks, and I'll be out of your way."

"Fuck, Mariana," he swore. "Do you honestly think that's what I want?"

She still couldn't meet his gaze. "You're a biker. The president of a club with very powerful men. Every girl in this club has her sights on you. I see how they look at you. I hear every dirty fantasy they voice about you and, believe me, there are many."

"Is that what's bothering you? Honey, I've probably had every single one of them at one time or another. If I'd wanted more with any of them, I'd have pursued it by now."

There was no stopping the wince. She'd only been with Jason, and now Thorn. Did he find her horribly inadequate?

"Get that look off your face now," he snapped. "Fuck!" He pulled her close, wrapping her up in his arms tightly this time. She felt his cock pulsing between them but was afraid to do anything about it. "Mama was definitely right. We should have talked more about this before I started fuckin' you regularly." He said it almost as if to himself.

"I don't wanna," Mariana muttered. "Just let me have this time with you without telling me again how temporary I am."

He pulled back sharply but didn't let her out of his arms. "What the fuck? I never said that! Not once."

She blinked, trying to step back, but he pulled her firmly back, growling as he did. "You said as long as I was with you we were exclusive."

"What part of that did you take to mean I didn't want you around?"

"It's not that, Thorn," she sighed, giving up trying to get away from him. "I just know the score. You'll move on. Like you always have. If I'm completely honest?" She looked up into his face, waiting for him to tell her if he wanted to know what she had to say. When he nodded sharply twice, she gave a shuddering breath before continuing. "I'm not sure I can compartmentalize my relationship with you. Even now, when it's all still new, I know I'll never forget you. Or what I've shared with you."

To her complete and utter horror, a tear leaked from her eye and rolled down her cheek. Mariana tried to duck her head so he couldn't see. Even better would be to duck under the water under the pretense of slicking her hair back. Unfortunately, Thorn wouldn't let her get away with either option.

"Look at me, Ana." When she stubbornly kept her head down, Thorn gently curled a finger under her chin and tipped her face up so he could look into her eyes. When he spoke, his voice was tender. And so filled with heat it stole her breath. "Why in the world would you think that I didn't feel exactly the same way about you?"

Mariana had to fight for air. Her throat burned, and she was desperately afraid she was going to start sobbing.

"I didn't want to admit it. Damned sure didn't know how to explain to my brothers. Mama was wrong about something, though. They know exactly why this is happening and who it's for. They are willing to fight for you because they know you're my woman. The one woman for me. They recognize you belong with me, and they've claimed you as their own as well. You're as good as an ol' lady. They know you'll be mine soon and they've brought you firmly under the protection of the club. Which includes protection from me if they thought you needed it."

"You'd never hurt me," she whispered, looking up at him in a kind of awe. She'd never known he could lay his emotions out like that. "You've never been this blunt with me before. Is this some kind of trick?"

Thorn grinned. "Why would I need to do that? I don't play mind games, Ana. With me, what you see is what you get. I'm laying my soul bare. My heart." He shrugged and gave her a gentle smile. "You hold both in your hands. The only question is, are you brave enough to take them?"

To her complete and utter horror, a sob escaped. Just one. When he pulled her into his arms, the dam broke. Mariana wasn't certain why she was crying. Was it for herself and all she'd lost over the past few weeks, even before she met Thorn? Probably. But she wasn't opening the door to that. Not yet. Not when the possibility she could be hurt again still loomed over her. She refused to dwell on it, because that way lay madness.

Chapter Six

Ana's tears were killing him. Thorn held her tightly, willing his body to be the shelter and comfort she needed. Though he wasn't exactly certain what had her upset, he had a good idea. She was a beautiful young woman who'd been betrayed in one of the worst ways possible, yet he was asking for her trust. It was probably too much for any woman, but his little Ana was especially vulnerable after everything that had happened.

Thorn knew he was a bastard. Knew the last thing she truly needed was sex. But when he had her in his arms, making love to her, bringing her to orgasm over and over, he knew she let herself go and just felt the pleasure he gave her. Reveled in it. She always clung to him so sweetly afterwards, and he'd come to crave that afterplay almost as much as the actual sex. Right now, sex with her was the only way he knew to get her to that warm, lethargic place where she let him take care of her and put her trust completely in him.

Moving them to the shallow end, he pulled at the strap of her bathing suit. He hated that she chose the one piece instead of a bikini to show off her beautiful body, but he knew she had scars from the attack. Though she never talked about it, he knew she was self-conscious about any lingering marks on her body. Lord knew she tried hard to hide from him sometimes. Thorn pretended not to notice because he didn't want her uncomfortable, but he knew the time was coming when he'd have to deal with it all. She would have to deal with it. Otherwise, it would fester like an abscess that never healed until she grew sick with it. Until they were both sick with it. Because Thorn had a feeling once she opened up to him, even though he knew exactly what had happened, he was going to share every single pain she had inside of her, and he wasn't altogether certain he could handle it gracefully.

Once he got Ana's bathing suit around her waist, Thorn lifted her to sit on the edge of the pool, wedging his hips between her thighs. Looking up into her eyes, he could see the sorrow and fear there, and it nearly broke him.

"Hey, hey," he said softly, cupping her face in his hands. Her gaze skittered away from him, but he ducked back into her line of sight. "Look at me, baby. Let me see your beautiful hazel eyes." Tears continued to fall, but she met his gaze with her eyes glistening in the scant lighting of the pool. "I'm not goin' anywhere. I'm with you like stink on shit." As he'd hoped, she let out a surprised giggle. Something that had been coiled and roiling inside his chest eased just a little bit at the soft sound. Yeah. He was so fucked. He wouldn't have it any other way. "No matter what, I'm always gonna be with you. You're part of Bane now. Soon as this little fucker is dea -- err, out of the picture, I'm makin' you my ol' lady. Believe me, that's not something I do lightly. I don't claim a woman then let her go. You're mine. Now. Always."

Her breathing had grown ragged. Something that looked suspiciously like hope blossomed on her face before she tried to mask it over. Then she let out a breath, her shoulders slumping just a little.

"What about you? Will you still be with the club girls? I know that, when you guys have parties, there's lots of sex. Other clubs or your own girls like to party, and it usually leads to sex."

He grinned. "Oh, I expect we'll both have lots of kinky, raunchy sex at those parties. But only with each other. Baby, I'm yours. You're mine. I'll always protect you, and I absolutely do not share. Don't expect you to share me, either."

Fuck. She looked up at him like he'd fucking hung the fucking moon. His chest swelled with pride and a possessiveness that nearly doubled him over in its intensity.

"Really?" she asked. "You mean that?"

"I never say anything I don't mean, Ana. You should know that by now." He dipped his head to take one peaked nipple into his mouth and she gasped, her hands going to his head to hold her to him.

"Thorn," she whimpered.

"Gonna love you all night, baby. We're gonna make love, and work out the details of what happens next, but we're gonna do it together. From now on, we're a pair. You're part of us now. The club. They'll protect you as fiercely as they protect me. They do it because they know you're important to me, but they also do it because you're important to them. And before you ask, they won't always take my side over yours. Hell, there's a couple of those bastards who'll automatically assume I deserve whatever you're mad at me over and kick my ass on principle." That got another giggle. "You understandin' me, babe?"

She sighed, urging him to continue sucking her breast, but he looked up at her, needing to make sure she knew he was telling her the absolute truth. "Not really, but I'm going to take your word for it. I have a feeling being with the president of a club like this I'm gonna have to do a lot of that. Just..." She swallowed, letting her pain show through just a little. "Just don't give me a reason to regret that decision. I'm willing to trust whatever you're doing with the club has a good reason, and some things I'm better off not knowing about. Just please don't bring another woman into the dynamic. Not for any reason, no matter how much you think the ends justify the means. I can't have another conversation with anyone like I had with Jason the day you and I met. But especially not with you. You have to know, I never cared about him anywhere near the way I care about you, Thorn. I find you with another woman, it would gut me."

"Never gonna happen, baby, so don't spend time even considering it. For now, I want you out of this bathing suit. I'm gonna spend the rest of the night worshiping your body. You'll be so exhausted tomorrow all you're gonna want to do is sleep."

"Which means you've got something planned for tomorrow, doesn't it?"

"Not ever gonna lie to you, darlin', so don't ask if you don't really want to know." Deliberately, Thorn wrapped his tongue around her nipple again before sucking strongly. His hand found her other breast and kneaded it lovingly.

"OK," she sighed. "We'll talk about it later."

Thorn chuckled before urging her to lift her bottom so he could pull her suit down her legs and toss it in a sodden heap on the concrete beside her. He pulled her knees over his shoulders then dipped his face to her bare pussy, inhaling the scent of her arousal.

"Ah, fuck, baby," he growled. "You smell like fuckin' paradise."

"Thorn." Mariana let her legs fall wide off his shoulders. "Lick me."

Was there ever a sweeter demand?

"My fuckin' pleasure," he growled. Then he set in.

When he first made contact with her clit, Ana screamed, arching her back off the concrete. Thorn was worried she might injure herself, so he lifted her so she sat astride his neck, his mouth firmly against her pussy. At first she squealed and clutched at his hair, the position awkward and new to her. But Thorn knew he could hold her there easily and gave her a swat on the ass to still her struggles.

It didn't take her long to simply let him take over. Thorn held her with his big palms splayed wide across her ass. Wasn't the most ideal position, but it was better than her scraping her back all to hell on the concrete. Besides, any position where he could get his mouth attached so firmly to her pussy was a great position.

Soon, Mariana had herself balanced, her hands in his hair, and rocked her hips over his mouth. Her little pussy wept with every stroke of his teeth, lips, and tongue over her clit. Her cries filled the night, echoing off the building and floating out to sea. Thorn loved that she was so abandoned. Everything about her was sensual and hedonistic. She just needed to learn to let herself go with him more often. Tonight, that was something he was going to encourage. Let her make all the fucking noise she wanted. His brothers would congratulate him for a job well done, and every single club girl on the place would know he'd claimed Mariana as his. Once her vest was done, she'd wear his property patch, and no one would bother her. Any club girl who didn't get the message from that would learn when they were banned from the clubhouse.

Thorn felt her body tense on the verge of her first orgasm and pulled back. He wanted her to come, but not yet. He wanted her mindless with need.

"Thorn! Let me come!"

"No," he growled against her clit once, smacking her ass again. "Not yet."

"Oh, God! Please, Thorn! Please!"

He let her slide down his body as his arms came around her. "Put your legs around me, Ana. Need to fuck you while you come."

"Yes," she gasped. "Yes, let's do that."

Had his cock not been so hard he was in actual pain, he might have chuckled at her little demand. The second she came, Thorn knew he was coming with her.

She did as he asked. Thorn took them out of the pool to one of the loungers and laid her on it. He sat in the middle, his legs over the sides. Her legs draped over his, and Thorn guided his aching cock to her entrance before gripping her tiny waist and pulling her to him at the same moment he surged forward.

"AAHHH! Thorn! Fuck!" Her screams were louder than before, her arms stretched over her head, her hands gripping the head of the chair. She again wrapped her legs around him to give herself leverage and met Thorn thrust for thrust.

How the fuck could Jason have said she lay unmoving beneath him during sex? This woman was starved for sex! Every single time he fucked her, she was always a giving and a bit of a demanding lover. She never balked at anything he wanted to do and always threw herself into sex with him. She fucked as good as she got fucked.

"Little witch," he bit out. "Cast a spell on me. Makin' me want to fill you with my cum. Is that what you want? My cum?"

"I do," she whispered. "Oh, God!"

"Well, you're gonna get it. But not in your pussy. Not this time."

She looked confused until he swirled a finger around his dick and gathered her creamy dew before moving his finger to her ass. He circled the little hole, coating it with her own juices before carefully pushing inside her.

"You ever been fucked here?"

She sucked in a breath, her cheeks going flush and her eyes wide. "I have a feeling I'm about to be."

"You have to answer the question, Ana. I need to know what you can take."

"No. I never have. But you stretch me. Prepare me. Do that, and I can take you. I will."

"Fuck! You're so fuckin' fierce!"

She hesitated, her eyes going even wider. "Is that -- Thorn, is that wrong?"

He barked out a laugh, surging into her once again a couple of times, needing her back into this. "Fuck no! Are you kidding me? I love that you want to do dirty things with me. Gonna enjoy showing you off during parties. I'll fuck you on the pool table in front of the whole fuckin' room. Everyone will be watchin', fuckin' their own women, and I'll be the luckiest son of a bitch in the whole Goddamned place because you'll put on such a wild show. Given' me everything I want and enjoying it so much you come 'til you pass out. You think you can do that?"

She was definitely turned on. Her eyes glazed over and her breathing quickened. More importantly, her pussy clamped down on him hard, pulsing around him until he wasn't sure he could keep from coming inside her.

Fuck it. She could make him hard again. Did just by looking at him. No time ever had he fucked her that he didn't get hard almost immediately after he'd come. He'd take her somewhere more private for round two, and use his fuckin' cum as a lubrication for her ass.

"Mother fuck!" he shouted. "You fuckin' come with me, Ana," he commanded as he surged into her hard and deep. "Fuckin' come now! Now!" He threw back his head and roared to the stars. Her screams filled the air while he emptied himself into her pulsing little cunt.

She clung to him, digging her nails into his shoulders. Thank God she did, too, because that little bite of pain grounded him. Helped him realize he had way more to accomplish in the next couple of hours. And he'd get it done, too, because the club was expecting company tonight. He wanted Mariana firmly attached to him before they showed. Mostly so she obeyed him without too much effort on his part. If there was going to be death tonight, he wanted none of it to touch his little Ana.

* * *

Emotions overwhelmed Mariana as Thorn urged her to wrap her legs around him. He stood and grabbed a towel, somehow draping it around her back so it covered her ass and tucked between their bodies. He was still semi hard inside her, and she could feel his cum leaking from her body.

"Keep your arms around me, baby. While I got no problem with my brothers and sisters seeing you, I know you're not there yet. Just know I'll always keep you safe. Do you trust me?"

God help her, she did. "Without question, Thorn," she answered immediately.

Because she did. He could have left her any number of times since she'd been discharged from the hospital. But just the fact that he'd stayed by her side the entire time, then brought her to his home, kept her in his bed, treated her like she belonged with him and he was keeping her, earned that trust. She knew he was going to kill Jason, and that was another reason to give him the benefit of the doubt. No way he did something like that for her unless she meant something to him. What he described during sex might seem a little over the top for her, but Mariana couldn't deny she was intrigued with having people he trusted watch them having sex. She knew she would never make a conscious decision to do it, but Thorn could cajole her into trying. He could make her so hot for him she'd sink down and give him a blow job in the middle of town if he promised to give her orgasms like he continued to do. He pushed her, but he never hurt her. Physically or emotionally. He always seemed to be careful of her even while showing her his wild nature. She was falling fast for the gruff MC president.

His arms held her to him like steel bands, holding the towel in place as he entered the common room. Naturally, they got cat calls and more than one brother hollering out that he was "leaving a trail of cum" in his wake. Both of them were bare-assed naked. She just had a towel around her because he knew she'd be uncomfortable. His whole everything was still hanging out. Hell, they could probably see his dick was still in her pussy as he walked. She thought she'd be embarrassed -- mortified, even -- but she wasn't. She saw several of the club girls in their walk from the pool. He had to take her all the way through to the back to the stairs where his room was on the floor above. Some gave her a thumbs up and a bright smile. More than one gave her venomous looks as if she were encroaching on their territory, even though the women were currently with a different patched member of the club.

Something else she noticed. More than one of the girls was topless. Beast was with Fleur, his hand around her shoulder and under her shirt. She made a halfhearted attempt to get him out as she waved to Mariana, but giggled all the same. He did not remove his hand. Vicious was with Lucy in a corner off to themselves, kissing like teenagers in a movie theater. He cupped a breast. She cupped his crotch. A club girl -- Topaz? -- knelt between Red and Tinker, a cock in each hand, alternating sucking them. She met Mariana's gaze and winked at her, grinning even around her mouthful.

It should have horrified Mariana. If she'd been the good girl her mother wanted her to be, it certainly would have. But Mariana had known for a very long time she wasn't a good girl. Now the thought of sex with Thorn, surrounded by his club, his brothers, didn't hold the revulsion it might once have. It was obvious his brothers didn't mind. Neither did their women. She thought about everything that had happened to her over the last month. What if she'd died the night Jason had beaten her? She'd have missed out on all this. Missed out on Thorn. On the wild and sometimes rough but always satisfying sex he shared with her.

Never again. She was not going to live the rest of her life trying to please anyone but herself and Thorn. If she was lucky enough to have a child, she'd include him or her in that circle, but she was going to experience anything and everything Thorn wanted to throw at her.

"Don't like you so still, woman," Thorn growled. Speak of the Devil.

"I was just thinking about what you said earlier."

"What was that, baby?" He'd reached his bedroom door and opened it, kicking it shut. He took the towel from her body and tossed it to the bed for her to lie on. The bed they shared was large and inviting, ready for their use like the comforting arms of a lover. Mariana already loved being here with Thorn. It felt like home. Definitely more of a home than she'd ever felt with her mother or with Jason.

Thorn didn't separate their bodies, just crawled up on the bed, still inside her. She felt him pulse as she clenched her muscles around him. "About you fucking me at a party with your club." They both cried out as his cock swelled inside her. Yeah, he liked that idea. A lot. "I saw Fleur and Lucy with their men. As long as it's something you want to try, I'm willing."

"And this is just one of many reasons why I love you, Ana." She sucked in a breath, the admission shocking her. He continued, dropping gentle kisses to her neck as he moved in and out of her, his movement lazy and contented. "You're willing to give my kinks a try."

"You -- you love me?"

He pulled back, threading one hand through her hair. "Baby, I'm pretty sure I fell hard at the diner. By the time I had you home?" He shrugged. "I was a fuckin' goner." Then he kissed her before she had the chance to say anything else.

His tongue slipped between her lips, stroking in time to the thrusts of his hips. It wasn't long before Mariana was panting and clinging to him, digging her heels into his ass to urge him to go faster.

* * *

Thorn built her slowly only to let her fall back without falling over the edge. He wanted her on the edge of madness before he took her ass. Just her willingness to try anything with him was the biggest turn-on he could think of. Not that he hadn't done all that with other women. He had. Many times. But

Mariana was special. She was the only woman he'd ever felt anything like love for, and she wasn't like any woman he'd ever met. Well, except for Fleur or Lucy. She was just like them in many ways. Most importantly, she was like them in that she was perfect for the man who'd claimed her. Him.

He snagged her hands where she gripped his back, clawing at him to move faster, and pinned them over her head in one of his. With his other hand, he stroked her body. Up and down in a lazy glide until he finally settled on her breast, cupping it. Squeezing. He took her nipple between his thumb and finger and tugged. Gently at first, then more aggressively, just to see how she'd respond.

Mariana cried out, arching her back. She clenched around him in a wet rush, her pussy sliding around him even as she clamped down.

"Don't you come yet, baby," he commanded. "Not until I tell you."

"Thorn! No! Please let me come!" She opened her eyes, giving him a wide-eyed look, obviously shocked. Why, he didn't know, but maybe because she'd slipped into the role of a submissive without realizing it. He could play the Dom if she wanted it sometimes. Just another aspect of their sexual relationship he was dying to test out.

"Not until I say." For emphasis, he slid his hand to her ass. When she raised it to thrust her hips at him, he smacked it sharply.

And, fuck, if she didn't clench around him so hard he was afraid she'd taken his cum from him again.

"Fuckin' hold still!" He gripped her hip. Sweat erupted over his skin, and he had to shake himself to get any semblance of control back. Once he did, he reached over to the nightstand and pulled out a tube of lubricant. "Now you're gonna get it, girl," he growled. "You ready to get that ass fucked?"

"Oh..." Her eyes, so expressive, widened, her pupils large in her excitement. "Oh, God..."

"That's right, baby. Just focus on me. Listen to what I tell you. I'll make this good for you." She nodded several times, her lips trembling. "Words, baby. You don't want to do this now, we'll talk about it at length first. Ain't sayin' I won't try to talk you into it, just sayin' we don't have to do it tonight."

"No! I mean, yes." She took a deep breath, squeezing her eyes shut. "I want this, Thorn. I want you to take me there."

He gave her a crooked grin. The grin he knew drove women wild when they saw it. "Where, exactly, do you want me to take you, baby? Hawaii? 'Cause I might be able to work something out, but it'll take a few days."

"Thorn!" She burst out with a nervous laugh. "You know very well what I mean!"

"Hmm... Alaska, then? Not exactly my thing, but I'll be happy to take you there if it's what you really want."

"My ass, you swine! I want you to fuck my ass! OK?"

It was his turn to laugh. He sat up, his cock still firmly in her cum-filled pussy. Then he unscrewed the cap of lube. "Yeah, I think I can manage that."

He pulled out of her until only the head was in her tight little cunt, then coated his cock with a long line before capping the tube and gripping his cock, spreading the cool gel until he was generously lubed. Again, he thrust into her pussy, fucking her slowly, watching as his cock disappeared into her.

"Love watching my cock fuckin' you, baby. Love knowin' it's my cum in your hot little pussy."

"Oh, God!"

"You ready, baby? Ready for me to fuck that little ass of yours?"

"Do it," she hissed out. "Do it now!"

Again, Thorn picked up the bottle of lube, this time squirting some in his palm. He coated his thumb with it good before reaching underneath her to find her little puckered ass. He stroked his lubed thumb over and over her hole before slowly and carefully slipping his thumb inside to the first joint. She hissed out, but held still, her pussy still pulsing around him occasionally. His cock was still firmly encased in her heat, feeling every single movement inside her, from his thumb in her back entrance, to her body clamping down on his in excitement.

"Hook your arms under your knees and bring them to your chest. That's it, open yourself to me." He growled at the sight of her bare pussy stuffed full of his cock. He pushed his thumb deeper, giving a few strokes to let her get used to the sensation. At the same time, he flipped open the cap to the lube again. Thorn withdrew his thumb and squeezed out more lube, this time coating two fingers on the same hand.

Again, he ran his fingers up and down her asshole, making sure she had plenty of lubrication and to give her time to prepare herself. Sometimes, the anticipation was its own reward.

Carefully, he inserted his middle finger first, then wedged his index finger in beside it. Not too deep, but enough to open her up a little. He had to be careful. Acutely aware of her inexperience with anal sex, he didn't want to hurt her, or, worse, scare her. The first he knew he could control. The second was a bigger challenge.

"How does it feel, Ana? Talk to me."

"Odd," she said, her breath coming in little pants. "But it doesn't hurt." As evidenced by the way her pussy was practically pulsing around him in time with her heartbeat.

"Want me to continue? If you want to wait, I can introduce this to you more slowly. Take days or weeks to stretch you out with plugs. I won't be mad or disappointed in you if you need to take a step back." Hopefully, his little Ana never knew what that concession cost him. He wanted to fuck her ass more than anything in the world in that moment. Not because he thought it would be better than oral sex or fucking her pussy. Because it was the one part of her no one had touched. And he wanted to be the first. Wanted to claim that last hole for his own. Stake that last claim on her.

"What? Yes! I want you to continue! Are you fucking kidding me?" Her voice was high pitched, almost desperate. His own barked laughter sounded nearly as desperate.

"Don't worry, baby. I ain't stoppin' unless you say so. Plan on fucking you here more than once tonight. Before I'm done, you're gonna be so full of my cum you may never get me out. I just don't want you to end up hating this because you weren't ready."

She gave him a soft smile, as if he'd just melted her heart. "Don't worry, Thorn. I might feel a little apprehension before we try something I've never done, but if you want to try it, I'm willing to try anything once. If you make me like it, I'll do it again."

As if to show him how much she wanted this, Mariana reached down to grasp her cheeks and spread them apart. Fuck. He had to actually see this.

Slowly, he pulled his cock free, taking the opportunity to apply more lube to his hard length. It was an awkward job, but he managed it because he had no intention of removing his fingers from her ass until he was ready to fill it with his cock.

"So fuckin' hot," he murmured, not even trying to keep the lust from his voice. He scissored his fingers as he fucked her slowly, stretching her ass. He wasn't a small man, and he was going to make her ready for him no matter how long it took.

"Rub your clit for me, baby," he ordered, still staring at the place where his fingers worked. "Want you to be so turned on when I get ready to fuck you that you don't mind the burn."

"Burn?" she squeaked, her eyes again going wide.

"Oh, yeah, baby. I ain't small, but you are. That's why I'm stretchin' you." He looked down at her. Her fingers worked her clit in small circles. "Dip your fingers into your pussy. Use two. That's it. Stick them in as far as you can."

She obeyed, seemed to welcome the direction. No doubt she did. It was obvious her experience had been limited, but, oh, she made up for it with enthusiasm. She seemed to want only to please him. To make him feel as good as she could. Thorn now had no doubt she'd follow through with her statement earlier. She'd let him take her in a room full of his brothers. She would do exactly what he told her to, keep her eyes on him, and let him be the only man in her world while showing off her lovely body. Hell, he might tie her up and spank her before he fucked her.

"What's that grin about?" she said through her ragged breathing. Her stomach muscles were bunching occasionally, showing off her lithe body. Her legs were spread wide, her glistening pussy on display. His fingers were in her ass while hers dipped inside her pussy. He pushed against the wall separating his fingers from hers, and her eyes widened.

"Oh, nothing you'd be interested in, baby." Again, she pulsed around him, recognizing a wicked, dirty thought when she saw one.

"You lie," she said, a smile tugging at her lips despite her level of arousal.

He chuckled. "Well, unless you'd be interested in me tying you to the bar in the common room, baring your ass for all to see, then spanking it until it's a nice shade of crimson before I fuck this little hole" -- he wiggled his fingers --"then I'm pretty sure you don't want to hear about it."

She groaned and let her head plop down on the bed, her fingers slipping out of her pussy. "You're killing me!"

He laughed then, a real honest-to-God laugh. "Fuck, you're sexy. I can give you every single fantasy you've ever dreamed of, Ana. Every single one, and you'd always, always, be safe with me. No one touches you but me. Ever. No one makes fun of you or makes you feel bad for acting on your desires or they answer to me. No matter if it's one of the club girls or my fuckin' vice president. I'm gonna give you every single dirty, raunchy sex act you've ever wanted to try."

"How 'bout we make a list? We'll check them off with a column of what I like and don't like."

"You're priceless, Ana. Just fuckin' priceless." He surged his fingers deep, squirting lube on them once more, adding a third finger to her ass. When she tensed and her face went tight, he soothed her. "Just relax, baby. You can take it. Just think -- once you're comfortable with these three fingers, you'll be ready for my cock. Do you want that?"

"Yes," she breathed, pushing out against him. "I want your cock inside my ass, Thorn." She nibbled her bottom lip, obviously undecided about something. He was about to coax her into talking to him when she made up her mind on her own. "I can feel your cum when I push my fingers deep." She did so, as if showing him what she was talking about. "I like feeling you when I fuck myself. Your cum. Your cock. When you finally get your dick inside my ass, I'm going to finger my pussy just so I can stroke your cock while you fuck me." She plunged her fingers inside her pussy once more. "Think you could feel me?"

"Fuck, baby," he rasped out, his mouth suddenly going dry. "You're gonna be a handful, aren't you?"

"That a bad thing?"

"Oh, no, baby. But it might get you spanked. You think you could handle that?"

"I'll certainly try." Then that sweet, dirty little-girl thing she had going on changed sharply. "But only if you put your cock in my ass. Right. Fucking. Now!"

Who was he to deny her?

"Just remember, you asked for it, baby. Gonna give it to you." He reached forward and snagged her chin hard, gripping her jaw so she had to look into his eyes. "You fuckin' tell me if you hurt. I'll slow down. Back out and start again. You don't, and we never do this again. Understand me?" Thorn tried his fucking best to sound mean when he was certain he probably sounded as horny as she did. "You get one shot at this. I hurt you, that's it. Your job is to make sure that doesn't happen. Get me?"

"Shut up already. I'm not gonna let you hurt me."

She reached back under her thighs and spread her cheeks apart once again. This time, he noticed her venturing closer to her back hole. He gave her a second, using the time to get himself back under control and to lube his cock once again. He was glad he did because she slipped one finger inside her ass and inhaled sharply.

"That's it, baby. You ever play with yourself there?"

"Not where anyone can see me," she muttered. "I like the way it feels. I've just never had anyone other than myself do it. And I only ever used one finger."

"Well, why stop now? I'm trying to get myself under control. Keep playing. Explore. We'll get you some toys, and you can experiment to your little heart's content."

She groaned, but sank a second finger inside herself, never breaking eye contact with him. Then she added a third, just like he'd done earlier.

"Fuck. Me," Thorn whispered, his hand absently stroking his dick. "Fuck!" He stared at her, mesmerized by the wanton sight she made. Legs spread, three fingers in her ass, Mariana was the most beautiful siren he'd ever seen. "Baby, I must have had sex with a hundred different women in my life. I could never reproduce what I'm seeing right now with any one of those women. Ana, you. Are. Perfect." When she gave him a shy grin, he'd had enough. "Move your hand, baby. I'm gonna fuck you now. You don't come until I say."

"OK," she said, her voice wavering a little. She was nervous. Understandable since he was nervous. He was the one with experience.

Her ass stretched beautifully for him when he pressed the head of his dick against her entrance. Thorn sent up a prayer to any god who would listen that he didn't come the second he entered her ass. Because it was entirely possible.

Chapter Seven

Had she ever been this turned on in her life? Mariana didn't think so. She and Thorn had been having sex regularly since she'd gotten out of the hospital. It wasn't her first time with him. But, God, she was so ready for this! As she spread her cheeks apart, she silently urged him to just shove into her. She knew he wouldn't, but in that moment, it was what she wanted. For him to just take her. To fuck her ass. Give her all the pleasure he'd been promising with every wicked thing he'd done to her up to this point.

The flared head of his cock stretched her hole. There was a burn at first, then a steady pressure. Thorn was careful to keep using lube and to work into her one slow inch at a time before backing out. After several shallow thrusts, he deepened his movements. Not long after that, she felt his abdomen against her ass and knew he was all the way inside. She let out a pent-up breath.

She looked up at him. "You're in all the way," she said. Not a question.

"Oh, yeah, baby. And it feels fan-fucking-tastic!"

With that, he began to move.

At first, the sensations were strange. Mariana couldn't tell if she was going to like it or not. It didn't hurt, but there was a slight burn that gave the pleasure just that extra bit of bite. Of course, Thorn noticed her indecision.

"Thought you were gonna finger-fuck that sweet pussy, baby?"

"Oh," she squeaked. "Yes. I was, wasn't I?" She slid her hand down her body, pausing to squeeze her breast once. Then she found her clit, circling it several times. The pleasure was instantaneous. She gasped, and Thorn raised the bottle of lube, squeezing a stream at the top of her pussy to trickle down to his dick as it sawed in and out of her ass. Taking a deep breath, she slid three fingers inside her pussy while continuing to circle her clit. "Oh, God!" Her eyes widened, and her hips bucked of their own accord.

"You like that, huh?" Thorn said, a smug grin on his face. She could almost believe he was as cavalier as he sounded, except that the strain around his eyes told a different story. "Keep going. Keep yourself on the edge. When I tell you, you're gonna come so hard the whole neighborhood hears you. Got me?"

She couldn't say anything, so she just nodded. She could feel the blood rising to her cheeks, making them hot. Sweat dotted her skin as the pleasure built and built to maddening levels. She thrashed her head and cried out sharply as Thorn sped up his movements.

Then he growled. "Need a better angle."

Without pulling out of her, Thorn backed off the bed so he stood on the floor. He pulled Mariana along with him so her ass hung off the edge but she was supported by the mattress. "Hold on, baby. Gonna to fuck the shit out of you in two seconds."

"OK," she breathed. "OK."

The second he had his feet planted and Mariana in position where he wanted her, Thorn surged forward, pulling her into him. He had his arms wrapped around her thighs for leverage. With every thrust, he pulled her with him, fucking her harder than ever. The longer they fucked, the faster he moved until he was pistoning in and out of her like he might fuck her pussy.

"No pain," she said, her voice shaking with the impact of their bodies. "No pain at all."

"You ready to come?"

"Yes! Thorn! Please!"

"Do it!" He hissed. "Fuckin' come around my fuckin' dick!"

She did. He followed, pumping stream after stream of hot cum inside her spasming ass. Her clit throbbed under her fingers, and she soon had to abandon it. With her fingers no longer touching herself, the pleasure began to dissipate, but, honestly, she was at her limit. This was all she could take. For now.

It took several seconds for Thorn to finish. When he did, he collapsed over her, his heavy frame pressing her into the mattress. She loved every fucking second of it.

"You good, baby? Did I hurt you?"

"I'm good. No pain, Thorn. I swear. I'll be sore, but it will be a good ache."

"Thank God," he said. "Not sure how I'd prevent myself from taking you again had you disobeyed me." He glanced at her quickly, as if suddenly realizing what he'd admitted to. "I would have, though. Never test me on that. I will never hurt you, Ana. Never."

She smiled. "I know." Mariana pulled him down for a gentle kiss, needing the tenderness after all the dirty, kinky sex. God, that had been fun! "I need to run through the shower."

"Oh, no. I'm running you a bath. Then I'm washing you very thoroughly. You're not going to be the least bit uncomfortable. Once you're clean, I'm gonna hold you until you go to sleep."

There was something in his voice. A note of something she couldn't define. "What happens after that? You're staying with me. Right?"

"I will as long as I can, baby. There's club business, but I swear, I'll be back as soon as I can."

"Are you leaving the clubhouse?"

"No, honey. I'll be in church or in the basement, but I'm not leaving the property."

She still got the feeling there was something he wasn't saying, but she chose to trust him. He'd tell her if she needed to know. She had no desire to know everything going on with the club. In fact, this was probably one of those times when the less she knew, the better.

Thorn did exactly what he'd said. He bathed her, dried her, then pulled her into his arms and cuddled her until she went to sleep. The last thing she remembered was him promising, "I'll never let anyone hurt you again, Ana. Not ever."

* * *

"I can get the little fuck from here," Beast said, sounding just a bit too eager. Not that Thorn could say much. He wanted Jason Harrison dead. No. That wasn't quite accurate. Yes, he wanted the man dead, but not right away. Eventually. But first, he wanted to show him what pain really was. He wanted -- no, needed -- Harrison to suffer.

"Put the fuckin' gun down, Beast."

"You said if we made a positive ID and he was anywhere other than the front fuckin' door we could shoot him! Do you remember sayin' that?"

"I do."

"And?"

"Put the fuckin' gun down."

"You're gettin' soft around that woman."

Thorn smacked the back of Beast's head. Hard. "Have you forgotten the last time we intended to take him down? I want him up close before we do it. There will be no mistakes. Besides, I want him to know it's coming. And know there's not a Goddamned thing he can do about it."

"Fine," the other man grumbled. "But he says one wrong word, makes one wrong move, I'll be takin' matters into my own hands. Man's got a lot of shit to pay for."

Thorn ignored that. He knew everything Jason Harrison had to pay for, and it was almost time. "How many did he bring with him?"

"We've spotted six. They're all packin', but they have no idea how to use their weapons other than aimin' and pullin' the trigger. Skipper said he saw one dumbass showin' another dumbass how to turn off the fuckin' safety."

"Good. Just don't underestimate them. They may be inexperienced, but they can still get a lucky shot off. Be ready for anything."

"On it, brother. This one's for your woman."

Thorn shot him a look. "Thought you were doin' it for me?"

"We are. Doin' it for her more. She's special, that one. Probably the only woman in the whole fuckin' state who'd have your sorry ass. You're lucky to have found her."

Thorn rubbed his chest where it felt too full. His brother's caring and Mariana's love filled up spaces he never knew were empty. "Don't I know it."

They watched the small gang gathering outside the clubhouse, trying to get their courage up. The Jim Beam they were currently shooting would certainly do that. It would also create its own problems.

"Maybe it's time to go out and greet our guests."

Beast snorted. "Guests. Right."

"Red. Tinker. You know this guy. I need you to make the identification. He baited us with a relative last time. Need to make sure it doesn't happen again."

"We'll both make certain," Red said. Tinker nodded. The two men fanned out away from the group as Beast, Vicious, Havoc, and Thorn walked together to greet the group of young men.

"Gonna need you to state your business," Thorn said briskly. "This is private property, and we like to keep it private."

"You were the fucker with my girl," the leader said.

Thorn had no idea why this prick was pretending to be Jason. That cat was already out of the bag. His words were slightly slurred which probably explained at least some of it. Instead of calling him on it, Thorn glanced at his brothers and shrugged. Let it play out. See what happens.

"I come to get her. She's carryin' my baby. You know that?"

At that all the guys laughed and nudged each other and Steve. It seemed odd, like the man had no idea about the extent of what he'd done. what he'd done, but Havoc didn't tell him. Apparently, Jason hadn't either.

"She's fine where she is," Thorn said, shifting his stance to be better able to reach his gun if necessary. He had no intention of shooting the little bastard. That would be too easy. "Besides, you and I have business to attend to."

He'd been about to wave the seven men inside the clubhouse where they could control everything, but Red's voice over his earpiece stopped him. "Can't confirm the bastard," he said. "I need to get closer. Lookin' for a scar over his right eye that I can't find.

I'm sure it's either Jason or the cousin Havoc warned off."

Thorn ground his teeth in agitation. He would make absolutely sure. Because this was going to be a permanent solution.

He looked at each man, noting who seemed relaxed and who was nervous. Most fell into the latter category, but two were actually checking out their surroundings like they might know what they were doing.

One of them said, "This an MC?" Thorn nodded, shifting to the balls of his feet in case he needed to move fast. Something was nagging at his instincts that he needed to be on guard.

"It is," Havoc said, his gaze shifting over the seven men as well as around the area. He wasn't the only one. Beast and Vicious had both moved farther away, looking around the front of the property as well as positioning themselves so they could see around the side of the building. "Which girl you talkin' about? Ain't got no girl here pregnant."

"Right. I know she's here," Steve said. "I seen you with her at Red's Garage, and I seen her outside here one night." He spat on the ground, and more than one of the Salvation's Bane members inside the clubhouse made their way outside. They draped themselves against the building or stood with their arms crossed and waited, a blatant show of force. The four men who looked so nervous backed up a step, glancing at each other. Steve, as well as the two bolder men, kept their attention on the Bane members in front of them. It was likely the final fight would be only between these three men and any of Salvation's Bane who wanted to participate.

"You got a name for the girl?" Thorn asked, setting his trap, letting the reality of everything that had happened reveal itself along with exactly how much this lot knew.

"Her name's Mariana, but everyone calls her Mari."

"Wrong," Thorn snapped, stepping forward. "No one but Steve calls her Mari, and she fuckin' hates it." To his credit, the younger man flinched but only took one step backward and only because Thorn crowded into his space.

He shrugged. "Well, we ain't calling her Mariana. It's a stupid name."

"That's one," Thorn warned. "Please keep going. The more beatings you earn, the better I'll feel."

"Right. Like to see you try."

Immediately, one of the two brave friends he had with him grabbed his shoulder, pulling him back a step. "Easy, man," he hissed. "You might want to think about what you're doing. Girl ain't worth dyin' over. Neither is Jason, or he'd be here himself."

Thorn was immediately hyper aware of the man looking at him with hate-filled eyes. He spoke up so the mic at his collar could easily pick up his voice. "Ripper, double check the security feeds. We might need to look for an intruder." He turned his attention back to his adversary. "You're not Jason Harrison, so you better fuckin' admit it right this fuckin' second. 'Cause that's all you got before I drag you inside. Once we have you there, you ain't fuckin' leavin' alive."

* * *

Everything had happened so fast. Mariana's head spun when she thought about everything Thorn had done to her body, playing it like a master. Hell, if he continued to give her the kind of pleasure his kink provided, she might be willing to call him master. He'd left their bed late that morning, but not before making slow, lazy love to her. It was almost hard to reconcile the two different sides of him, but Mariana knew she loved both of them. She also knew he'd made an effort to give her tender to offset the rough and kinky. She'd never admit it to him -- at least, not yet -- but she was beginning to suspect she enjoyed the rough and kinky even more than the slow and gentle. At least, with him she did. Probably because he took his time and made her enjoy every single dirty thing he did to her. She shivered and grinned just thinking about it.

She'd seen Thorn a few times throughout the day. Always, he took time to pull her into his arms and kiss her. Always, his brothers catcalled and whistled, but he just grinned, kissing her all the more enthusiastically. The first time it had happened today, Mariana had tried to push him away. He'd swatted her ass and kissed her again before letting her go. He'd winked at her, and then she'd listened to his brothers. Really listened. They were ribbing him about being so gone on her he couldn't even wait to get her into private before kissing her senseless. None of them had said a negative word about her. In fact, all the men and most of the club girls had congratulated her on finally semi-taming him.

She'd been a little bemused, but hey. When in Rome, right? Besides, she couldn't help but think about all the filthy images he'd put in her head the previous night. Him fucking her in front of his club at a party. Or even just whenever he took the notion. She wondered what would happen if she bent over at the waist to pick up something she'd dropped while wearing a short skirt and, oops! She forgot her panties!

Yeah. That'd get her fucked, she'd bet. What a whirlwind of a day!

She'd waited until the club girls were done with the pool, then made her way there. It was hot and humid tonight, the moon bright. Knowing Thorn would know she was in the pool -- he probably had Ripper keeping tabs on her all the time, which should have freaked her out but just made her feel safe -- she wore only a towel wrapped around her. The second her naked body slipped beneath the water, she groaned. Was there any more sensual feeling than skinny dipping? And really, why was that? It didn't feel the same when she bathed, and she certainly didn't wear a swimsuit then.

God, how her life had turned around! For the first time in a very long time, happiness blossomed in her chest. Thorn made her happy. Made her feel safe. He accepted her as she was, brought her into his life without reservation. How long had it been she'd felt that kind of… of family? The only people who'd been remotely sour toward her were Mama and Pops. Mostly Mama. And only when she was trying to get her and Thorn together. Though the other woman gave her an uneasy feeling, Mariana still wanted to tell her she understood. She wished the couple hadn't left.

Oh, well. She'd make up for it later. Maybe Thorn would take her to visit the other club, and she could thank them both in person.

Mariana had made a turn and kicked off the side of the pool, swimming laps, when an arm grabbed her, hauling her down beneath the surface.

She struggled, trying to see if it was Thorn messing with her, but even though the underwater lights shone brightly, she couldn't see whoever was behind her, snaking an arm around her neck.

That definitely wasn't Thorn. Mariana struggled in earnest now. Thank God she was a strong swimmer and could hold her breath, but she was out of shape from her recent ordeal, and there was no way she could last like this more than a few seconds.

Realizing she wasn't going to get free using strength or clawing her way out, she reached back with one hand down low, looking for the crotch of her attacker. The second she found it, she squeezed with all her might until he let go. Even then, she didn't release him until he stabbed her hand with a knife. He'd drawn blood, but, thankfully, hadn't been very accurate.

Lungs burning, heart pounding, Mariana took off swimming as hard as she could until she reached the wall, hefting herself out of the water. She turned to find her attacker still in the water, but recovered from the pain and shock and coming after her. She let out a sharp scream, so out of breath a long, sustained scream just wasn't possible. But she did run around the edge of the pool to the pool house the club was building. Their tools were all put away, but there were stone and bricks. She picked up a rock in one hand and a brick in the other.

By this time, she was able to focus on her attacker. Not one of the club members. Jason!

"Thorn!" she screamed as loud as she could, still out of breath and growing more and more short of air as panic seized her. In her mind, she was back at the hotel, Jason standing over her. Kicking her over and over.

"He ain't here to save you, bitch." Jason sneered. "You're on your own, 'cause nobody in this shit club gives a damn about their president's whore." He stalked toward her, knife still in hand. "That's what you are, ain't it? A fuckin' whore?"

Mariana threw the rock at him. Jason batted it away into the pool. "Stay away from me!" She needed to make as much noise as she could. "Help! Thorn!"

"That's right, bitch. Call out for him. He don't care about you. You're just another piece of pussy. You got any idea how many bitches he's had? Hell, he'd probably be glad to replace you with someone who can actually fuck. He'll get used to shocking you, then you'll be just another boring piece of pussy who doesn't know how to fuck a man."

He had almost reached her when there was a war bellow from the other side of the pool. Thorn had climbed the fence from the front side of the property and was charging toward them like a bull. The look on his face was pure, unadulterated rage. Her avenging angel.

Jason took his focus from her, turning to face the oncoming threat. Like she wasn't a threat. He wouldn't think so because he'd already beaten her once. Had nearly killed her.

Had killed her baby...

Something inside Mariana snapped. Without a word, she picked up another brick and swung it two-handed into the back of his head. He fell like a stone onto the concrete, mashing his face as he did.

But Mariana didn't stop there. With an angry scream, she pounded the brick into Jason's head over and over. Blood and brains splattered over her arms and up her bare legs. Every time she pulled the brick free, there was a sickening squish. Once, a piece of bone stuck into her shin with the force of her beating. Blood was everywhere.

A woman was at her side, trying to soothe her, rubbing her back over and over until she finally gave one final hit with the brick only to throw it down on his head one last time. There wasn't much left of Jason's head. She turned to see Fleur and Lucy reaching for her, fierce looks of understanding laced with worry on their faces.

Mariana looked around her for the first time. Several club members, along with the ol' ladies, a couple of club girls, and Thorn stood all around her, protecting her from the outside world. Then she saw three unfamiliar men. One looked exactly like Jason. Steve. His first cousin. They looked nearly identical except Steve's hair had slightly more gray in it, and he didn't have the scar over his right eye Jason had from a fight as a teenager. This man's forehead was smooth and unmarked.

She addressed Steve. "Did he talk you into coming here so you could distract the club long enough for him to kill me?"

* * *

Normally, Thorn demanded he be the voice of the club. Not this time. His ol' lady was doing a smashing job. No pun intended. He was angry with himself he'd let that little fuck get close enough to her to actually get his hands on her.

"Well?" she snapped.

"We, uh..." Steve looked around him nervously. Mariana was naked as the day she was born. Covered in blood, brains, and a few pieces of bone. She looked like something out of a horror movie. Of all the people around those three men, she was probably the least dangerous, but Steve's gaze kept returning to Mariana, and not with lust, either. "I told him I didn't want to come here, but he said he just wanted you back. Never figured that big guy was serious when he said he'd fuckin' kill me if I helped Jason." He shuddered. "Guess the Jim Beam made this seem like a much better idea what it was." He glanced at Mariana before shuddering again and looking away. "Ain't like he was mean to you or anything. He loved you. In his own way."

"Do you have any idea what happened between us? Do you know what he did to me? To my baby?" She sobbed out the last word, but took several deep breaths and got herself under control. Thorn had eased over to her side, needing to protect her, but also wanting the other man to know she was Thorn's.

"He said you just up and left. I --"

"Fucker!" she screamed, turning once again to Jason's body and kicking him soundly. Thorn winced. That had to hurt her bare toes, but she just kicked him again before turning back to Steve. "He's a lying sack of shit! He kicked me out! Then, when someone showed me some attention, acted like I was important, Jason attacked me! His ego wouldn't let him let me be happy! Did you know he killed our child?" Her hands went to her belly, as if protecting the unborn baby instead of mourning it. "Did you know?"

Finally, she left Jason's body. Thorn jerked his head, and two prospects immediately moved to cover Jason's body in case someone was able to get over the fence to investigate the noise. But he'd be Goddamned if he'd make her be quiet. She needed to get this out of her system if she was going to heal. To his surprise, someone did, in fact, get through the fence. Coming to stand with Mariana, Pops handed Mama a blanket. The older woman draped it around Mariana's shoulders.

Instinctively, Mariana clutched the light material over her body.

"I -- I didn't." Steve got a panicked look as realization dawned on him. "Oh, God! That was you and Jason? At that motel. I heard on the news, but they didn't give any names."

"Yeah," Mariana snapped. "That was me. He left me there to die, Steve. Then he came after me tonight to kill me. I don't pretend to know why, but he'll never hurt me again." She lifted her chin high, facing Steve and the other two. "If you're here to hurt me, I'll make sure you never get the chance to."

Fuck, but Thorn was fucking proud of her! She was fierce as an MC president's ol' lady. Right up to the point where she burst into tears. It broke his heart. He pulled her into his arms, wrapping her up tight. "I swear to God, Ana, no one will ever fuckin' touch you again. Not as long as any member of Salvation's Bane is alive. This will never, ever, fuckin' happen again. We will fuckin' fix this."

Red stepped over to them, resting his head on top of Mariana's damp head. "You can count on us, little sister," he murmured.

Thorn nodded once, his eyes stinging suspiciously, like he might show a tender emotion in front of the club. "Take Mariana up to my room. Have Fleur and Lucy sit with her."

"We can watch over the child as well," Mama said. "She's a good girl." She shook her head. "A good girl."

"Why are you still here, Josephine?" Thorn had to know. He wasn't sure why his aunt had been so upset before.

"To make sure you and that girl finally got the stubborn out. You need each other."

"I knew that," he said, scrubbing a hand over his face, still unwilling to let Mariana out of his arms. She was far too fragile for that at the moment. "I was taking care of it when you lost your temper."

Mama gave him a rueful smile. "You were the only one of my boys who could rile my temper."

Papa snorted. "Because he's just as stubborn as you. I told you to let him do it his own way."

Thorn chuckled softly. "You and I always did butt heads. But you have to know I love you. You might not have given birth to me, but you were my mother in every way that mattered."

His aunt actually blushed and blinked several times, probably trying to prevent any tears from leaking. "Well, then. I'm glad we slipped past Red when he thought we got on the plane."

"Why did you come back?"

She shrugged. "Maybe to apologize. Maybe to make you apologize."

"You haven't changed a bit since I was a kid. And I hope you never do, Mama."

"Good. Now. Pops can carry her to your room. The girls and I will get her cleaned up and into bed. You take care of the trash." She glanced at the three men standing there. Now that Thorn looked at them closely, only Steve looked worried. The other two looked angry. Like they'd been just as deceived as Steve had and were royally pissed about it.

"I've got it. You take care of her. She's the most precious thing in my world."

Mariana looked up at him. "Please don't leave me too long, Thorn. I'm so sorry about this."

"Honey, why in the world would you be sorry?"

"I killed a man. In your clubhouse. I'll take full responsibility. I don't want the club to take the heat for this."

"For what, honey?"

"For..." She gestured to where Jason's body lay under a tarp. "For that."

"Sweetheart, by the time Blood is finished, no one will know he was ever here. We started covering his tracks before he got here. There might be something on the news if anyone bothers to report him missing, but no one will find any trace of him." He tipped her head up to his. Blood had splattered over her cheek, and there were a couple of spots on her forehead, but he ignored it. Cupping her face in his hands, Thorn kissed her softly. "You go with Mama and Pops. Lucy and Fleur will help you clean up and get you into bed." He winked at her. "If you want to seduce the pair of them, just make sure you don't let their men in there. I'd hate to have to kill my brothers."

"Thorn!"

He laughed, kissing her nose. "I'm kidding, honey. I'm kidding."

"Oh, you're such a hound dog!" She slapped at his chest, and a grin tugged at her lips even as a tear tracked down her cheek.

"Hey, what self-respecting man wouldn't want to watch three hot chicks going at it?"

Fleur snorted. "You're just like Beast. He thinks he's cute, too." She put her arms around Mariana's shoulder and guided her to Pops. "Come on, honey. Let's go."

Pops lifted her carefully, Mama making sure the blanket didn't slip. Then all of them left the pool area and went inside. Thorn hated leaving her, but he had to deal with this. He had no idea how deep these three men were in with Jason Harrison, but he was about to find out.

"Here," one of the two men with Steve said, holding out his phone to Havoc, his other hand out in front of him in surrender. "Call him yourself. He'll vouch for us. We were only here to make sure you guys got the job done."

"What job?" Thorn was pissed beyond measure. Now that Ana was safe, he was ready to kill a motherfucker.

"The job of killing Harrison and deciding if his cousin needed killing, too."

"And the other four? The ones who high-tailed it outta here when the heat cranked up?"

"Never figured they'd get far. They wanted to be hardasses, but they weren't. I've already got men picking them up," the man said.

Havoc took the phone but made no move to call the person in question. "Says El Diablo sent him. Says Jason made contact with Black Reign the same day you left with Mariana from Red's."

"I take it he was trying to put some kind of hit out? Who on? Me?"

"Yes. He said you'd kidnapped the girl and were having your club rape her repeatedly."

Havoc snorted. "Can't imagine a man like El Diablo appreciates that his reputation has gotten around enough that little pissants are looking him up to put a bullet in someone's brain. I'd think that was a bit beneath him."

The other man scowled. Now that he thought about it, both men looked familiar. "Wait. You're El Segador. The Reaper." The man nodded. "What the blue fuck are you doing associating with these assholes?"

El Segador's partner spoke. "We were coming to make sure Jason didn't live through this, and to see how much Steve knew."

"Jekyll's brother is a cop here in Palm Beach," El Segador said and nodded to his companion.

"I contacted Beau the second Jason brought this to us. Kid don't know jack about Black Reign except that the authorities consider us rivals of Salvation's Bane. Don't think he expected us to actually check out his story. Guess he thought we'd just roll in, guns blazing. But we dug. Didn't take long to uncover what happened. El Diablo sent us here to put that fucker out of Mariana's misery if you hadn't already. When Jason got with Steve over there and put this shit plan together, we figured it would be the perfect way to see exactly how much Steve knew."

"You took a chance we wouldn't kill you, too," Thorn said.

"No," El Segador said. "You guys are a lot of things, but you're disgustingly moral on some issues. You don't shoot first and ask questions later. Might should have in this instance, but we knew you wouldn't. Even know about your little raid on Harrison's apartment. If you'd been like us, you'd have just walked in and shot the motherfucker and worried about the collateral damage later."

"I don't kill innocents," Thorn said. "Not if it's avoidable."

"We know. Which is why we took this chance," Jekyll said. "After Mariana's questioning of him, I'm convinced Steve didn't know as much as we first thought he might. Not sure it's enough to get him off the hook, but he did seem to have been deceived."

Thorn snorted. "Would help if we could question Jason, but that ship has fuckin' sailed. And good riddance."

"What do you want to do?" El Segador raised an eyebrow, giving Thorn the impression this was all his decision when Thorn knew if he didn't do as El Diablo thought he should, El Segador would take matters into his own hands.

"Kill him," he said, acting on instinct. "Beatin' him didn't make an impression and Havoc didn't pull any punches last time." He nodded at Jekyll. "No one will ever find the body. Or, rather, the pieces."

Steve made a whimpering sound where he stood on the concrete next to Jason's covered body. At first, Thorn thought he was afraid of what was about to happen to him. Instead, the man was looking down at the pool of blood and trembling. "I can't believe she killed him. I-I never thought she would ever hurt a fly. She was always so sweet to everyone."

Thorn reach out and snagged the young man's T-shirt and dragged him two steps away from the body. "Your cousin there beat Mariana until she miscarried her baby. The child Jason conceived with her. I have no idea what their relationship was like, and I'm not asking her, because I can't kill him again. But trust me when I tell you, he got off easy considering what he did to Mariana."

Steve nodded quickly. "I never thought he'd hurt her. If he did before, I never knew about it. I'd never have let him get the others involved. I especially wouldn't have let him get Black Reign involved." He glanced over at the two patched members. "Can't say I don't deserve this since I never bothered to question Jason. He's my family. You're supposed to side with family. Right?" In that moment, Steve looked like a teenager, confused as to what to do. Thorn thought he was genuinely sorry about what had happened. Too bad he realized it too late.

"Damn shame you didn't look into Harrison's claims before you decided to go after Mariana. Even if you thought she'd been held here against her will, you should have made an effort to find out before puttin' out a hit on someone."

"I know," Steve said, softly. "You're right." He took a shuddering breath, then looked up at Thorn, his face a hard mask. "Do what you have to. Ain't dyin' like no fuckin' coward."

That took Thorn by surprise. Judging by the way Rycks' eyebrows shot up, it had him too. Thorn nodded to the Black Reign men. "I'd like to hear your opinion on this. Your club was at risk, same as ours."

Rycks shrugged. "Not sure about that. I think we coulda took you if we needed to."

Havoc snorted loudly. "If a buncha pussies like you guys managed to get a shot in, then I suppose we'd deserve to have you kick our asses."

Jekyll bared his teeth, but stayed quiet. Beast cracked his knuckles and grinned, as if he was looking forward to a rumble.

"We'll take him," Rycks said at length. "What happens tomorrow depends on him."

"Keep me informed. And Rycks? Next time El Diablo decides to run an op against my club, he better fuckin' give me a heads up or I will shoot first."

Epilogue

The following few days weren't the easiest of Mariana's life. She had nightmares about the police arresting Thorn because he refused to let her take responsibility. Sometimes, she tried to kill the men who'd come to arrest Thorn. Other times, she kept screaming she did it. She was the one to kill Jason, and she was glad she had. Always, there was blood on her hands.

Each time the nightmares came, Thorn was there to coax her awake, then make love to her until she was passed out in an exhausted sleep. He was always patient with her, but he wasn't always gentle. The man seemed to have a sixth sense about what she needed from him. The first time she told him she didn't need sweet and slow but hard and rough, he'd flipped her over onto her belly, swatted her ass, then proceeded to fuck her until her lungs heaved and her throat was raw from her screams. Even then, he'd cleaned her, then turned her into his chest and cuddled her close, murmuring how much he loved her and how fucking sexy she was. After that, she'd gone to sleep with a big smile on her face.

Today, he'd told her he wanted to take her back to the diner. "Marge and Elena been askin' 'bout you, and I promised I'd bring you back. Today is peach cobbler day, and it's kind of my favorite, so we're goin'." She laughed, hugged him, then agreed to go anywhere he wanted.

Another thing he'd started doing a lot of was taking her on long bike rides. Most of the time, his brothers flanked him. Red always followed in what they called a "cage" but was really just a big Ford truck with a trailer that housed all kinds of tools, spare parts, oil, and plenty of room to haul a bike should one break down. Mariana was surprised how the show of solidarity made her feel safe. She never worried about anything happening to her or Thorn because the other members of Salvation's Bane wouldn't let anything happen. They were a solid wall of muscle and fury when it came to protecting their president, and they'd included her in that circle of protection. She saw it every day in how they treated her. They truly thought of her as their "little sister." Mariana loved the feeling it gave her.

Now, they all pulled into the diner. Marge stuck her head out the door and yelled, "How many you got this time, Thorn?"

"Eight or ten. Nothing you and Tito can't handle."

"Well, give a girl a heads up next time! I thought you were just bringing Mariana!"

As they filed in, Marge had already started Tito on the orders. The woman knew what all of them liked, apparently. She eyed Mariana with a critical eye, then a sad expression. "I think someone needs a Marge special, Thorn."

"You're a miracle, Marge. Don't let anyone tell you differently."

He urged Mariana into a booth then scooted in beside her. Beast sat across from them. Vicious and Havoc sat in a booth next to them, one on each side of the table. The others found room and started flirting with Marge in hopes of getting a free milkshake. A notion she might have encouraged by telling them they all had to outdo Red if they wanted to get a free Marge Special. Marge basked in the attention, but still ran a tight ship, never missing an order.

The bell to the door rang, and Mariana's gaze automatically swung in that direction. The second she did, she froze. Thorn, ever the attentive, wonderful man he was, noticed. He dropped his arm around her shoulders and scanned the room until he found who she was staring at.

Adelaide Everly. Mariana's mother.

Adelaide's eyes narrowed as she saw her daughter. Thorn leaned down and brushed a kiss over Mariana's temple. "Don't you back down from her, woman. You're the ol' lady of Salvation's Bane's president. You don't back down from no one. Got me?"

Mariana turned her face up to his and gave him a smile. "I got you." Then she cupped the side of his face and pressed her lips lightly to his.

"That's my girl." He hugged her before sitting back and stretching out his legs in a lazy pose. Mariana could see him ready to pounce if need be. But, really. What could her mother do other than berate her? And even her mother might think twice, seeing her with this lot.

After the initial recognition, Mariana forced her gaze to Beast. "I never got the chance to thank you and everyone else for coming to my rescue. I want you to know I appreciate it."

He winked at her. "Any time, darlin'. You're one of us now. We protect our family."

"Mariana." Her mother stood beside the table, her arms stiffly at her sides. Her clothes were immaculate, and she looked fresh as the morning even though it was pushing a hundred degrees and humid as hell outside. "I need to speak to you immediately."

She glanced at Thorn, who shrugged. He wasn't going to fight this fight for her. At least not yet.

Mariana knew it was only because he knew how much she needed to do this herself that he held back. Beside her, his body had tensed, as though he might protest should she try to leave him.

"I think you said all you needed to a few weeks ago when you left me stranded on the side of the road after I called you for help."

"You will come with me this instant, young lady," her mother insisted. All she needed to do was stomp her foot for good measure, and Mariana might have burst out laughing. Of all the nerve! Why in the world did she expect Mariana to just drop everything and do what she was told?

"No, Mother. I won't. I'm about to be served the best cheeseburger, fries, and chocolate malt in the whole world. I intend on eating them while they're fresh. If you want to talk, you have my phone number. Call. I'll answer if I'm not busy."

Her mother turned every shade of red before settling on purple. "How dare you disrespect me this way?"

Mariana shrugged. "I'm sorry, is there a point to this?"

Her mother leaned in slightly, giving a wary glance to both Beast and Thorn. "You're ruining our family's reputation!" she hissed. "You will come with me this instant. I've found a place where you can give birth to that ill-conceived child, and no one here will be the wiser. You can put it up for adoption immediately, and we can get on with our lives."

OK, that hurt. Fortunately, sensitive to her as ever, Thorn intervened.

He stood. Adelaide backed up a step only to bump her ass against the table where Vicious and Havoc sat. That prompted her to give a little cry of surprise and to jump back straight into Thorn. "That's enough, Mrs. Everly. If you'd care to sit, I'm sure Marge would be happy to serve you whatever you want."

Mariana thought she heard Marge mutter under her breath, "That'll be the day," but she wasn't sure.

"Otherwise, it might be best if you moved on. Mariana's had a rough few weeks after she was attacked. Losing the baby has been exceptionally hard for her, and I'm sure she doesn't want to talk about it with you."

To her complete and utter dismay, Adelaide actually looked satisfied. "Well, at least I won't have to worry about those rumors." She looked back to Mariana. "Now, you still need to come with me. One problem has been solved. Now, you just need to get back into church and behave like a young woman should. Come along, dear."

"Did she just call the fact that I was beaten until I miscarried a... problem? One that she needed solving?" Mariana couldn't believe this. "She actually said that, didn't she?"

"Babe, I can make her leave if she's upsetting you."

"She's pissing me off!" She turned to her mother. "Why are you here? Because I damned well know it's not because you care about me. What's happened for you to decide I'm suddenly worth saving?"

Marge smacked her gum as she set Mariana's chocolate malt on the table in front of her. "I'll tell you what happened. Someone told the folks in the women's Sunday school group that you weren't actually dead, Mariana. That Adelaide lied because she was embarrassed you were expecting. I think the preacher's wife had a good long talk with her. From what I heard, Adelaide, you were supposed to ask forgiveness of your daughter and welcome her back into the holy flock. Not browbeat her and tell her you were glad she lost the child she was carrying."

At this point, both Tito and Elena came around the bar, out of the kitchen, and into the dining area. "Adelaide Everly," Elena said, disapproval in her voice. "If you think I won't tell Brother Samuel and his wife how you're acting, you should think again. You're hurting yourself and your child. You should be horrified that your only grandchild perished in such a way!"

"I have my reputation to think of, Elena." Adelaide sniffed as she looked the other woman up and down, like she found her lacking in every way. "Unlike others here, people actually look up to me and depend on my goodwill to keep them going."

"Rubbish!" Elena said, her fists going to her ample hips. "You're no more important than the rest of us, you're just too self-centered to see it. Brother Samuel's wife asked you to make amends with your daughter to help your poor rotten soul. As far as I'm concerned, you're a lost cause." Elena turned up her nose and went back to the kitchen.

"I really think you need to leave now." Thorn's voice was deep, the deadly side of him not far from the surface. While Mariana knew he'd never hurt her mother, she could almost wish he was the type of man who would, just to give her mother a brief glimpse at what her daughter had gone through. But then, the reason she loved him so much was because he wasn't that kind of man. She could see he wanted with everything in him to rough up her mother for the way she treated Mariana. But he wouldn't. Instead, he escorted her to the door with a hand at the small of her back. As he urged her outside, he gave her a hard look. Her mother stepped back.

"We need to get one thing straight." Thorn didn't shut the door and joined her in the parking lot. He obviously wanted witnesses to what he was about to say. "Mariana is my woman. She's going to be my wife. How much, if any, role you play in her life is completely up to her. At the moment, you're at exactly zero percent. I'm good with that. But I have a feeling that, one day when you're old and alone with no one to check in on you or call to say 'Happy Mother's Day,' you'll regret what you did here today, and the day you left your pregnant daughter on the side of the road in the oppressive heat. If you never get to the point where you do regret it, then she didn't need you in her life to begin with. Good day, Mrs. Everly."

Thorn shut the door and turned his back on Adelaide Everly. Mariana talked with Beast while Thorn was busy with her mother. She tried to pretend she didn't care what he said, that she was engrossed in her conversation with Beast instead of hurt and angry at her mother. If she showed either, her mother would have won. She'd obviously come there to punish Mariana for getting a lecture from their pastor's wife. If Mariana pretended indifference to her mother, then Adelaide wouldn't feel like she was the center of Mariana's attention, devaluing her in Mariana's circle of importance. That was exactly the impression Mariana wanted to give.

When Thorn sat down, Beast reached over and squeezed Mariana's hand. "I'm proud of you, little sister. You're going to make the best ol' lady for Thorn."

"I'm going to try," she said softly, looking up at Thorn. "It's the least I can do since you're so good to me."

"Honey, I'll always be good to you. I fuckin' love you. Any day you can't feel that when you're near me, I have a fuckin' problem." He hugged her close to him and kissed her soundly.

Marge put their plates in front of them and grinned as she smacked her gum. "Don't you worry about Adelaide none." She winked at Mariana. "Them Baptist church ladies can cut you to shreds if you don't behave the way they think you should. Adelaide's in for a big surprise when she gets to Sunday school tomorrow. Got a feeling the lesson and Brother Samuel's sermon will revolve around something along the lines of loving your family and not lying and telling the church your only daughter died just because you disagree with her life choices."

Mariana giggled. "Would serve her right, but I honestly don't care. Thorn's right. She's run off every single person who's ever cared about her. I was all she had left. And she's pushed me away too. I thought I'd feel even worse about it when I saw her walk through that door, but, honestly, it's kind of freeing to know I never have to deal with her again."

"Damned straight you don't," Thorn growled. "You just gotta deal with me."

From the kitchen, Elena yelled, "She don't gotta deal with you if she don't want to. Honey, he gets outta line, you send him to me. I'll make sure he knows how to treat his woman."

"Uh, oh, Thorn," Tito said with a big grin on his face. "That's the first time I ever heard my Elena less than pleased with you."

"Not fair, Elena," Thorn called with a grin and a wink at Mariana. "I ain't done nothing!"

"Just making sure you don't. Mariana's a sweet girl. You don't treat her right, you answer to me." There was a pause then she called, "If Thorn is mean to my girl Mariana, the first one to tell me gets the Marge special and the Elena special on the house!"

The diner erupted in laughter. Mariana knew she'd found her home. This club. This man. These people. They were good and kind. They might be rough around the edges, swear too much, and party hard, but they looked out for her and all the women that belonged to them. They were a family. And she was a part of it. She looked up at Thorn with tears in her eyes and a smile on her face. "I love you so much, Thorn."

"I love you too, honey. I always will."

Mariana knew she'd always love him, too.

Marteeka Karland

Erotic romance author by night, emergency room tech/clerk by day, Marteeka Karland works really hard to drive everyone in her life completely and totally nuts. She has been creating stories from her warped imagination since she was in the third grade. Her love of writing blossomed throughout her teenage years until it developed into the totally unorthodox and irreverent style her English teachers tried so hard to rid her of.

Marteeka at Changeling: changelingpress.com/marteeka-karland-a-39

Changeling Press E-Books

More Sci-Fi, Fantasy, Paranormal, and BDSM adventures available in e-book format for immediate download at ChangelingPress.com -- Werewolves, Vampires, Dragons, Shapeshifters and more -- Erotic Tales from the edge of your imagination.

What are E-Books?

E-books, or electronic books, are books designed to be read in digital format -- on your desktop or laptop computer, notebook, tablet, Smart Phone, or any electronic e-book reader.

Where can I get Changeling Press E-Books?

Changeling Press e-books are available at ChangelingPress.com, Amazon, Apple Books, Barnes & Noble, and Kobo/Walmart.

ChangelingPress.com

Printed in Great Britain
by Amazon